The heir of a Duke, betrothed to a daughter of his king, Jeremy Nottingdale thought he knew what life had in store for him until his uncle threw him overboard. Accustomed to a life of privilege and pampering, Jeremy is suddenly faced with the challenge to survive. Cast Away tells of Jeremy's transformation from a spoiled aristocrat to a respectful nobleman not only because of his time marooned on an island, but also because of the woman he finds there. Beautiful, intelligent, and resourceful Sanura is an enigma. Rather than seduce her, as would be his usual wont, he finds himself acting as he knows a gentleman should. Over time, the challenges and dangers of their life of exile draw them closer. They find they can express through love what they cannot in language.

Jeremy's greatest desire is for a rescue so he can see Sanura safely to her family, whoever and wherever they are. Yet the granting of this greatest of his wishes would mean he must part with her and never see her again. When the time comes, will he be able to cast her away?

Cast Away
Copyright © 2019 Amelia Dalton
ISBN: 978-1-4874-2594-4
Cover art by Martine Jardin

Published by eXtasy Books Inc or
Devine Destinies, an imprint of eXtasy Books Inc

Look for us online at:
www.eXtasybooks.com or www.devinedestinies.com

CAST AWAY

BY

AMELIA DALTON

DEDICATION

To you, dear reader — Keep living, keep loving!

CHAPTER ONE

Jeremy Nottingdale stared into the black waters he was soon to meet with the brittle twists of rope sinking their tiny barbs into his wrists. A larger, cold pricking at his throat held ready to plunge at his first move. He smelled the tang of sweat and metal on the hand under his chin. It was a hand he had recently clasped in friendship, a hand he had placed his own beside in the working of the ship, and a hand he had trusted. He had been taught better than to trust. *A man of monarch's blood can trust no one.* The lesson came back to him, sharp and poignant as the blade at his throat. He had set that wisdom aside, as he had many things, seduced by the adventure of the sea and the camaraderie of sailing men.

He had spent—wasted—his privileged childhood yearning for the sea. He had grudgingly been allowed to fulfill his dream, but not until he had sworn an oath to abandon it afterward and assume the duties of his birthright.

Yet the sea was a jealous mistress. She would see a man die before allowing him to set her aside. Even he, regal man-child that he was, would not be forgiven.

Jeremy's gaze moved from her undulating bosom to meet those of the man who approached. "You'll not get away with this, Ombreux," he said calmly, despite the ice floe in his innards. "My father will see you all hang for this."

The barrel of the man's chest swelled under his graying beard. He threw his head back, and the deck of the ship rang with his laughter. "Your father!" he scoffed. "Your father will never see this vessel again unless he grows the balls to

1

command a ship in battle."

This remark elicited laughter from the men.

Ombreux looked down at Jeremy, his eyes colder than the sea. "He used what little he had to burden my sister with your ungrateful carcass. I think, my nephew, that was more than a feat for him."

A hot spark ignited above the frigid darkness of Jeremy's gut.

"He was right not to trust you. The only reason he did was because he loves my mother so much."

"It is because *I* care for her it pains me to do this, but it is the penalty she must suffer for betraying the family and marrying a duke rather than a king. Now *my* son will be the one to marry royal blood, and the true monarchy will be revived."

"Justice will find you!"

Ombreux laughed again. "It hasn't yet, and here's a parting secret for you, nephew." He leaned to whisper in Jeremy's ear. "I've done *far* worse than this."

Jeremy stared at his uncle's smug, jovial face. Slowly, he became aware of what Ombreux was suggesting—the most sinister of deeds.

Ombreux's expression melted into a scowl. "Overboard with him!"

The men cheered. Jeremy lanced Ombreux with his gaze as strong hands turned him and shoved him to the railing. Even as frigid terror washed over him, he refused to show it. He was of noble birth. He would be noble in death as well.

The inky water sent crested tendrils splashing up, eager to seize, engulf, and drag him down to the gate of hell itself. He closed his eyes, and his legs went numb. The man that held him wrapped an arm around his chest. The man's other hand, still bearing the dagger, seized his wrists as another man bound Jeremy's ankles.

"Stop squirmin', ye scoundrel!" the man said loudly,

though Jeremy barely had the power to stand.

Jeremy felt the blade slide along his wrist in their struggling movements. The tension of the rope eased, and cold metal pressed onto his palm.

Hot breath blew against his ear. "*Bonsort*, my liege."

The ship left his feet. He made a quick gasp of fear and anticipation. An explosion of cold jarred his body, seizing him in an insensate hand of silence and terror. He swirled about in the wake of the passing ship. The surface was lost, but his senses weren't. He resisted the urge to struggle so he could more easily rise to the surface. All he could hear was the rush of water and his heart pounding. Panic closed in on him just before the black hand of the sea uncurled from over him and he burst through the surface.

He took a tremendous breath, coughed violently, and another wave immersed him. The sea was pulling him down, but he remembered the dagger. The blade cut into his fingers and palm, but he didn't dare loosen his grip.

The sea broke once more, and he took a deep breath, putting the hilt between his teeth. When the next wave sent him under, he bit as hard as he could into the soft leather and put the rope on his wrists to the blade.

The rope had already loosened. A few hard rubs frayed it apart, and Jeremy wormed his hands free. He took the blade firmly in his right hand, surfaced for a breath, and put the blade to the rope around his ankles. The next time he surfaced, spitting seawater and contempt, he looked around for the ship. Her lights could not be deciphered from the stars, and there was no moon to betray her. He was alone in a black sea.

Anger overrode the fear that threatened to paralyze Jeremy. "With the stars and any god that commands these waters as my witness, I swear to you, Ombreux, I will have my vengeance against you. I will live, and everyone will know the crimes your black heart has committed. I will not die until I see you die first!"

Sunlight and the sound of water gently lapping woke Jeremy. He was not sure if sleep or unconsciousness had taken him. For a moment, he could not remember what had happened. Then his mind was flooded with the memory of being taken from his bunk and flung into the sea. He remembered the cold and fatigue that had threatened to claim him for the waters. He remembered the sudden wash of warm water around him.

He had come upon the great river in the sea, used by mariners to speed them from the tropical climes bearing the cargo of paradise to their temperate homes. With the stream was the litter found in any thoroughfare—the flotsam and jetsam of shipwrecks, rubbish thrown overboard, debris washed from far lands by storm and flood, masses of seaweed, and the creatures that thrived within them.

Jeremy had found and struggled upon what might have been a broken section of a dinghy or other small boat. Flat with smooth boards nailed together and sealed with sap, it was large enough for two of him to lie upon.

He stared above into a bright blue sky dotted with dollops of meringue clouds. Ah, what he wouldn't do for a bowl full of dobs of the sweet foam *pets*.

Jeremy rubbed his eyes. Once typically an easy feat, sitting up was a challenge at that moment. After grimacing and trying to stretch the muscles that complained the most, he took a look around. It really wasn't worth the bother. The view was the same on all sides, water and sky. Jeremy took a deep, somewhat sore breath and let it out as he drew his knees up to lean upon and ponder his situation.

He was angry, betrayed, and fearful, not only for himself but for his family. Had Ombreux insinuated what Jeremy thought he had? Had the intensity of the moment spawned paranoia in his mind? There had been worse crimes in the history of nobility, but the possibility that a family tragedy had been caused by one of their own was unthinkable.

Jeremy took a moment to feel confused, hurt, and sad, thinking of his parents, his mother. He was sorry he would not return to them, at least not right away. They would think him dead. Would they ever know Ombreux had done this deed? If they found that out before Jeremy returned home, they would have to bear that as well. Were they in danger from Ombreux? Jeremy had to get to his father as quickly as he could to warn him, but at the moment, that was not likely to happen.

He sat in a whirlpool of emotions and feelings until another took his attention. Apparently, one part of his body had not received the news of the previous night's events. It was demanding the release of water, though there would be none to replace it. Jeremy sighed and moved the balance himself on his knees as close to the edge of the makeshift raft as he dared. As he watched his foolish body cast into the useless brine what it would soon be demanding most, he tried to formulate ideas for escaping his predicament.

He had just tucked the family heirlooms back into his breeches and tied the laces when more than an idea caught his eye. His previous surveillance had missed a dark smudge on the furthest horizon to the northwest. It could have been a growing storm or a bank of fog, but it could also be land. The merchant stream was carrying him north. He took his place back in the center of his raft and sat, waiting, his gaze fixed upon that faint chance of hope upon the horizon.

The sun rose, the clouds swelled, and the mirage did not fade. Instead, it became more solid, although it drew no closer. It drifted along the western horizon. Jeremy was convinced it was not a vapor of any sort. If it was land, it was not big, but then anything was better than a plank of wood no larger than two of Jeremy.

The current showed no indication of carrying him closer, and he was not about to let it pull him further from it. Jeremy lay flat, dispersed his weight, and dipped one arm into the water. He paddled first on one side and then slid over to the other to do the same. His eye was quick to return to the horizon, but it also searched the debris around him. It was not long before he found a shard of wood, just over a meter long. Slightly wider than his grasp, it would do. Jeremy re-centered himself and used the wood as a paddle.

The sun reached its zenith and began to roll down the western sky. The clouds swelled, and their feet blackened, but they did not shed rain. They brought increasing relief to Jeremy's sunbaked skin. Though he had a shirt and breeches, his arms were warming past the elbow and his legs past the knee, where his clothing did not reach. His face and the back of his neck also grew sensitive, though he dunked his head now and again to cool it. He found being able to immerse himself in water but unable to drink it an increasingly maddening paradox.

His palms started to ache, became sore, and then threatened to become raw. Having an epiphany before he opened them to bleeding blisters, he cut strips from the end of his shirt with the dagger and wrapped them about his hands. That made the constant work a bit more tolerable.

Jeremy's growing physical complaints were counteracted as his hopeful vision solidified. The sight of a peak of rock sprouting from a bed of thick jungle grew more detailed with each stroke, driving him to the next and the next.

The sun lowered to hide behind the rocky crag in the center of the island, which Jeremy guessed to be perhaps two hundred meters high. From his vantage point, he guessed the beach stretched for four or five kilometers. It was of good size, and that was promising. If there were no human settlements, there was at least a good chance of finding food and water.

At long last, Jeremy came to the island. He let the raft ride a mere swell of a wave onto the shore and stumbled off of it, sprawling onto sand as soft as his mother's rose-scented powder. He stared up at yellowed clouds suffused with late-day sunlight high above. He was only aware of his own body panting and throbbing for a few minutes. After a time, though, he heard the soft hiss of waves on the shore and the rustle of the breeze in the leaves of the forest.

Grudgingly, he sat himself up, nearly failing in the attempt. After a few breaths, he unbound his hands, which weren't quite as sore as he had feared. The cloth left white bands on his otherwise red skin. From there, he found his way to his feet. He had enough wits left to pull his raft further onto the sand and make his way to the edge of the trees. Plant life, especially as thick and green as that before him, would need water, and lots of it. Rain surely provided much of it, as he guessed the island lay just within the tropical climes, yet that rain had to have somewhere to go when it was not sucked into the soil.

A look up and down the beach gave him something of interest to investigate. It was not too far of a walk to a jumble of rock vomited out by the forest onto the sand. There he found more than he had hoped for. A stream ran out from the trees, dancing among the rocks to meet with the sea. A few meters under the shadow of the foliage was a ledge of solid rock, forming a dam and creating a small pool of fresh water that spilled into the brackish mire swirling among the rocks below.

Jeremy plunged his head in, immediately surfacing to begin scooping it into his mouth with his hands. In a few moments, he went from being dried out to waterlogged to a bit nauseous. After the heat and salt of the day, the cool, fresh water was a shock. He sat on the rock ledge to let the sensation pass. His wandering eye caught his own reflection in the water. He turned to take a closer look, not approving. Sailor and soldier though he was, he still preferred clean overall. He used his fingers to comb his hair into some semblance of the way he liked it. Thick and dark with reflective hints, one day it would have the speckles of steel his father's had. He had to undo the tie at the nape of his neck to master it into the short tail that was the fashion of the day.

His eyes were his mother's, blue as the sky on a spring morn. Though reddened by sunburn and shadowed in stubble, he could see the defined jawline and high cheekbones that made him a Nottingdale.

He wasn't quite satisfied with the appearance that met him and decided a bath was in order. He proceeded to strip and stepped over the high ledge to immerse himself in the water. It was just deep enough, perhaps being a meter in depth, all that Jeremy needed. He had never had the need to experience such relief. With it came happiness and gratitude to the forces of fortune that had taken him there.

Refreshed in a way he never thought possible, Jeremy climbed out, knowing that to stay and become cold would be foolhardy, no matter how warm the water seemed. He considered how to don his clothes without a towel to dry himself when he had a thought. Why dress? No one was around. There were no maids who would blush and giggle, no servants to whisper about his brazenness, no elders to admonish him for indecency. Better yet, it was not within the confines of walls. He was alone, with nothing between him and nature, a token reward he would accept for his suffering of the day. He slung his clothes over his shoulder and was able to find a bit of contentment as he made his way back to his landing spot. Although, he thought on his way, he wouldn't have minded if a maid or two were there to catch a glimpse.

Though tired and sore, Jeremy was able to summon the last of his strength and drag his raft to the tree line. He found two trees that had the right distance between them and propped the wood panel against them on their forest side. In looking it over, it was more of a small human gesture to claim one's sleeping spot than any sort of real shelter. If it rained in the night, which glimmers of light on the darkening horizon told of a coming possibility, it might give him a bit of a chance to stay dry.

He wasn't too keen on the fact that it was on the edge of the forest. He could imagine any sort of creature deciding to come and investigate in the night, yet there was no place to make his shelter on the sand, and the thin, grass-like cover of the forest floor seemed to be a bit more comfortable and certainly cleaner than sand. So, Jeremy Nottingdale, the son of a duke, sat himself on the grass under a broken piece of boat and called it home.

At first, he looked to the eastern horizon, watching night rise in the sky. He searched for specks of light or the outline of a shape that could be a ship on the merchant's current, but he saw nothing. He heaved a sigh, disappointed, and remembered what an unhappy position he was in. This was emphasized the next moment when his body told him he was hungry — very hungry. Appeased of the need for water, it presented the next of Jeremy's problems, but of course, gave no suggestions for a solution.

Once again, Jeremy rose and walked the beach along the trees. His luck held. He soon found fruit-bearing trees among the collection of foliage with fruits he recognized, likely the descendants of fruits cast overboard for being rotten or washed ashore after shipwrecks. He found several oblong fruits, *pahpahs*, cherished for their juicy meat. Anticipating a messy meal, he went to the pool, sat on the edge, and took his knife to his finds. Whether by lineage or by Jeremy's deprived state, they were the sweetest, most tender of the fruit he had ever had. He spared as much of the meat as he could when he scraped out the seeds with his knife, leaving him many mouthfuls of the luscious orange fruit.

Later, content and once again clean after washing away the sticky juices, Jeremy sat under his shelter again. A suddenly full stomach forced him to lie down, only to get up in a few minutes and hastily search for a secluded spot away from his camp. Apparently, the rest of his system had not been consulted before his stomach's adamant demand for food. Of course, he had been a bit greedy in his indulgence. After a day of not eating and hard labor, it was hard to resist. Relieved, he picked up where he left off when he returned by lying down. That was the last he remembered until sunrays prodded his eyes.

If moving had been hard after he landed, Jeremy found it excruciating the next morning. Even after his military training at home and time aboard ship, he was not conditioned for what he had done the day before. His hands refused to curl into fists. His fingers made a weak attempt but refused to bow to his command. His skin was hot and tight where the sun had scorched it. At times, it felt as if he were being pricked by tiny metal pins. As maddening as that was, he could not scratch. It would cause his skin to burn anew, raw and sore with a deeper torment that made his teeth ache.

That was the least of his concerns, too. His arms felt like lead weights, sending searing pain at the mere thought of moving them. His legs, chest, and abdominal muscles complained in a similar form. After lying in misery for a few minutes, Jeremy managed to get himself turned over and his feet under him. With grunts, groans, and tottering steps, he paced around on the sand. After moving and stretching a bit, the pain subsided, and he found a rock sit upon.

He was keenly aware that no one was going to bring him a pot of tea and a plate of ham, eggs, and toasted bread with sweetened fruit preserves. Oh, how he wanted it, too, yet, he reminded himself, he was in a much better place than he was upon waking the day before.

Another more conservative meal of *pahpahs* and a wash had him feeling a little better. The sun was already warming the sand and doing its best to make a hot, humid day. Having nothing else to do, Jeremy slowly moved his shelter down the beach to the pool and arranged it in similar fashion as he had before.

He kept his rowing stick close, as well as the strips of cloth from his hands though spots were worn and needled with splinters. These items and the knife were the sum of his possessions. He frowned at them, though not ungrateful, turned, and sat under his shelter to watch the eastern horizon for a speck of white that wasn't a cloud.

His mind troubled him by noting that if he did see a ship, he had no way of letting it know he was there. Fire would be the only way. The ship could see the smoke by day and the flame by night, which was a bit of a problem. Jeremy had never been very good at making fire. He had never thought he would ever need it and scoffed at the lessons of his military survival training. He had always assumed if he ever did find himself in need of fire with no flint, he could rely on someone of his entourage who was sure to be with him.

Of course, he was in his current predicament because his entourage had turned on him. Jeremy looked over the blade with a sigh. Well, not everyone. Why had his savior joined the rest of the traitors? Had he been paid? Threatened? He had taken great care to hide what he did. Was he the only one who cared about Jeremy? Perhaps he wanted rebellion, but not at the cost of the future duke's life.

Jeremy soured and tasted bitterness at the mere thought of his uncle. Why? He had never been close to the man, but they had always been friendly. They had no loyalties to one another other than that which blood-ties required. Even those were not good enough, apparently. Jeremy had not understood the wary countenance his father assumed around the man. Uncle Ombreux had always seemed so genial, laughing often and bold in his speech. Of course, now Jeremy saw it all for what it was—a ruse to influence people to trust him. His mother did not even need the show. She always was delighted in the presence of her older brother, eager to please and serve him. For what reason, Jeremy could not say. He mimed his mother's reaction simply because he loved her. Until the night before last, he had never had a reason to share his father's aloofness.

His father had been right. He protested letting Jeremy go away, but Ombreux offered his presence on the expedition as a comfort. It was his mother who had finally persuaded the Duke. Now his father was without a captain, less a merchant ship and crew laden with cargo, and without a son and heir.

Angry, Jeremy stood. He *would* make fire. He *would* get home. Anything else was unacceptable.

Two hours later, Jeremy threw his stick to the ground and gave a sweeping kick that sent it and the rowing stick across the sand. He groaned, clutching his shoulder and hopped gingerly on the leg that had kicked. It had not taken long for his tortured muscles to mutiny. His arms had complained as he whittled the end of a small, thin stick to a sharp point. He used the knife to twist a small hole in the rowing stick. Being flat, hard wood, he thought it would work fine. With a bit of dry grass in the hole and plenty more close by, he had felt pretty clever.

He rubbed and rubbed and rubbed. He had made fire, all

right, but only in his arms, back, and chest. The worst part was smoke appeared very soon after he started. The grass smoldered, but try as he might, he could not get a flame to leap to life.

He sat, then lay in the shade of his lean-to. When he had caught his breath, he rose gingerly, stripped, and eased himself into his personal bath. He lay floating, watching the lambent sunlight dancing through the canopy above, trying not to think of anything that would make him angry.

The water felt good, as it always did. As hot as he had been when he got in, the water had not been a shock to enter. It was cool, but not cold, perhaps because of the tropic environ. Yet, there were charted islands in the area with volcanic hot springs. It was possible, especially with the rocky crag standing over the island, that this water had a hot nativity. He would have to hike inland one day and investigate.

In the meantime, his stomach began another pesky demand for food. At least his fire endeavor wasn't completely wasted. It had given him an idea to help him with his present, recurring problem. He left his bath and took a moment to dunk his clothes. He spread them over two large, white rocks on the beach. Between the sun and the heat of the rocks, they would be dry shortly. Next, Jeremy took a short walk into the woods, a pleasant experience with just himself, although he kept a very sharp eye out for insects and where they intended to land. He did not have to go far to find some dead branches and vine. He broke off smaller limbs until he had eight sticks of similar size in hand and one twice their length.

Back at his camp, he lashed the sticks together with the vines. It took a little while, but when he was done, he had what looked like an eight-legged tent frame that stood to his waist. It was crudely made and a little uneven. He doubted it would hold the weight of canvas to make a tent, but it would serve the purpose he had made it for.

He found another stick of harder wood in his search that was perhaps a meter long. Using his knife, he sharpened one end to a point. It took longer to make than his useless fire stick, but he hoped that one would serve him better. Once he was satisfied with its point, Jeremy made his way to the water.

The beach was rockier than where he had landed. As he made his way south, the beach rose and become a wall of rock. Coral, most likely, or perhaps it was a frozen lava flow, shorn clean by the gnawing ocean. Whatever it was, it created a good place to fish. There were no waves to speak of, even though the tide was rising. Jeremy waded in and followed the wall, which rose another half-meter or more above his head. Broken segments made channels and paths through the miniature canyon. Jeremy had to take care not to step on broken rock and shell. The water was clear and only softly undulating, so he saw every step he took and the quarry he sought.

Flashes of white, grey, and yellow betrayed the fish as they grazed on the sea greens growing on the submerged rock. Some were tiny and hardly worth a look. Others, probably feeding on the little ones, warranted a cautious lifting of the stick from Jeremy's shoulder before they flitted away. The water lapped at his thighs, with larger swells sometimes becoming cat paws swiping at his dangling mouse-toy. The water actually felt a little chilly when that happened, a fact to which his manhood made a visual protest. It didn't seem to want any part of the goings-on and would try to hide from time to time. Jeremy ignored it, intent on silencing the other troops of his body that, for once, were clamoring louder than it was.

He approached some of the larger fish and concentrated on moving very slowly. They still kept a wary distance, but no longer fled at his approach. Jeremy found a pocket in the rock, an open space perhaps five meters across. He ventured in and waited, intending to catch as many fish as he could and dry the meat on the crude rack he had made. It would take a few days for it to dry properly, but the sun and wind would do the job well.

In the meantime, he would eat more *pahpahs*, look for other plants, and he was sure he could easily spear or catch the crabs he'd seen foraging on the rocks and on the sandy seabed between them. Those he could eat right away. He could also eat fish raw, but he intended to keep trying to light a fire. The cool of evening and night would make the work a little less torturous. As soon as he had a fire, he wouldn't have to wait for the fish to dry.

"Ouch!"

Any sense of security the fish were gaining vanished at his shout and the subsequent sloshing stumble that nearly put him under. Jeremy gritted his teeth against the sharp pain in the ball of his foot. He hobbled over to the rock wall and pulled his foot up to rest against his knee. He reached down, felt a hard, sharp edge embedded in his foot and through the shimmering water could see a white triangle of broken shell right under his big toe.

Jeremy braced himself and pulled. It came out easily, but not without pain, leaving a wisp of red to float and bob in the clear water.

He was relieved to have the shard out, but the cut itself, immersed in saltwater, stung like hell. He knew it would pass. He'd had much worse. He pinched the pad of his foot to close the slice and try to discourage the bleeding. It was stubborn. Red ribbons still drifted lazily from his foot. He sighed, already over the pain and getting impatient. He wanted to get back to fishing.

After a minute, he let go, but he still bled. He stretched his leg, which was still sore and greatly protesting, and pulled it back up to keep pressure on it. He did this a few times. Each time he thought he had stopped leaking and let go, the red trail poured from his foot again. After the fourth or fifth time, he gave another impatient sigh, pinched, and looked up to have his anger replaced by fear.

A shark had entered the pool, a big one, a meter and a half or so. It tossed its head and tail back and forth, tasting the water for the scent.

"Gods!" Jeremy forgot his foot and remembered his spear. A quick glance up the rock was enough to tell him he could not scale it. There were nooks for footholds, but no place to grab. It was too high to jump and reach the top. Jeremy eyed the beast as it cruised along the opposite wall. It turned and made an oblique approach in his direction. He didn't know a lot about sharks, but he did know enough to know the danger he was in.

Jeremy licked the salt of the sea and sweat from his lips. The tang of fear was stronger on his tongue. He held the spear ready, watching the shark, gauging the distance, searching for a mark. He would have to make a damn good strike. Where was the best place to hit a shark? The eye, obviously, but those were only small, wavering spots to him. The head? He guessed so, but could his stick go through?

The beast moved past him two meters away and made a sharp turn back directly at him. Jeremy hefted the spear, sending a prayer to whatever gods might hear him, and tensed to deliver the blow.

"Hai!"

Jeremy was startled enough to turn and look up to see a face with two arms reaching down to him. He threw the spear on top of the rock wall, made a lunge, and grabbed. A frenzy of grunting, grasping, and pulling himself up ended with Jeremy flat on hot rock, looking up at the sky.

Two gasps preceded a whoosh of relief, and his brain began to think again with *what the devil?*

Jeremy looked up and then sat up, amazed. A woman, bare from the waist up, sat on the edge of the rock, looking down into the pool. Her skin was the color of dark clover honey glowing with the light of morning. She curved everywhere, but her legs, her arms, and her waist all flowed, undulating smoothly, declaring femininity and strength. Her raven-dark hair fell in a thick veil to nearly touch the rock, and about her waist was a linen that must have been a dress at one time. Rather than hide her, the red cloth embellished the strong legs it covered, enhancing them for the eye to notice.

Jeremy had never seen a woman like this before. She turned, and he forgot about her body.

He had never cared for hunting deer. The dark, dewy, heavily lashed eyes of the creatures always made him pity them. The eyes that met his banished all sympathy he had ever spent on the beasts. Widened still in alarm, the doe-eyes before him made him wish to comfort her, though he was the one who had been in danger. Her face was as smooth and flowing as the rest of her, with high, firm cheekbones and a long, narrow nose. She reminded him of the delicate and exotic black-masked faces of those cats from the mysterious shores of the Eastern edge of the world. Her lips were thin and wide, deep as pomegranate and looked as sweet.

One of her hands reached out and laid long, slender fingers on his leg. Her voice came, sultry and full, not yet deepened by age, but it was also not the voice of a child. The part of Jeremy's brain that still functioned noted she must have been close to his age, perhaps a little older. Of course, he paid no attention to that part of his mind. He could only focus on one thing at a time, and he was working on the part attempting to decipher what she had said. Unfortunately, it had nothing to offer him. As he was starting to formulate a reply, her gaze looked him over, probably much as he had done to her. He hadn't a stitch of clothing on and had gone through a scare in cold water to boot.

Her gaze had returned to his face. She offered another phrase which Jeremy still did not understand. His brain caught up, though.

He countered with, "Do you speak my language?"

She gave no hint of comprehension. Jeremy tried again with another of the Empirical languages. Again, there was no recognition, but she did speak in response. He did not know the words but was able to note they were of a different tongue than she had used before. She was putting him to the same test.

He sat up, taking on a more dignified pose than splayed-out-in-surprise. He queried her again and again, starting to tap into languages he was not fluent in but knew enough of to get by. She knew nearly as many as he did. This was an educated person, or at least well-traveled. He had originally used the most common languages in his life. Then, making an assumption based on her appearance, he offered those of the *Ladinari* descent of the empire south and east of his homeland. He scraped among the eastern and then far northern tongues. Then, his ear caught a word among those she offered.

"Dai-noss."

"Dainoss?" he repeated. She looked at him hopefully.

Yes, of course, the tribal people of the far west across the ocean from where the most valued goods in trade came. He had only learned a few words and phrases and knew any merchant worth his trade could speak the language. First, he wanted to make sure he understood her. He said a few words he knew in the language for wine, meat, fruit, necklace, fish, ending with, "Dainoss, yes?"

Her face lit up. "Dainoss! *Ahu, ahu!*"

Jeremy was elated at her double yes response but had to let it fade. He had expended most of his vocabulary, with the exception of *I will trade,* and a phrase that, put politely, meant *that is a very appealing woman.*

18

The appealing woman before him offered a sentence in the language, but Jeremy had to shake his head with a shrug. He could only offer the weak explanation, telling her *speak trade* in Dainoss, which used the remainder of his non-object repertoire. He could only hope it translated at least half as well as he intended.

She understood they were at an impasse, nodding with comprehension. "Speak trade, *ahu*." She looked away in frustration and contemplation.

Jeremy wanted to ask her a thousand questions, but he didn't even know how to ask her name. At least he could get around that. "I am Jeremy," he said, causing her to look up again. He tapped his chest. "Jeremy."

His words and actions brought a smile of understanding. "Zher-ah-mee?" she repeated carefully, with a hint of a roll to the *R*.

Close enough. "*Ahu*."

"Zher-ah-mee," she said again. She placed her hand on her chest. "Sanura."

The way she said it, it came out in three clipped syllables, the *R* almost rolling again, but even less, so that to Jeremy's ear it could have been a *D* or a *T*.

"San-oora." Jeremy's tongue automatically melted the syllables together. His language was the most legato of those of his knowledge. He knew it was considered genteel and romantic. He had often used it to woo women who didn't know a word, speaking nonsense about their imbecile brothers and pompous fathers who were stupid enough to leave them unescorted with Jeremy Nottingdale on the prowl.

The more insulting he was about the men who brought the women to the manor as baubles to show off, the warmer those women got between the thighs. His accent, what had always been his ally, his weapon, his spell, he found himself uncomfortable with for the first time. That certainly wasn't how she had said her name. The way she said it was — well, the way he was accustomed to saying things. It was a simple word that implied deeper, exotic, sensual things. The word itself was a pleasure.

He tried again. "Saw-new-rah."

The second syllable was closer this time. How could he make an emphasized *U* staccato?

She accepted it, though, smiling and nodding. "*Ahu*, Sanura. Zher-ah-mee."

Jeremy nodded. They at least had that much, but what about the rest of it? What was she doing there? How had she survived, and for how long?

Sanura rose. She went to what looked like a segment of netting that had four *pahpahs* in it. A couple more of them had rolled out. She gathered them back and lifted the bundle. She was foraging.

Jeremy stood and almost ended up on his back again. Sanura turned in alarm at his bark of pain. He had forgotten his foot. He put his weight on the heel and managed to stay upright as she came to him, concerned. He immediately waved her fear away. She took his arm to steady him, asking something. Her face translated that she was asking of the problem.

To show her and to check it himself, Jeremy lifted his foot and saw the bottom covered in red. Apparently, it had not much appreciated scaling the rock wall.

Sanura exclaimed, but Jeremy again dismissed it. "No, no, it's nothing." He lowered his foot and made to begin his return to camp.

"Zher-ah-mee . . ." She seemed to want to protest but did not know how.

"It's not far." He pointed toward his camp as he retrieved his spear. "Just there." Although she didn't know the words, he was sure she gathered the meaning from his gestures and tone. She slung the net bag over her shoulder and took his arm with her other hand. He used the spear to help him keep balance and made his careful way over the rock.

He had caught no fish, but he might have found something much better.

CHAPTER TWO

Jeremy dipped his feet in the pool of fresh water and couldn't help a sigh of contentment. He carefully cleaned the cut in his foot as best he could. He had managed not to get any sand in it. To make certain, he encouraged it to bleed again. He gave Sanura the opportunity to drink and had a bit himself before he took a quick dip to refresh himself and wash off the saltwater. She submerged her arms and splashed a bit on her face as he bathed. After, she sat on the rock ledge looking out to the sea thoughtfully.

When Jeremy emerged, he immediately wrapped his foot in the strips of cloth he had saved. He found his clothes and made himself decent. Sanura watched, seemingly out of having nothing else to do, offering neither looks of approval nor disappointment as he covered himself. His ego slightly bruised, Jeremy sat beside her with a sigh.

"Well, now what are we to do?"

Sanura sighed herself and made a statement of some sort. She stood, looking over his tiny settlement, and gave a gasp, pointing to where his knife lay on a rock under the lean-to. She spoke again. Jeremy retrieved it, not sure of what she wanted.

"This?" he asked. "Do you want to see it?" He handed it to her.

She seemed very pleased, her body language conveying excitement as she took it. She turned it over, feeling the blade. She grasped it in her hand, testing the weight and making a few motions with it that were surprisingly adept. She made a statement, obviously approving, as she handed the hilt to Jeremy.

He couldn't help an intrigued smile. "You are familiar with blades? That's unusual."

Most women he knew were trained to blanch and flutter their fans at such horrible things as weapons. Of course, when he had them alone with a sword at his side, he knew the fluttering was only to quell the hot flush the heroic image brought to them. They would never let anyone else see that, though, and not a one would ever hold a blade. He had offered before. The most any ever ventured was a gentle touch to the hilt before blushing and turning away. This one looked as though she wouldn't hesitate to stick it between his ribs and knew exactly how to do it. It was his turn to feel a slight flush at the vision of the person before him enacting the drama of a duel or defense. He decided he would have to dwell on that later.

In the meantime, Sanura had gone to his drying rack. She seemed to be trying to figure out what it was.

"For the fish I wanted to catch," he said. "For *dago*," saying the closest word he knew for what he meant in the best way he could, hoping she understood he meant fish.

Her face furrowed in thought, and she bit her lower lip. She offered a word he didn't know, said *Dago*, then another few words, pointing inland. When it was clear he didn't understand, she gave a small sigh and went to pick up her net bag. She motioned for Jeremy to follow, stepped up the low ledge, and walked inland along the stream. Jeremy tucked the blade carefully into his waistline at his back and let her lead him into the jungle.

The environment was immediately different. The smell of decaying leaves and rich soil hung in the still, humid air. Myriad plants and flowers climbed over one another, competing for sun, soil, and water. Jeremy and Sanura both waved at bugs now and again. Jeremy had felt them at the beach but was largely able to ignore them. Either there were fewer there or the ocean breeze blew them away. Here, the humans seemed to draw them.

Jeremy was largely distracted by the array of plant life that surrounded him. As he had seen before, there were some he recognized, but there was a good deal more he had never seen before. Naturally, he wondered which might be edible, usable, or poisonous. Perhaps Sanura knew some of them. He tried thinking of ways he might ask her at some point.

Then, "*Pistanos!*" he exclaimed, using the ancient word since he didn't know the Dainoss word.

Sanura stopped and turned as Jeremy stepped carefully into the plants and plucked a small bunch of the long, thick-rinded yellow fruit. The one he separated was a touch green and hard to snap open at the stem, but once started it would be easy. He saw a few more that were ripe and took them, as well as one that had fallen to the ground recently. The rest were black and rotten. Sanura smiled as she opened her net bag.

"Thank you." Jeremy set the *pistanos* in, keeping three for himself, and they continued. The fruit had a bit of the dry, tart taste of the rind, but it was delicious. The white meat inside was soft and sweet. Chewing on the candy-like fruit, surveying a tropical paradise, following a beautiful woman to who-knew-where, Jeremy actually felt a touch of contentment, perhaps a little excitement. It was the closest to happy he had felt on the island so far. His confidence that his fate would be satisfactory in the end was on the rise.

They followed the stream as it wound its way through the forest. There were more fruit plants, many flowers of all sorts, thick trees, waving ferns, and tangled vines in a tapestry as intricate as any that hung on the walls of his home. Though there were sounds of small animals all around—high and low—Jeremy didn't see a one. Birds, however, were in great abundance, all vocalizing in a cacophony of song, chatter, and screeching that made one incoherent melody through the trees.

As they went, the ground rose under their feet. Most of the trip was made stepping upwards on the path, gradually, but enough to gather the sense of elevation.

Sanura stopped at what appeared to be a wall of broken rock. A stream danced down, nearly vertical, ricocheting among protrusions and boulders before tumbling into a small pool only a stride across before continuing down the slope in a more civil manner.

Sanura knotted two corners of her net bag together and said something. She pointed up the rock and put her head and one arm through the bag, keeping its easily bruised bundle in front of her. She climbed upwards, using the rock as stairs.

Jeremy looked up the shaded rock with some doubt. As interesting as the walk was, it could not distract him completely from the pain in his foot. He had been walking with most of the weight on his heel and had a limp in his stride. He wondered how far they had to go and how much more painful it was going to get.

It was not so steep as to warrant true climbing, but each step took effort and many times a grab to the rock to pull oneself forward. This grew wearisome, and the soreness in Jeremy's arms and chest turned to pain quickly, the rest of his body following suit. He gritted his teeth and pushed on. At first, Jeremy watched Sanura to find the next place to grab or step. As he got the feel of it, despite his discomfort, he found he appreciated this angle of vision. He admired the way Sanura's body moved, strong and confident in spite of the physical demand. The rounded curves of her muscled rump moved enticingly under the red linen, suggesting only enough of what he could not see to make it even more alluring. Sunbeams danced off of her silky cascade of hair as it waved back and forth over her back and down to her waist. When she turned at the right angle, he could catch a glimpse of her breasts, firm and round as any *pahpah* and most likely just as sweet upon the lips.

Jeremy averted his eyes, blaming the tropical heat for the flush in his cheeks. Now was certainly not the time for that. He paused to let her get a few more steps ahead, letting himself feel his foot throb to distract him. He then watched where he stepped instead of the vision of empowered womanhood before him.

At last Sanura came to level ground. She turned to Jeremy with a smile as he summited, turned about to face east, and gasped with awe at the scene. The tops of trees waved at the height of his waist. Before him, facing east, a slope of deep green leaves rolled down to turquoise water, marbled with jade that stretched halfway to the horizon, deepened to blue, and further, the near black of deeper water.

Jeremy turned about, seeing for kilometers to the east, north, and west. The view to the south was blocked by the naked peak of rock, towering high above, still wide and dominant even at this height. Before it on the ledge was a pool. This one was much wider and longer than Jeremy's bath. It was large enough that it would take a few strokes of swimming to get from end to end. It was narrower side to side, but still more than a leap across.

The water at its rocky edges was clear and darkened going down to the center which appeared to be quite deep, as Jeremy could not find any defining bottom. The end of the pool spilled over the end of the ledge. It was the headwater of the stream that fell down the rocks and made its way to what Jeremy considered his pool.

Sanura turned away, and Jeremy followed her. At the base of the peak was a jumble of rock that melded into the solid body of the crag. A jagged shadow betrayed a cavern at its base. Sanura stepped around the boulders and between the parted curtain of rock. Jeremy entered the mountain with her and was again amazed. Though uneven, the floor of the cavern was smooth, perhaps a lava flow frozen in the moment of its birth. Two men of Jeremy's height could lie foot to foot and touch the walls with their outstretched fingers. Going back, the cave went further. It narrowed at the far end but did not quite close.

This was not the greatest source of his wonder, though. The very fact he could see these details was. He was being helped by a small flicker of flame sitting in an indentation near the mouth of the cave.

"You have fire!"

Jeremy's exclamation was enough to make Sanura turn away from where she had gone toward the end of her small home. Her smile did so much more than words at conveying that she knew how important it was, how hard it was to make, and how exciting it was to see it. Jeremy mirrored her expression, his happiness swelling exponentially. Yes, his day of fishing had been lucky after all.

Compared to Jeremy's lean-to, Sanura's cave was a palace. As Jeremy looked around, he concluded she had been there for a little while. A pile of large, green leaves was against the wall opposite of where she was placing the fruit from her bag. They overlay a gathering of what might have been long, dry grasses. He could not quite tell. She had the fire and wood to feed the fire.

Along the other wall where she knelt was a collection of fruit as well as halves of coconut husks stacked together, fraying palm leaves, shells, an assortment of other items of the like, and two large oblong bowls of some sort.

Curiosity overcoming him, Jeremy approached to find they were turtle shells, big ones, but not too large to lift, obviously.

They were turned on their backs and held water up to the brim. Jeremy thought it odd. Why bring water in here when there was a whole pool of it outside? His musing was interrupted when Sanura picked up one of the husk halves and laid leaves of some sort within. She scooped a small amount of water into it and crushed the leaves with a rock.

She said something to him as she worked, but he had no idea what. Then, she pointed to his foot and made a motion for him to remove the bandage. Jeremy sat on a rock and obeyed. She guided him to lay his foot against his other leg and poured some of the mixture over the cut. Jeremy gritted his teeth at the sting, but it passed quickly. She handed the bowl to him, taking out the leaves and motioning for him to drink as she took the cloth to rewrap his foot. Surprised and intrigued, Jeremy could only comply, hoping she knew what she was doing. Her bearing certainly exuded confidence. She laid the leaves against his wound and bound his foot again.

She stood, saying something more, seeming pleased. She presented a question. Through hand and body motions, he gathered she was asking if he could walk more. His tortured body wanted nothing more than to lie still for a full day, yet his interest was sparked to do anything she suggested. He nodded and made the same motions.

She smiled and went back to her collection. Jeremy helped himself to a couple of scoops of the cool water as she rummaged around. She came back with something that looked like a cord of thin rope or twine. She held it up and made a statement, her smile showing she didn't seem to mind that he didn't understand. She took up her net, put a flat piece of shell the size of her hand in it, motioned for him to follow, and led the way out of the cave.

They descended from the rock ledge on the west side. The going was perhaps a little easier, but just as rocky. A few unfortunate steps made Jeremy wince. Otherwise, the pain in his foot was subsiding, and he kept stride with the vivacious woman before him. When they reached more level ground, Sanura kept on through the trees. They came to the end of the trees a bit sooner than if they had taken the eastern path back to Jeremy's spot. Here the beach was a little different, not as rocky, and wider. Ankle-high swells lapped the sand in shallow water for many yards beyond.

Sanura turned south. Jeremy could see that the island bent from a north-south direction towards the southwest. At the inner elbow of the curve, the beach was widest, and there appeared to be a marsh or tidal grassland. They walked the edge of the trees, side by side.

Jeremy watched Sanura as she scanned the ground and forest for anything of interest. Either she had been taught how to survive in such a place or she had learned quickly. Jeremy desperately wanted to know her story. Surely there were people in the world who missed her, loved her, and were heartbroken, thinking her dead. Parents, siblings, then he thought, a husband? A lover? Children?

He cast a quick glance to her exposed midsection. No, certainly no distortion or marks of childbearing there. Of course, she was an unusually fit woman in his eyes. Perhaps if women were active to the extent that she was, the scars of pregnancy were erased. Women of Jeremy's world were shaped well but did lead sedentary, pampered lives. They kept their figures as long as they could, and only became fuller as children and fine living accumulated on them. Not one of them would or could trek through the jungle and climb rocky paths, and they certainly wouldn't pull a strange man from an imminent shark attack and give him a tour of the island half-naked.

Jeremy became aware that his thoughts were making him smile. He tried to quell it and focus on the seriousness of the situation.

It worked, but only to a certain extent.

A few times he caught her sending a glance his way, until she saw he noticed and pointed to his foot. "*Tayna?*"

He nodded, "*Ahu, tayna.* Good."

She nodded as well and went back to her searching.

It was not long before they reached the crook of the land. Sanura set her bag down by a tree and took out the flat shell. She looked out at the grasses, and a thoughtful frown settled on her face. She looked from Jeremy's foot to the marsh and seemed to make a decision.

She said something to him, clearly instructing or giving an order. It was clarified as she lifted her hand before him, her palm out. She wanted him to stay there. Not having the slightest idea of what she was doing, Jeremy nodded and found a bit of sandy grass by the tree to sit on. Satisfied, Sanura waded into the grasses that reached to her waist. This made an intriguing illusion. Jeremy found his smile was creeping up again. A few meters in, she bent down and disappeared. He heard grass being struck with much rustling and hacking. Grasses waved and jumped. Now and again Sanura surfaced for a moment, moving something, and dove in again.

After a few minutes, she rose and lifted a bundle of the grass over her shoulder. She made her way back to Jeremy and dropped it at his feet. He could see why she had told him to stay. Her feet and legs were covered in sandy muck halfway to her knees. She said something, taking a good handful of the grass at the base where she had cut it with the shell. She went to a large tree, a kind whose root dropped down from the branches and grew to become part of the trunk. Jeremy believed they were called *banian*. Regardless of its name, Sanura flogged it with the grass. After a few good whacks, she pointed to the base of the tree where the chaff and some insects had fallen. So, they were threshing the grass. Jeremy nodded. Sanura handed the clump to Jeremy and motioned for him to follow suit. He complied, and she wandered back into the marsh.

As he flailed the innocent tree, Jeremy found his thoughts beginning to question himself. What *was* he doing? Not only with the grass, but with this woman. Just because they had met didn't mean they were obliged to stay together. He certainly didn't have to follow her around and do her bidding.

Jeremy sighed, turning the grass in his hand. No, he didn't have to. He wanted to. This was survival. People had a better chance of surviving with other people. It was also the gentlemanly thing to do, to help a damsel in distress. Although—Jeremy thought with a look toward the marsh—he seemed to be the one to have been in distress.

Besides, he continued to reason, she had helped him, probably had saved his life. He was intrigued by and interested in her. It was nice to know he wasn't trapped on the island alone. No, he decided, he shouldn't question himself. They needed each other, and they both knew it.

Jeremy stayed to the shady side of the tree as the sun, already a good way to the sea when they arrived, lowered further. It did not take long for him to become wet with perspiration. His sunburn prickled maddeningly. With oncoming thirst also came the reminder that nothing but fruit for two days was no way to sustain a man.

Flies and insects buzzed around him, making his skin crawl. His face especially itched from dirt, bugs, sweat, and the incoming beard he was unaccustomed to. Worse than all that was the mutiny by every muscle in his body. Every one burned and ached. He found himself pausing quite often to stretch or to rest and let the ache subside. Had any of his marching comrades been there to witness his performance, they would surely have many emasculating comments to add.

It was getting to the point he almost felt dizzy when Sanura came with yet another batch. He had already gone through a large pile she had collected. He was trying to come up with a way to ask how much more she was going to cut when she grabbed a handful and beat it against the tree. He was immediately humbled as she seemed to attack the tree where he might have been using painting strokes. Well, if he had help and if they were almost done, he could bear it a bit longer. She was just as sweaty, dirty, and bug-pestered as he was. If she could stand it, so could he. As he worked, he couldn't help but study the image, taking notes on this new sub-category of female he had found.

Finally, the last of the grass failed to shed. Sanura stacked it on the rest, blowing a breath. She looked at Jeremy with a smile, a pleased statement, and untied the knot of her skirt to let it fall. Before Jeremy could react, she left him, walking across the sand, the sun casting a shadow as long and dark as her hair behind her. He needed no instruction for this. Jeremy also shed his clothes and followed her to the water.

It was very shallow. Even at ten meters or so from shore, it only came to his thighs. It was enough for them, though. They fell in gratefully. The water, though warm, cooled them. Jeremy turned to sit, reclining on his elbows with the water to his chin. He sighed in relief. Sanura knelt, splashing her face and scooping water over herself a few more times. She sighed as well, wiping drops from her face, looking distantly into the water.

The sea, shocking turquoise against the land, was gin clear all around. Infused with the light of the lowering sun, it made the distorted curves and angles of her body shimmer. Her hair floated on the surface, undulating lazily as though some kind of satin seaweed.

The part of Jeremy's mind that still hadn't realized he was a castaway thought if he weren't so tired, hurt, hungry, sore, and thirsty, he would likely have a hard time controlling himself at that moment. Even so, he could probably forget about all of that if necessary.

Sanura's focus locked on to something, and she moved forward slowly. He watched, curious. His angle was such that he could not see what she was doing. After a minute or two of intense observation, she moved forward quickly, had a brief chase, then lifted a squirming cluster of legs from the water.

Jeremy exclaimed in surprise and delight. It wasn't the biggest crab he had ever seen, but it was a crab. That was the only important thing. He looked around. It was not long before he pulled a blue water spider from its feeding grounds. Sanura, in the meantime, found a second. They were both standing now. After sharing tremendous smiles, they walked to land, still searching the water for more.

Sanura exclaimed and pointed with one of her flailing catches. Jeremy soon had a crab in both hands as well. Careful to hold them at a safe distance from their bare flesh, the two slogged their way out of the sea and to the tree line. Sanura only had to put one down for a moment as she popped the other in her bag. Though attempting to escape, the first was quick to follow, with Jeremy's right behind. She found some large leaves from a tall bush nearby, nearly as broad and long as her bag. She slid them in, lining it and enclosing the crabs and her other finds in them. When she was done, she tied it and gave Jeremy a smile, pinching at him playfully with her fingers. Jeremy laughed and nodded. Yes, very clever.

He had clothed himself as she had taken anti-pinching measures. She wrapped her skirt about herself again, which Jeremy saw was one length of cloth, and searched in the trees. She gave a look to the sun to see where it was in its journey to the sea, picked up another leaf, and showed it to Jeremy.

"*Pistanos*," she said, using her hands to show the size she desired and looked around.

She was looking for the broad leaves of the fruit tree. Jeremy nodded. "*Ahu, pistanos.*" He searched as well.

She found some thick, woody vines and used her shell to cut several lengths as they searched.

"Ah, there!" Jeremy pointed when he saw the long, wide, deep shiny green leaves they sought.

The plant also had a few ripe fruits. Sanura plucked two, handing one to Jeremy. He peeled it and nearly swallowed it whole as Sanura ate hers, looking over the leaves. She held the long, round fruit in her mouth, raising Jeremy's eyebrow, and cut one leaf off at the stem. She took another bite, examined, held, and cut. She did this a few times, discarded the peel and cut more.

When she had nearly a dozen of the leaves, she gathered them at the stems and tied them together with a length of the vine. She handed the cluster to Jeremy, who slung them over his back. She picked a few more *pistanos,* and they made their way back to the beach.

Sanura used the twine she had brought to bundle up the grasses. Jeremy set his burden down and helped when he could. She made loose loops in two places toward one end on a flat side of the bale. She sighed, cast a look to the sun, then pointed to Jeremy and to their two bundles. He understood and went to the grass. It was heaviest. He started to pick it up, but Sanura stopped him, motioning for him to kneel. She set the bundle up long-ways at his back, brought the loops up on either side, and guided his arms through. He stood with only minimal strain to himself, appreciating her innovation.

Meanwhile, Sanura quickly made a few loops around the end of the leaves and dropped the loops over her head, clasping it at her chest with one hand. The other took up her treasure bag, and they made the trek back up the beach.

It was not easy. It was not comfortable. They slowed when

they turned into the jungle, then more as they scaled the rocks. They stopped a few times, Jeremy's thirst going from torment to torture, his body protesting with agony. He knew Sanura had to be as uncomfortable, though perhaps not in as much pain. They pushed on, Jeremy envisioning the pool of water at the end of the trail.

When they finally reached the flat ledge, Jeremy gladly wormed out of his burden. He made straight for the pool.

"No, no!"

Though not the same as Jeremy would pronounce the word, Sanura's exclamation startled Jeremy enough to stop him. She took his arm and led him into the cave. They indulged in several husks of water from the turtle shells. Jeremy sat and leaned against the wall when he'd had his fill, slightly nauseous but relieved.

Sanura had apparently learned better and paced herself. Between slow gulps, she looked him over. She gave a gentle touch to his shoulder and made a comment. He winced slightly. The seared skin was still very sensitive. She took a last gulp and rose, going to her stockpile. When she returned, she had a husk with thick pointed spears of a plant that Jeremy immediately recognized.

"*Aloe!*"

He was no herbologist, but he knew the benefits of it. He helped her to squeeze the gelatinous innards of the leaves out into the husk. She smeared it over his raw skin as he continued to milk the plant. The cool contrast of the *aloe* against his hot, itchy skin made Jeremy's back teeth feel as if they were cringing. He clenched them and kept working, reveling in the relief the plant brought.

They had used all of what she had brought when Sanura finished covering his scalded skin. She rubbed the residue off of her hands onto her own arms and stretched them with a sigh. Jeremy grunted when he tried to do the same. Sanura saw his pained movements and made an inquiry. He had no idea how to answer. He was too tired to try to think of a way.

She motioned to his foot. "*Tayna?*"

It was throbbing with the rest of his body. He shook his head, making a weary motion at it which included his physical being in general.

Sanura immediately got up and again went to her collection. She came back with a husk and the leaves she had used before, pouring water into the husk. She repeated the treatment she had given him earlier. She gave him more of the liquid to drink than before. Jeremy tolerated it, as it seemed to have helped him through the afternoon. When she was done, Sanura cast a glance to the coloring light outside. She went back to her corner, and Jeremy watched as she did something strange.

She emptied the collection bag, leaving the still squirming crabs within its confines after the leaves were removed. She took a coconut husk and tore bits and pieces of different things from her collection—a rind of *pahpahs*, a bit of *pistanos* peel, a small handful of nuts or some such thing, and some leaves she had collected. She also took the sharp rock and cut off one of the smaller legs of the crabs. She went to Jeremy. She pointed to his knife, making a pleading query, it seemed.

"This?" He handed it to her.

She seemed to utter a gratuity and offered a hesitant question, pointing at him, but above. He had no idea what she wanted, looking behind him as if it would give him a clue.

Sanura reached out and touched his head, taking a pinch of hair. She inquired again and made a motion with the knife.

He made the gesture himself. "You wish to cut my hair?" Jeremy had thought this woman could be no more of an enigma.

Apologetic, Sanura nodded, taking a pleading pose.

Jeremy knew that asking why would get him nowhere. The

only way he would find out was to see. He shrugged and nodded.

Very carefully, Sanura cut a few strands of his hair, setting them carefully on a small leaf in the coconut. She took it, the knife, and the coconut she had been drinking from with more water in it and went outside. Since he had a small investment in this activity, Jeremy couldn't let it go by unobserved. He rose slowly with a few grunts. His exhausted and starved muscles were already starting to stiffen. As he struggled to his feet, Sanura returned. She took a few small sticks from her store of firewood and held a splayed branch of dead leaves in the fire. It caught quickly, and she carried it outside.

Jeremy followed her to where she had set the two halves of coconut. She knelt beside them, laying the branch on the ground before her. She laid the other sticks on top of it. Sensing an air of gravity, Jeremy lowered himself on a rock to observe.

Sanura watched the setting sun before her as she encouraged the fire. When the bottom of the orange orb touched the water, she lifted a flaming stick, holding it between her flat palms. She closed her eyes, lowered her head, and spoke in a tone of address with an even, measured cadence. After her statement, the stick was returned to the fire, and she took an item from the husk. She held her hands out to the sun with the item in her cupped hands and recited another phrase. Her hands opened, dropping its contents into the fire.

She repeated the action and recitation with another item, then another. She did this several times and took the knife, holding it the same way. Jeremy grew concerned that she would drop it in the fire. It wouldn't hurt the blade, but he didn't want the leather hilt to be damaged.

Sanura only passed it over the flame, however, and set the knife aside. She knelt as she was, watching the sun in the fast seconds before its last sliver slid into the water. For a few seconds, he was hypnotized into watching the sun melt into the sea, then it was gone. Sanura picked up the other husk, repeated the gesture with a longer statement, and poured the water out over the fire, dousing it. She picked up the husks and knife and rose. Going to Jeremy, holding the knife out, she made motions with words that led him to believe she was asking for the use of it for another task. He nodded wearily, motioning what he hoped was understood as a grant of her request. She uttered the phrase he thought was a gratuity and went into the cave.

Jeremy sat, fatigued and pondering. It was obviously a religious ritual of some sort, but of which following? His exhausted and starved mind offered no answers, producing only vague recollection of what religion was in the first place. His culture had its belief system, an omnipotent god and a myriad of demi-gods one wasn't allowed to call gods — people who were once alive and presumed to have abilities influencing the lives of mortals now that they were long since dead. That had always confused him, but when he was old enough, his father had initiated him into the world of powerful men and told him the truth. People could tolerate the misery of life if they believed another waited if they were patient in suffering. It was a political card to be played throughout one's career as a noble. One morning once a week spent in a show of humility was a small sacrifice to make to appease the masses. A strong following, sometimes taking a leader to deity status himself, could be achieved with public displays of piety. With that, any political blunder or quest for dominance could be justified as the will of an invisible hand, and the people would rally to its cause.

Even so, Jeremy still held a deep respect for the unexplained. He had yet to wholly disregard the idea of forces and powers beyond human awareness. It had been easy to abandon the gravity of the rituals and pontifications once allowed to see them for the fearmongering they were. The god was not as simple to dismiss as the religion, though.

He was aware of the numerous religions that existed, and he was aware there were many deviations within each. Sanura's beliefs might be one of those. He sat and wondered what religion it was she practiced. Of course, that necessitated the question of where she came from, who she was, and why she was so different than any woman he had ever met.

A thought struck him. She held the confidence of a woman of power and influence. Thinking back on her faithful monitoring of the sun that afternoon, he realized it had been of utmost importance to her that she return for this ceremony. Perhaps she was a priestess of sorts. It certainly would explain a few things. Her natural inclination to lead, to protect, to help, her self-sufficiency, her intelligence, her proficiency with languages all indicated it was a strong possibility. Of course, for all the questions it answered, it created many more.

Suddenly, Jeremy lost his train of thought and turned toward the cave, taking a tremendous sniff. His stomach cinched, twisting painfully and released with a vociferous growl that seemed to shake all of his innards. He had contended with hunger pangs for most of the time since he woke up floating on a panel of wood. The smell of food, real food, awakened a roaring beast within.

Moving presented a challenge, but he would have made his way to the cave if he'd had to crawl there. The fire within outlined the mouth in a warm, comforting glow in the darkness that was settling around the island. He made a stiff but determined entrance to find Sanura kneeling before the fire.

She had spread it low and wide. A smaller turtle shell nestled in the flames. Within it, varying pieces of fruit were mixed with some water and leaves of some sort. Sanura was using the knife to coax the edible parts of an open crab from the shell and dropping them into the carapace. She used a rock to crush a part of the crab shell and continued to dig with the knife.

Jeremy was caught between wanting to help, wanting to plunge his face into the concoction, wanting to eat one of the crabs as it was, and wanting to simply watch her in fascination. Luckily for him, Sanura again took charge. She rose, saying words he wasn't sure if he would be able to understand even if she spoke his native tongue. He was so hurt, tired, and hungry he wasn't sure which ailment troubled him more.

Sanura had him sit against a nearby rock. She had a coconut bowl with wads of dark green leaves or other sorts of plant parts. She took a short stick whose end burned in the fire and stuck it into the bowl. The leaves smoldered and smoked. She took a deep breath of the incense it made and blew to encourage the leaves to burn. She motioned for him to smell the vapors and gave him the bowl and stick, indicating he should continue to promote the burn and breathe of it.

Not unfamiliar with the practice of smoking that had been brought with the *Conquistadores*, Jeremy appreciated the improvisation but thought it an odd time to indulge in the luxury. It smelled and tasted different than what he was used to. Of course, many sorts of leaf came from all parts of the world, insufflated in many different ways, so here was another curiosity to add to the list.

After a few good breaths, mostly to be polite, Jeremy lost interest and set the bowl aside, returning the stick to the fire. His attention never left Sanura's hands as they worked, quickly cleaning out the crabs and filling the cooking shell with a torturously tempting concoction.

Sanura was clearly aware of this. Her smiling dark eyes reflected the flames as she looked over the fire, gesturing for him to be patient. Jeremy found it wasn't hard to do. His exhausted mind disengaged, and he simply stared, thinking of everything and nothing, trying to be patient.

Then it hit him. His pains were eased. His body no longer throbbed with the toil of the day. The pain in his foot, which felt as if it had another shell in it, had abated. His tempestuous mind was at ease. The burning leaves were medicine. Obviously, Sanura had found this plant and knew of its healing properties. He had no idea what it was, but then, unless a plant had fruit on it, he usually didn't. Again, this was the mark of a priestess.

Jeremy took a deep breath, welcoming the relief, and did his best to help it by relaxing and trying to stretch his sore muscles now and again. Finally, Sanura seemed pleased as she stirred her concoction with her stick. She took a coconut bowl and dipped it in, careful not to touch the mix or the turtle shell with her fingers. Jeremy sat up eagerly. Sanura handed him a short, hard stick with the bowl, warning him to mind the drip and to be careful as its contents could be hot. Had it burned a hole in his tongue, Jeremy wouldn't have cared. Sanura had been mindful of his eagerness, though, and only warmed his dish.

It was rapture in his mouth, his tongue cloaked in flavor. The table of the king had never had such ambrosia. He barely chewed and hardly needed to. The meat and fruit were as soft as warm butter. Sanura had her hand out for the husk when he had poured the last drop of the juice down his throat. Another helping disappeared as quickly. This time, Sanura took the husk and set it aside. Before he could protest, she shook her head and put her hands on her belly and made a face.

Jeremy burst into laughter.

It was spontaneous, perhaps a little unwarranted, but it burst from him as an outlet for the immense amount of pleasure he had been filled with. Yes, he well remembered the lesson of his first night after stuffing himself following starvation. It was the contrast, though, of Sanura, so lovely, so poised, making such a face that brought the humor of irony bubbling forth from him.

Sanura laughed too. The sudden sound of an angel's song evaporated his mirth but only added to his pleasure. He leaned back again, gratitude buoying his contented smile as he watched her finish her own meal with the delicate refinement of a lady.

No more could be expected of Jeremy after that. As the medicine and food sated his torments, the need for sleep came upon him swiftly. He was sitting in a drowsy haze of bliss when Sanura was suddenly before him, taking his hand. She implored him to stand. Nothing but good came from her directions. He gained his feet and followed her outside, wondering what the name of the god she served was so he could worship properly.

At the edge of the pool, she motioned for him to strip. He could not hide his surprise, and he tried to refuse politely. He was in no mood to jump into cold water just then. He crossed his arms and held them in a pantomime of cold. Sanura smiled and took his hand. She knelt, taking him with her and put his hand in the water.

It was hot.

"Not a priestess, a goddess," Jeremy breathed. He could not strip fast enough.

She helped to steady him as he negotiated the rocky edge of the pool in the dark. Her motions showed him a ledge where he could sit and lean back, his head resting on the lip of the pool, up to his chin in steaming water. The hot water on his burned skin was painful for only a few moments. The relief it brought to his muscles trumped any discomfort.

After dunking his whole head a few times, Jeremy closed his eyes and hoped not to open them for fear he would wake under the lean-to sunburned, insect-gnawed, dirty, and starving. His religious skepticism waned as he hoped there was a heaven and imagined it as a place that felt exactly like this. Of course, the stories of his people offered no angel such as this to minister to his pleasure.

He was vaguely aware that Sanura was dunking his clothes in the water. He undid the strips around his foot, careful to keep the leaves, and set them on the rock ledge behind him. He slowly flexed his foot, letting the heat work its magic to ease the pain. Soft movement in the water made him turn his head. His half-slit eyes caught the shadow of female curves in the starlight. Now she was a mermaid, ducking under and surfacing, gliding with only soft ripples, swimming across the pool. Jeremy watched her, the tiny, lucid part of his exhausted mind wishing he had his full wits about him to properly enjoy the vision. Then again, it was just as nice in a dream-like state, his entire mind and body at ease, simply watching and admiring the scene he found himself immersed in.

He wasn't sure if he slept or not as he watched Sanura bathe, using some sort of concoction in her hair and on her skin that must have acted as a soap. She ran her fingers through her hair to detangle it and sat with a sigh as contented as those he gave now and again.

After a while, much too soon for Jeremy, Sanura emerged. She coaxed him from the water as well. They used the wrap of her skirt to dry their bodies. She wrung out her hair as he dried, and they went to the cave. Jeremy's clothes were spread on rocks by the fire which was piled high with wood. The turtle shell had been pushed to the side. Sanura sat Jeremy on another rock beside it and, to his delight, lifted the shell, set it in his lap, and gave him an eating stick.

He made short work of the remainder of their dinner and heaved a massive sigh when the shell was empty. He set the bowl aside and looked to see that Sanura was doing something with the grass and leaves they had brought up from the beach. He wished he knew how to ask if he could help. Of course, he wasn't sure how much assistance he would be. He had to concentrate to go to the water shells to have another shell-full now that he knew why he couldn't drink from the pool. After, he went outside and watered a bush on the side of the ledge.

When he returned, Sanura had made a second pile of leaves near the first he had seen when he had been brought to the cave. She was arranging the *pistano* leaves over the mound of grasses they had collected.

"How do I ask to help?" he mumbled.

Sanura said something, took his hand, and pulled him down onto the leaves. Of course. It was a sleeping place. Without a second thought, she had made a place for him, a stranger, in her home. His body gave him no choice but to lie down. With the last of his consciousness, he brought Sanura's hand to his lips in gratitude. He would later have no recollection of letting her hand go.

Jeremy dreamed of the Duchess Nottingdale. She was a fair woman. Her hair was the color of chestnuts. Her eyes, the same warm shade, glowed with happiness and love. She was fond of friends, devoted to her family, and enjoyed her elevated social position to the utmost. She loved parties. She would dance like a butterfly in a garden through the crowd. Her laughter was the song of a violin over the orchestra of the guests' voices.

He did not dream anything in particular. He only saw her radiant smile, her elegant gown, her glittering jewels, and her dancing eyes full of love for him. He was sad, knowing grief would come upon her soon. Only once had he seen her merry fire doused. The death of her parents had brought a grief upon her blacker than any cloud that shrouded the sun. Death in itself was a tragedy enough, but they had died together, murdered.

The memory brought Jeremy a dark vision not so distanced

by time.

He woke with a start and could not remember where he was. White rock walls were illuminated in orange light. He was naked, but warm enough on a bed of polished leaves. Then he remembered something that only drew his dream nearer.

Anxious to set it aside, Jeremy rose as quietly as his stiff muscles allowed and stepped outside to relieve himself. When he came back into the cave, he tested his clothes for dampness. Being so close to the fire, they were dry. He must have slept for quite a while and had every intention of continuing. He slipped on his breeches. The damp of the air gave it a sense of coolness. Sanura's skirt was spread out by the flame as well. Jeremy looked over at her.

She was partially blanketed in shadows that danced with the fire. She lay on her side, half curled up, her arms close, one around her waist. For a moment, another part of him marveled that he had no thought for what he would have done in this kind of situation any time prior to this. Even as that part of him played out the idea of lying beside her and running his hand over her naked body, the other part of him, the new him, it seemed, dashed the very thought away, aghast. This wasn't a game. It was about what she *was*, and she was not anything like that. In that moment, it gave him more pleasure to care for her, just as she had done for him.

Jeremy took the soft cloth and went to her, laying it gently over her before he quietly took his place again. Neither the soft touch nor the gentle crackle of grass woke her. Jeremy drew a deep breath and returned to the land of dreams.

CHAPTER THREE

Jeremy's nose woke him. His stomach woke a second later, knotting in hunger at what he smelled. His eyes opened with a deep, full smell of what could have been roasted game hen. Warm yellow light filled the cave, seeping in from the morning outside. He could just see a blue sky full of the melodic bird songs coming from waving green treetops.

Sanura was sitting by the fire, leaning against a rock. She was lazily stirring something in the smaller turtle shell that had been returned to the fire. Jeremy took a second to collect himself. His whole body ached. His foot pained him. His hands felt sore, having unusual demands placed on them for two days in a row. He was rested, though. He also felt stronger, having had something decent to eat. He was definitely up for that again. After a careful stretch full of bliss and agony, Jeremy rolled over and got his feet under him. He couldn't put his weight on the ball of his injured foot, but he managed well enough.

Sanura gave him a brilliant smile as he came to lower himself across from her. "*Sabailkeer*." Good morning, he guessed.

He tried to imitate it. "*Sabelkir*," he replied and added in his language, "Good morning."

"*Tayna*? Zher-ah-mee *tayna*?"

Good? Compared to the state he should have been in versus the state he was in, he was fantastic. He didn't know the word, though. "*Tayna*," he said and smiled. "*Tayna, tayna, tayna, tayna.*"

This broadened her smile. She had watched him closely as

he moved. She offered him the small bowl of leaf wads and a burning stick. Although the smell wasn't entirely pleasant at that hour, Jeremy knew it would ease his physical pains. He took a few deep breaths of the smoke. When he couldn't stand the thought of another, he set it aside. He sat back to let it work. Sanura had two bowls she had half-filled with a variety of cut-up fruit. She had been up for a while. Jeremy hadn't heard a thing. She held a bowl over the cooking shell, speared some sort of firm, white meat peppered with an herb, and filled the husk bowl with it.

Jeremy accepted with gratuity and waited politely for her to serve herself. He couldn't help taking a smell. It still reminded him of roast game fowl. He trusted anything she gave him but was curious as to what it was. He had no idea how to ask but decided to try and hoped she interpreted the query.

He pointed to the bowl with the eating stick. "What is this?"

She seemed to understand and considered how to answer. She set her bowl aside. She held her thumbs together, raised her fingers, and waved them together. It was bird after all.

Jeremy hoped his smile conveyed he was pleased, grateful, and impressed. "*Tayna*," he said and added, "Sanura *tayna*."

Not exactly the eloquent praise that naturally flowed off of his tongue, but it was the best he could do.

Sanura gave him a modest smile. "*Shokrahn*." Her gratuity.

Jeremy lost no time and helped himself to the reward of her labor. It was shortly thereafter when Sanura pushed the shell out of the fire with a thick stick and divided the rest of its contents between them. When they were finished, Jeremy was cognizant enough to put the husks into the turtle shell and take them to the pool outside to wash. He might be the son of a duke, but his time in the military had taught him the ways of communal living.

Sanura, meanwhile, made several trips to the pool with

husks, filled them, and returned to the cave. He found she was filling the larger shells with the water when he followed her in. Yes, that would make sense. In a while, it would be cool enough to drink a full amount without risking a belly-ache.

He sent a momentary prayer of gratitude for the island's fresh water. Of course, as he had thought when he found the pool on the beach, it was not uncommon for freshwater springs to bubble up on the shallow-water islands in this region. Larger islands, many more kilometers wide and long were in the area. It was not impossible that their runoff fed underground rivers that flowed below the shallow sea. That was the theory, anyway.

He only knew of one man with that theory, though, the Consult of Nature to the King, a man with whom the Duke liked to keep in company. Jeremy talked to him as often as he could. He found the man's ideas to be fascinating. There was no way to prove his explanation for island water, but it made sense to Jeremy.

Springs flowed in flatlands many kilometers from mountains in his land. Why would it make a difference if the ground they traveled beneath was dry or submerged? Hot springs tended to be found in volcanic regions, and this area certainly was known for it. Jeremy was just glad he had found a place where all those factors met. He decided he wanted to take advantage of it again.

He stripped and lowered himself into the hot water, letting it and the medicine lull him into calm once more. This time, however, he did not have sheer exhaustion clouding his mind. After a few minutes, he stretched his aching muscles, weary of being hindered by them. Sanura came and sat nearby, lifting her skirt enough to dip her legs in up to her knees. She watched him, seeming to want to say or do something, but unsure of it.

Jeremy turned sideways, resting one arm on the rock edge of the pool. "I know," he said, "I wish we could talk, too."

Surely, they could learn from one another, but where to begin? Of course, sitting naked – again – in a pool wasn't how he wanted to start a language lesson. It was just then, though, that Sanura gave them a small opportunity.

She lifted her right leg from the water and pointed. "*Kha-dum*," she wiggled her foot, "Zher-ah-mee *khadum tayna*?"

He laughed inwardly that they had been in the same frame of mind, but then, it was natural for people to want to communicate.

He nodded. "*Ahu, kha-dum tayna.*" He took advantage of the chance. He pointed to himself and lifted his foot from the water saying, "My foot is good. *Tayna*, good."

"Goot," she repeated. "Foot goot."

"Yes," he answered. "*Khadum tayna.*"

She held up her hand in an obvious motion to indicate correction and made a statement using *khadum* and pointed.

Jeremy repeated the phrase. It had to mean *Your foot is good* or something similar.

They shared a smile.

"Well," said Jeremy, "that's a start."

She spoke again, making signs, asking if he wanted to walk with her.

He answered similarly, "Yes, I will walk with you."

It would help him stretch his legs a bit. There was a breeze that dried him even before he had gathered his clothes to don them. He took a minute to wrap his foot before he dressed, giving the leaf more time to work. Sanura was ready when she emerged from the cave. She had her net bag and a stick that was not unlike the spear Jeremy had made. She gave him a smile and they started down the path she had led him up from his landing camp on the east side of the island. On the way, they collected more *pistanos*, a few *pahpahs*, and several assorted handfuls of leaves Jeremy did not know. When they got to the beach, Jeremy's camp was as they left it, such as it was.

Jeremy sat on the edge of his pool and took a couple of handfuls of water. He wiped his face with his hand and turned to see that Sanura had her back to him, looking out over the sea. He could not help but pause to look her over in admiration. One leg peeked out from behind its linen curtain. Lined with the curvature of muscle, it only drew his eye more, since the rest was concealed. He had a brief vision of running his hand over the rounded calves, feeling the firmness of her thighs under his fingers as he drew them up to grasp her rump. Would she like it? Would she freeze in anticipation, begging him to continue what she could not verbally permit? Was she the kind to mirror his touch, her fingers setting flame to his flesh, clothed or not?

Jeremy tore himself away. He felt a glow of the same heat upon his manhood, and he quickly dunked his head in the cool water to quell himself. A woman who served a god or gods wouldn't serve the needs of the flesh—hers or his. He didn't want to make her uncomfortable, or worse, fearful. Her life was hard enough in this cruel place. He wanted her to know she could be around him without his soldier springing to life every time his mind wandered for a moment.

He mastered himself as she turned and went to the spear he had made before, picking it up and handing it to him.

She spoke and made motions to say, "Let us go hunt fish in the rocks over there."

Jeremy nodded, forcing his mind to tend to the business at hand. He had his knife this time and another person with a spear. A shark would not be so much of a threat. Nonetheless, he trod even more carefully than before.

They spent some time between the shaded walls of the broken rock. Sanura speared two fish, each about a half meter

long, and put them in the bag slung over her back. Jeremy
tried and missed several times. Sanura did not try as often,
but only missed twice. Once, as Jeremy lined up to spear into
a fish, its mottled coloring making it nearly imperceptible
against the dotted shadows in the rock, Sanura caught his
arm, shaking her head.

She pointed and said a word. She clasped her midsection,
making a distressed face much like the night before and
closed her eyes and let her head fall to the side.

"Poison?" said Jeremy. "They're poisonous?" He motioned. "Fish no *tayna*, poison." He mimed her act. "Poison."

She nodded. "Yes," she said, using his word and startling
him. "Feesh poi-sun."

He couldn't help a grin. "You are delightfully savvy, my
dear."

Though she didn't know what he said, she knew it was a
compliment. She smiled and went back to stalking fish.

They had another fish, thanks to Jeremy, and a crab in the
bag when Sanura suddenly looked up. Jeremy paused too,
watching as she listened very intently. She cast her eyes
above. Jeremy did as well. Bleach-white clouds billowed up
into the azure sky. Sanura frowned at them and motioned.
They should leave. It wasn't until they were on the beach before Jeremy heard it. A distant throbbing boom warned of a
storm brewing. Out of the shade of the rocks, Jeremy felt the
humid heat adhere to his skin, trying to burn it off. It was not
surprising that the weather would react in such a way to the
tropical conditions.

After having a drink at Jeremy's camp, Sanura motioned to
his drying rack, asking if he could dismantle it. She used *tayna*
among other words to let him know they could use it. It made
him feel a little better about himself. He easily took it apart,
tied the sticks together in a bundle, and laid it over his

shoulder. They moved briskly up the mountain, eating fruit along the way. The air under the trees was cooler but had warmed since they had come through earlier. One could nearly taste the water on the air, and they were both sweating through their clothes.

When they reached the top, a breeze greeted them. It was refreshing, but they could see the streaks of black and grey that marched across the water to the west. The horizon was nearly full of them. The towering white clouds stretched far above. Even as they looked, shots of yellow licked along the surface of the sea. They set their burdens down at the side of the pool.

Sanura wasted no time in asking for the use of the knife and gutting and cleaning the fish. Jeremy reconstructed his rack, then knelt by Sanura, motioning that he wished to help. She set him to de-scaling the fish with a sharp stone she had fetched from her cache in the cave. Together, they made short work of the chore. They moved the rack, fish, and the rest of their belongings into the cave as the sun was blotted out by the storm. The rumbling and booming had gotten louder, preceded by strained crackling at times. They laid the meat out on the rack and hurried to the pool to clean themselves.

Jeremy got in first. Sanura paid no mind to him as they washed. She cleaned the grime from her hands, slipped out of her skirt, piled her hair up, dipped herself in the water, and was out, taking her skirt and going to the cave with nary a glance to him. He sighed as he emerged and used his shirt to dry himself. She was admirably devout, but surely, he was worth a look, wasn't he?

He donned his breeches, and his eye caught the movement of his reflection in the water. He knelt and took a look at himself. Yes, he was much rougher than he liked, but he would still draw attention from the female kind at home. Shirtless, it was hard to ignore the trim physique he had earned as a soldier and sailor. To see him with no shirt made the women at home forget their coy games. To see him unclothed made them forget everything else.

To have a woman of such pure beauty show such disinterest was a blow to his pride. He would have thought that even the most pious woman would be prone to a stare or two. He was not arrogant or vain, but he was aware of the advantage of his youth and enjoyed playing upon it. If he didn't earn a second look, then the men of her land must be veritable Adonises — or her disinterest could be from something completely different.

Jeremy sighed and rose as a gust of wind blew a cold mist upon him. He took his shirt and hastened to shelter. A clap of thunder ushered in a wave of pounding rain outside. Jeremy laid his shirt over the rocks by the fire and fed the flames a few dry sticks. Sanura was tidying in her collection corner. Jeremy felt tired and refreshed. With nothing else to do, he went to his bed and lay down. In minutes, the storm lulled him to sleep.

When Jeremy woke, it was still raining. The thunder had calmed to lazy rolls now and again. He stretched and looked around. Sanura had followed suit and was lying on her leaves under her skirt-sheet. Jeremy lay still, his arm under his head, staring at the rocky ceiling and thinking. He dozed now and again, but always returned to planning when he became conscious.

Sanura had a fire. If they used it well, it could be their way to get off of the island. Was the ledge high enough for ships in those far lanes to see? Perhaps there was a place higher up the rocky crag to place a beacon. Would those ships mistake a fire for volcanic activity? They would have to be close enough to get a fair look with a spyglass. It would depend on where they were. Surely, though, if he could see sails, the crow's nest could see him. Of course, perhaps Sanura had tried already.

A new thought occurred to him. Perhaps she wanted to be here. She had made no indications of desire or effort to hail a ship. Perhaps she had chosen a life of solitude to serve her god or gods. Perhaps she was in the midst of a rite of passage in a quest for priesthood or serving a time of solitude to hone her skills as a priestess. She certainly knew how to survive. Perhaps this was her final test of training.

He looked over at her for a moment. Her form was more seductive in a veil than if she had been naked before him. Naturally, thinking he could not have her made her even more enticing, yet it wasn't just her looks. He had curtailed his pursuit of beautiful women before. It was usually a characteristic of their personality or a mannerism that would avert him. He liked to have at least a few minutes of pleasant conversation as he seduced them. This was what made the mystery of Sanura even more appealing.

The question of her origins aside, she was intelligent, resourceful, and confident. He was sure he could engage her in conversation and find it just as interesting as the games of lovemaking. Of course, even if they could talk, it would be *sans* seduction, given her spiritual status. Actually, Jeremy decided he didn't think he would mind too much. He would only like to talk to her.

It would be best to leave it at that. There wasn't much sense in becoming involved with her, except perhaps for a brief affair. Once Jeremy set foot on civilized shores, he was obliged to become an adult. Long before his eye was even caught by females, his parents had made arrangements for him to meet, court, and marry Princess Regina, the king's third daughter.

Jeremy's grandfather and father had worked hard to establish and keep relations with the royal family. Jeremy was obliged not only to maintain those relations, but to enhance the Nottingdales' position in court. If all went well, his grandson or perhaps his son would be a successor of the throne. Jeremy had mixed feelings about being a family stepping-stone, but he had no other options or aspirations.

With the idea of being a merchant sailor completely out of the question, he would do as expected. There were much worse fates than being a duke of the court. He could even be king, should a series of misfortunes strike the royal family. It would have to be a lot of misfortune, but the possibility was still there.

Once Jeremy returned home, all that responsibility awaited. He had met the Princess a few times. She hadn't turned his head nearly as much as some of her maids or other court visitors of the time. They had exchanged only the pleasantries of greeting and no more. It was hard to tell what sort of companion she would be.

It didn't matter. Her job would be to produce heirs of the Duchy and the royal bloodline. He only had to make his own contribution and had no more obligations to her than that. He hoped they could at least be friends. The rest of his life was sure to be less pleasant than his previous years if not.

Jeremy sighed, shaking off the melancholy thoughts. In half-dozing, he woke almost wishing he didn't have to go back, wanting to be a priest on this island with Sanura. If he could find a way to send a message home, then justice would find Ombreux anyway. It didn't have to be through him. His father could find another heir for his tangible and titular estate. Jeremy could stay and forget it all existed.

Reason took command a half-second later, and he quelled the thought. He rose to try to find a half-dry place to stand outside to urinate. The sleepy part of his mind still courted the misty fantasy of staying with Sanura.

The fish made an excellent meal. Jeremy wouldn't have minded a little salt, a block of cheese, and a loaf of bread to go with it, but he was grateful still. Sanura had worked her magic to add flavor to the dish. They moved the rack with the remaining strips of fish to sit over the low fire to dry it until they could put it back in the sun.

The rain had eased a bit as Sanura performed the sunset ritual, this time at the mouth of the cave as the light faded. Afterward, the rain came back in drumming torrents. They set their dishes out in it to clean them. After putting them in their place in her collection, Sanura came to sit by the fire. It was cooler and damp that night. She wrapped herself from the underarms down in her skirt and brought it together just above her bosom. She twisted the ends around each other and knotted the remaining lengths of fabric together behind her neck. Had Jeremy not seen her do it, he would have said it was meant to be a dress and nothing more. It went nearly to her ankles, so she wrapped her legs in it as she drew up her knees so she could rest her arms on them. She blinked into the fire, using her hair to cover her shoulders.

Jeremy wished he had something to offer her but was doing well to keep himself warm. He watched the flames, too, wishing to be in his room where his fireplace took most of one wall. Thick tapestries could be moved to trap the heat in the area around his bed. He also had thick velvet curtains that hung from the canopy. He could get lost under thick blankets and bedding stuffed with goose down, and a least a half-dozen fluffy pillows, also down. It was like sleeping on a warm cloud on cold winter nights. He had enough room to sprawl and still have someone else there. It even had room for two other someones, as he had been delighted to find one special night when a royal daughter and her maidservant from beyond the *Tijir* River visited. Yes, that had been a *very* special night. He still wasn't sure if he liked it better when they paid attention to him or when they paid attention to each other.

"Zher-ah-mee?"

Jeremy came back to the present to find that grin on his face. He blinked, and it faded. He looked up from the fire to see Sanura had a small, curious smile on her face. She made a motion, her expression questioning what brought him a smile.

How to explain *that*?

"I, ah, I was thinking of home," he said. "Ah, home," he repeated, trying frantically to think of a way to express himself.

He took a small stick from the fire and blew out the flame on the end. He thought for a second and drew a crude structure. It certainly did not do the Nottingdale chateau any justice. He decided it wasn't worth attempting any of the details, drawing it long and rectangular with two square turrets on the sides. They were there more in homage to medieval castle design than for actual use. He drew two rows of small rectangular windows down the length and one big horseshoe-shaped door. He did add lines and angles to make it three-dimensional at best. Below, or outside depending on the perspective, he drew a figure. It had no features but was decent enough for a caricature made with a burned stick. Pleased that his studies of art weren't wasted, he drew two more figures, one in a long dress. He drew two lines from the two figures that converged at the first figure.

He pointed to the single figure and looked up to Sanura who was smiling broadly. "That's me," he said. "Jeremy. This is my mother and my father. We live here. This is our home." He pointed appropriately and tapped the building again. "Home."

Sanura took the wrist of his drawing hand with a brief squeeze and a small smile of compassion. She clasped her legs and set her chin on her knees, looking at the drawing. A couple of times she took a breath as if to say something but did not.

She pointed. "Zher-ah-mee. Zher-ah-mee hume." She tapped on the female figure. "Zher-ah-mee – ?"

"Mother," he replied.

"Muh-ter," she replied carefully and pointed to the male figure. "Zher-ah-mee?"

"Father."

"Fah-ter." She nodded. "Zher-ah-mee hume, muh-ter, fah-ter." She puzzled a moment and said, "Zher-ah-mee hume?" She pointed in all four directions.

"Well, uh," Jeremy considered. He wasn't quite sure where he was but had a rough guess. "My – Jeremy – home is that direction." He pointed northeast. He asked her in turn. "Sanura home?"

She frowned and thought. Apparently, she had less of an idea of where she was because she pointed east, drew her arm south and dropped it with a shrug. That was little help. Her appearance and mannerisms had already led Jeremy to conclude she was not of one of his brethren cultures. Was she from the great wild lands of the south, the mysterious mountains of the east, or from one of the innumerable islands in the area here?

Jeremy drew again. He hoped it looked like a map of the known civilized world. He pointed to a spot north and west of the sheltered sea in the center. "Jeremy home," he said, "Sanura?"

She frowned at the picture, contemplated, shook her head, and shrugged. Jeremy shrugged as well. They would have to work on that when they could communicate more effectively. He did have something else he could try to discuss.

"Fire," he said, pointing at it. "How?" He rubbed his drawing stick between his hands as he had in his own failed attempts to create a flame.

She shook her head and rose. She went to her sleeping place and pawed under the grass on a top corner. She came back and handed Jeremy a necklace. Hanging on a chain of finely braided gold was an amulet. It was a sun half the size of his palm, the heart of it made of convex glass. The waving arms of the rays were made of polished gold. It was beautiful, very finely made, though he could not guess the style of craftsmanship. He wasn't sure why she had shown it to him, either. Perhaps she had misunderstood.

"Fire?" He pointed and held up the necklace.

She nodded and made a series of motions and explained, but the words were lost on him. Was it a magic talisman she used to summon the power of her gods? He showed he didn't quite understand and motioned for her to set one of the sticks of firewood ablaze. She shook her head and explained some more, pointing upwards. Perhaps her god only granted special favors after a certain ceremony.

Superstition again rose in his mind. Perhaps she had found a true god or gods. Of course, their power would work for her, the one who was connected to those gods. He, a non-believer, would have to generate fire the hard way and couldn't even do that. If she was the servant of a god, a real god, she had powers—powers he wouldn't even know about because he had never seen anything like this. Was religion only a political move for his people because they worshiped a false god? Had they drifted from the true gods, lost the benefit of their power, and corrupted what was left?

He had asked these questions to himself before. They surfaced again with the chance of proving their validity. Of course, it seemed he would have to be content to observe at the moment, renewing his curiosity about who she was and where she came from.

He watched her as she sat, looking at the amulet thoughtfully. She spoke, a reminiscence of some sort, it seemed. It didn't seem to matter that he didn't understand. It was probably nice to have someone to talk to. He listened politely, wishing he did speak her language. When she concluded and got up to put the necklace back, he remembered he had made a start. What was that word?

"*Khadum*," he said as she sat down again.

She made a query.

What, he thought most likely and pointed to his injured foot, repeating the word.

A smile graced her face, brightening the cave more than the fire ever could. "*Ahu, khadum*." She said, "Foot, goot."

"Yes," he said, fighting to remember the phrase in her language and recited it.

She made only a minor correction, which he repeated. He reached out and touched her foot. "Your foot is good." He moved his hand to his foot. "My foot is good. My foot, your foot," he said, moving his hand accordingly.

"My foot," she started with her hand on his foot. Jeremy shook his head and moved it. He led her to repeat, "My foot, your foot," appropriately.

He could tell she understood then. He went to hand, arm, leg, head, and stomach. She gave him the same lesson in her language. He was not sure how much time had passed, but it was very dark outside when they finally stopped. He actually needed to have a minute or two alone outside, even though it was still misting. Well, so be it.

He rose, saying, "Excuse me" to Sanura and took off his clothes to keep them dry. After a few minutes in the dark drizzle, he was cold, as he expected, and hastened himself to the pool. It wasn't as hot as before, diluted by the rain, but it was enough to soak the chill from his skin. It also felt good on his muscles. The discomfort receded to an ache. His sunburn had improved as well, with constant application of the *aloe*. Though his foot was very sore, the cut did seem to be healing thanks to Sanura's leaves. As he was taking inventory of himself, he suddenly was conscious of scratching his rapidly bearding face. He could amend that.

He went to the cave for his knife and some *aloe*. He had to shave by feel with no mirror and no reflection in the pool. It took a little longer, but he didn't mind sitting in the warm water the whole time. When he was finally satisfied that every hair was gone, he rubbed more *aloe* on his face. He was surprised that during his time at sea, his hair had ventured past its usual place as a short curl tied at the base of his neck. It now waved downward, trying to rest between his shoulder blades. He didn't mind it so much but did take the blade to shorten the ends a bit. That accomplished, he tied it as he liked at the nape of his neck and sat back to enjoy the warmth for a while.

When he returned to the cave, Sanura wasn't at the fire. He glanced around and saw the bulge in the bed of *pistano* leaves. Jeremy was again sorry they didn't have more. As he sat by the fire to dry, he dearly wished he could lay her in his bed at home. He wasn't even thinking of putting an intimate hand on her. Just then, the need was for comfort, warmth, and rest. He contemplated until he was dry, then he dressed and crawled under his own *pistano* leaves. They were not made of down, but, he reminded himself, they were a sight better than a broken segment of boat or nothing at all. With this in his mind, the grass and leaves seemed a luxury, and he quickly fell asleep listening to the drip outside.

CHAPTER FOUR

Jeremy was the first to wake in the morning. After trying to stretch out his sore muscles, he got up, trying to keep the rustling to a minimum. Jeremy laid some grasses and small sticks on the remaining embers of the fire to reawaken the flame and added thicker branches. After a visit to his favorite watering place, he went to the east side of their ledge.

The horizon was full of pink and purple, the crown of the sun just visible over the dark, still water. The scene was breathtaking. Jeremy leaned against the stone and watched the rise of the brilliant orb, understanding in that moment why some cultures worshiped it.

Perhaps Sanura was one of those. Her sun amulet and nightly ritual to the sun were good indications. Of course, he thought it was typical for people of such faith to greet the return of their god each morning. The cacophony of morning birdsong was enough that it should wake her if she was expecting it.

The ochre disc had lifted itself free of its watery bed when Jeremy sensed movement behind him. He turned as Sanura came to stand beside him.

"Good morning," he greeted her.

"Sabailkeer," she replied. Her eyes blinked heavily at the sunrise, and she rubbed her hands on her arms with a yawn.

No, there was certainly no religious ceremony here.

"It's beautiful," he said. At her questioning look, he made a circle of his hands and lifted it. "Sunrise. It is beautiful." He didn't expect her to understand the word, but he intended for her to remember this later when he used it again.

She pointed to the sun. "Soon-risse."

He nodded. "Yes. Sun." He made the circle. "Rise." He lifted his hands.

She gave him a groggy smile. "Soon-rise," she said a little more clearly.

"Yes." He smiled too.

She gave him her word for it. He repeated and tried to set it to memory.

Sanura smiled, "*Ahu,*" but her gaze lingered on him with an intrigued smile. She saw he noticed and rubbed her face.

"Oh, yes," he rubbed his own, now smooth as it should be. "I had a proper bath last night."

Her look lingered a moment more, then she gave another glance to the sunrise as she turned and went to the end of the ledge and stepped through the rocks to follow the base of the crag. A few meters alongside the steep wall was a spot they used as a lavatory.

He stepped back to let the rock wall block his view to allow her privacy and continued his observation of the new morning. When Sanura reappeared, she went to the pool, splashed some water on her face, and dried it with her dress. She went to the far end of the pool, where the top of a *banian* tree rose high and reached over the rock ledge.

"Zher-ah-mee." She beckoned him over.

When he arrived, she smiled and pointed up into the branches. Within the woven maze, a little way above, Jeremy could see two birds. They seemed to be caught in a web spread between the branches.

"So, *this* is how you have birds to eat!" Jeremy smiled down at her.

She continued to grin and climbed the branches as easily as those creatures he had recently learned of called *monkeys.* As he watched her disentangle her catch, he realized it must be a part of a fishing net that had washed ashore, most likely of the same stock as her bag. She was certainly resourceful.

It took a little time, but another hot breakfast was well worth the wait. When they were done, the sun was high enough and warm enough to set the rack of fish in its potent rays.

Jeremy took on the task, moving slowly and carefully, lest the entire thing fall apart. It held, and he was proud of himself as he set it in a suitable place.

In the meantime, Sanura used one of the smaller turtle shells to scoop up and pour ash from the fire over the ledge. She used a small dry palmetto branch with the frond cut short to sweep the ash into the shell. Jeremy would have liked to help, but there was no use in it. She had their fireplace tidy in short order. She placed more wood and a burning branch she had set aside, and soon their fire was revived. She had done the chore nude so as not to soil her skirt. When she went to wash off the dust and dirt, Jeremy followed and sat to put his foot in the water.

She was quick, and Jeremy refrained from staring at her until she stepped out. He gave a furtive glance at her luscious curves shining in the sun as she stepped past. He risked a backward look and drew a deep breath as he forced his gaze from the forbidden fruit, looking, instead, to the blue line of water and sky just visible over the tops of the eastern trees. He searched it for any speck of white but saw none. It led him to ponder what he had in mind to achieve at some point that day.

"Zher-ah-mee."

Sanura's voice brought Jeremy from his plotting. He turned to see she was dressed and beckoning him. As he approached, he saw she had made a small pile of grass and twigs beside the rock wall outside of the cave. He sat at her direction, and she knelt, smiling, showing him the amulet.

Always curious, he said, "Oh, yes, I'd nearly forgotten."

Sanura held the amulet out to the side, squinting up at the sun briefly, then fixed her gaze on the dry tinder. She said something in a tone of supplication, but the words held a firm confidence as well. As she did so, Jeremy exclaimed as a wisp of smoke rose from the grass.

Sanura smiled at his reaction without letting her attention leave the grass, holding herself very still. Her concentration led Jeremy to refrain from querying her. He, too, fixed upon the process before him. The grass smoked, and Sanura leaned down to blow gently as she introduced more grasses where the others smoldered. In a few minutes, licks of flame flitted briefly and took hold. Sanura repeated her incantation now and again as she waited. The flame came to true life. She laid thicker sticks over it, and once they caught, she lowered her arm and smiled at Jeremy.

"Fire," she said, handing him the amulet.

"By the gods," he said, "it's a magnifying glass."

He caught her infectious grin as he examined his enlarged palm through the glass. He handed it back to her. "Of course, this only serves to feed my curiosity." He continued to smile. "I find you truly remarkable, my dear."

An idea sparked in his mind just as the flame had. He turned and looked up the steep rock wall to where the peak stood hidden from view.

"This also amends a complication with an endeavor I am planning. I wonder how I am going to explain it to you."

He looked back at the flame, thought for a moment, and withdrew one of the sticks, blowing out the flame on its charred end. He proceeded to draw, as best he could, the rudimentary plans in his mind. He hoped he conveyed to her that he wished to build a fire, a big one, somewhere at or near the top of the peak. As were his original intentions from when he first landed, he wanted to make a fire to signal ships by its smoke or flame. When he was done, he looked to Sanura, hoping to see some excitement at the idea meant to enable their escape.

He was deflated to see no reaction of the sort. Perhaps she didn't understand, yet she didn't indicate such. She almost seemed troubled by it. Was his idea that she wanted to be on the island correct? Even so, he would expect she would be excited for his sake. Maybe she didn't want him to go? The idea gave him a flutter of something. Hope? Excitement? He couldn't dwell on that at the moment. He was too confused. If she sought solitude, why would she not want him to leave?

He had no answers. The expression on Sanura's face led him to think she was trying to formulate a way to give him some. She drew her knees up and wrapped her arms around them. She stared at his drawing for a minute, then seemed to resolve some inner conflict, straightening as she did so.

"*Tayna*," she said, "Zher-ah-mee fire good."

He brightened. "Excellent!" He stood and turned to look up the rocky wall before him. He put his hand to his chin, thinking. "It shouldn't be too difficult to find a way. I don't doubt there is somewhere suitable to build our pyre. Well, then, there's no time like the present."

He clapped his hands together and went to the end of the ledge where the slope of the crag was easier. He found a foothold in the broken rock and began to climb.

"Zher-ah-mee!" Sanura grabbed his ankle before it lifted out of reach.

Surprised, Jeremy turned back to see concern in her black eyes. She took a couple of breaths, trying to speak and finally gave up and said something that included his name.

"I'll be careful, if that's what you're saying," he replied.

His smile loosened her grip, and she stood watching as he scaled the crag. It was easy going, hardly different from the climb from the jungle floor to the ledge. He worked his way to the side of the peak that ships in the current would see. He gauged he was past halfway to the top when he found a swell of stone, perhaps two meters across, smooth and round as a sword pommel. Where it connected to the spire above, there was a meter and a half of relatively flat rock that sloped toward the base of the rock.

Jeremy had to work his way around the smooth swell of rock to climb up and stand on the flat surface behind. If the view from Sanura's ledge was magnificent, there it was astounding. The world was under Jeremy's feet. He stood upon a dais of leafy green. Before him on all sides was water so blue as to hurt his heart with its beauty. Beyond to the east was the dark ocean. Before him and west the waters were swirls of blue and green. He could even see other small islands nearby. A haze in the far northwest suggested a larger island, much larger. Cotton-puff clouds cast scattered footprints over the scene, dotting the vibrant colors with islands of shade.

"This will do quite well," declared Jeremy, setting his hands on his hips. "Yes, quite well indeed!"

He carefully made his way onto the swell of rock. At its edge, he knelt to one knee to look down. He could see the bathing pool of the ledge. It was a cobalt blue in the sun with a center black as night. There was no doubt it went deep, perhaps even to the center of the earth. Then Sanura came into view. She was shading the sun from her eyes, looking up the rock. Was it anxiously?

Jeremy raised his arm and waved. She waved back. He looked around again. He wished she could see what he did. Would she make the climb? Were it any other woman, he wouldn't bother to ask. She probably would. The thought made him smile.

On his way down, Jeremy noted several places that would be strategic in moving tinder up the crag. He safely reached the bottom. Sanura greeted him, her face asking questions she did not know how to ask.

"Methinks you will see soon enough." Jeremy smiled at her and went to get a well-earned drink of water.

The rest of the day was spent foraging for food and wood. They made several trips from the ledge to the forest for the latter. Jeremy also found some vine that would serve him. Several crabs went into the bag with a few clams as well. Sanura plucked leaves and flowers now and again as Jeremy collected his wood. He noted one tall, bushy plant she collected from that he thought was the medicine plant. The rest were to season their meals, no doubt.

The end of the day found Jeremy in the bathing pool watching as Sanura performed her ritual. She had again asked for some of his hair. She had done so every evening. She only took the end of a few hairs. He again pondered its meaning as she made her offering.

His mind and body were relaxed from a few lungfuls of the medicine plant smoke. His thoughts wandered lazily as he admired the beauty of her, from the way the fabric of her skirt conformed to her body, the smooth lines of her back that showed her strength, to the shimmer of her raven hair as it swayed in the glow of sunset. Her movements never stopped, flowing seamlessly from one to the next. *Legato* was the word that came to his mind, a word used in his lessons on the violin.

He imagined tracing his fingers over her arms, feeling her strength under her kid-leather skin. He pictured what it might be like to gather her thick soft tresses in his hand to draw them aside to rest his lips on her neck, to smell and taste her nape, to feel her cringe with pleasure at his touch. He wanted to rest his body against hers, to feel her, all of her, as he held her in his arms. The arms of his imagination caressed and explored in response to other desires that were awakened within him.

Suddenly, Jeremy realized his imagination had gotten the better of him. Relaxed, surrounded by warmth, and with such erotic stimulus before him, Jeremy's manhood had responded accordingly. With a quick breath, he tore his gaze away, turning to sit low in the pool. He resisted the urge to grasp himself. That would only make it worse. The midst of a religious ritual hardly seemed the time to relieve his needs.

It wasn't his religion, but he respected her belief. He also feared her reaction, religious ceremony or no. He could not frighten her. A few deep breaths helped to subdue him. He knew she was nearing the end of her ceremony. He didn't have much time. On impulse, he took a few laps across the pool and back to distract himself.

Just when he had conquered his urges, though, he was dismayed to see her getting into the pool. He didn't think he could trust himself to sit with her nude only a few feet away. Gods, no, he couldn't. She sat and gave a sigh of pleasure that almost doomed him. He nearly leaped from the pool.

Sanura had to sit up to keep from getting a face full of turbulent water. Though his soldier was no longer at attention, it was still noticeable that he was ready for combat. Jeremy grabbed his shirt and used it to conceal himself under a weak guise of trying to dry off. Thankfully, he didn't think she caught sight of him in the commotion.

"Zher-ah-mee."

He turned his head to see she was pointing to her skirt to offer for him to use instead.

To rub the cloth that had clung to her body over himself—

"Sweet gods, no." He just couldn't free himself from dangerous waters. "No, thank you."

Keeping his back to her, he hastened away. He couldn't even bear the thought of her glance upon him. He hastily spread his shirt before the fire, slipped into his breeches, and paced back and forth a few times. Ah, the blessing-curse of being a virile male in the vigor of youth. Jeremy knew there was only one way to relieve this itch. He would have liked to go for a walk, but there was no traversing the rocky paths off the ledge in the dark. There was one place he could go for solitude.

He made his way along the east side of the rock wall carefully, fatigue and the smoke making him slightly dizzy. When he was a comfortable distance away, he sat and leaned against a rock. Only then did he release his mind to wander forbidden paths.

Sanura was feeding the fire when he returned to the cave. She looked up quickly when he entered. Sleepy, hazy, and greatly relieved, he had only one goal in mind. The glossy leaves were actually comfortable when he lowered himself onto them. Sanura sat with her chin on her knees, her arms around her legs, staring at the fire. Moments later, he was asleep.

The next day began routinely. Jeremy moved the drying rack from over the fire to back outside. The meat upon it appeared to be curing satisfactorily. He helped Sanura to prepare their breakfast. Eager to begin work on his project, he thought deeply on it as he worked, hardly noticing what he was doing. He was grateful for the meal, though he ate quickly. He left the rest for Sanura, finishing before she was even half done with a first helping.

He immediately went to his pile of sticks and vine. He spent some time knotting ends of vines together with sturdy sailing knots until he had the length he needed. He coiled it like a rope and slung it over his head with an arm through it. He climbed up the side of the rock and found a place over the cave entrance. Wrapping an end of the vine around a rock, he threw the rest over and was thrilled to see it land on the ground.

Jeremy descended, added another few lengths of vine, and wrapped it around a bundle of branches. He went back up and pulled the tinder up. In steep places, he pulled his bundle up in the same fashion, or he made a pack of it as Sanura had shown him and carried it. After the second load to his selected spot, Jeremy sat in the shade of the peak and took off his shirt. He was sweating profusely in the rising heat and humidity. He wiped it away with his shirt and took and minute to catch his breath. Scrutinizing his amassed cargo, he guessed he would need to make two, perhaps three more trips to compile enough wood to create a fire of the size he wished for. A look up confirmed his plan. He would have to wait until later that afternoon.

The sun burned fiercely above. Jeremy hoped he would be able to complete the task. Puffy clouds seemed to be conspiring to join to make rain. Not only would that keep him from working, but it would make the firewood ineffective until it dried.

Jeremy sighed. Well, he was still going to try. He stood and went to the eastern side of the peak. He shaded his eyes and scanned the horizon. He only saw a flat blue. Still full of hope, he descended.

When he reached the ledge, he found Sanura wasn't there. She must have gone foraging. He was surprised and perhaps a little disappointed. He would have liked to have gone with her. Of course, he'd had no way of telling her how long he had intended to work. No matter what, they could not stop gathering food.

Jeremy had a long drink and decided to do his share. He took his spear and descended into the dark but steamy hot forest to look for fruit and perhaps catch a fish for them at the water. He had luck with both in his outing, spearing a nice fish and finding some *pahpahs* and a few other fruits Sanura had introduced him to. He kept his eyes and ears sharp for her, but she must have gone to the west side of the island. He had taken the eastern path. He was a bit lonely, but confident and pleased he was doing something to get himself, and this woman who had saved him, off of the island.

After catching his fish, he sat at the pool he had found on his first day. He stared thoughtfully at the panel of wood, still leaning against the trees, and pondered his situation. He would have to be very careful when they were found. He could not confess who he was until he knew he was in safe company, and even then, he should remain secretive. His uncle could have any sort of plan and any number of supporters. He didn't doubt that if he were brought into his uncle's presence, he would get steel in his gut as punishment for surviving.

"Bastard." He glowered.

He would do well to exact his revenge before even breathing his family name. He wanted his parents to know he was alive, but word traveled fast and assassins just as quick. No, he would be careful not to sabotage himself. His caution might even protect his parents. If Jeremy was near them, his uncle's men could hardly be expected to spare them in an attempt on him. Ombreux might even give the order to take Jeremy's father in order to protect himself. Jeremy could very well find out his father was planning his own retribution for Ombreux's treachery. That was, if he knew.

Jeremy felt a pang of sorrow for his mother. All in her family seemed set on destroying one another, and she didn't even know the worst of it. Would it ease the blow to lose her brother if she knew he had killed their parents? Or would it worsen her grief? He could not imagine having to contend with such knowledge. Had he not been the very one to have been thrown overboard, he would have to grapple with the idea of Ombreux being a murderer.

Jeremy sighed, again looking over the wood panel, his last

connection with the real world. It had only been four days, but it felt as though he had been on the island for much longer. Sanura was as much, if not more, of an enigma than when he'd first set his eyes on her. He wanted to know more about her. No, he wanted to know *her*. Even if a ship came that minute, he still wanted to know her. He decided he would spend the hot part of the day doing that very thing.

When he arrived at the cave, he was delighted to see her there. He was vaguely aware that she seemed a little downcast. He already had something that would cure that. He set his load of the day down and sat beside her with a smile. He held out a flower he had found, a bright pink bloom as large as his hand with five crinkled petals.

"For you, my dear," he said.

She was hesitant, perhaps a little puzzled, but took it, saying, "*Shokhran.*"

"It is a flower," he said, "a flower for you, from me." He gestured. "The flower is beautiful. Remember beautiful?" He made the signs again. "Sunrise beautiful. Flower beautiful." He took a chance. "Sanura beautiful." A shy smile edged onto his face.

Her own smile appeared. She tucked her hair behind an ear as she looked at the flower bashfully. "*Shokhran.*"

"The flower is a gift," he said. "I give a gift to you. I also give . . ." He turned and got his shirt which he had tied to make a satchel of sorts. "Fish." He pulled it from the folds.

Sanura exclaimed, delighted.

"And I give fruit." He produced his gatherings as well.

She continued to smile. "Zher-ah-mee good. Zher-ah-mee give good flower, fish, fruit," she repeated carefully. "Zher-ah-mee . . ." She faltered and failed.

"I know." He turned to face her more. "I want to talk to you too. I want to learn. I will teach you to talk to me, and you can teach me to talk to you."

She didn't know the words, but with his gestures, she guessed his meaning. "Yes," she said, "yes, talk."

The afternoon passed quickly. They gutted and cleaned the fish as they worked at their language lesson. After, they hid in the shade of the cave, sitting across from each other on their sleeping places, and exchanged words and phrases they would use on a daily basis.

A rain shower passed, ending as abruptly as it had started. Jeremy looked outside as a cool breeze drifted in. The heat of the sun was waning. He had some time before dark.

"I should climb now," he said and signed.

"Yes," she replied in a voice he had found to be as light and sweet as honey when used fluidly. "Eet ees no hot."

"It is *not* hot," he corrected.

"Eet ees no-t hot," she repeated and gave him the phrase in her language.

He echoed her, and they shared a smile. The afternoon had been quite productive. The lessons he had learned entertained him as he worked and climbed. The happiness their communication brought made his steps light, even when burdened. He was pleased when he finished, adding the third bundle of the afternoon to the pile of tinder he had made. It was not terribly big, only standing to mid-thigh in the center, but he thought it would do the job. He coiled his vine-rope and looked to the sun, hoping to have enough light to get back to the ledge. What he saw made him take in his breath and pause.

The sun, red as a poppy, was a perfect circle hovering over still, dark water. Its distorted reflection floated just below, giving an impression that there were two suns, one below the sea. The sky behind was a brilliant rose, the blue mists of night settling down from above.

How Jeremy wished Sanura could see. It would be gone

before she was halfway up. Sun-worshiper though he was not, it seemed a sin to Jeremy to leave with this scene before him. He sat and watched as the sun's aquatic mate melted into a shimmering orange river that flowed to meet the sinking orb. It sank into the water, leaving a pink dust in its wake. Jeremy sighed in contentment and stood to begin his descent. He was reluctant to leave but knew he would be putting himself in danger if he stayed.

Sanura had food ready when he entered the cave. He noticed she had left her ritual fire burning and was curious until she greeted him with the knife and the query for his hair. He felt guilty, realizing she had been waiting for him. He hoped he had not caused her to displease her god. She did not seem upset, thanked him, and went outside to complete her duty.

As they ate, Jeremy did his best to tell her what he had seen. He was only successful enough to convey sunset, reiterate beautiful, and perhaps give her an idea of the word color. Their evening routine progressed as usual. Sanura had apparently bathed earlier. She stayed by the fire when Jeremy went to the pool. He stayed a while, letting the heat of the water loosen his tired muscles.

He planned to climb the peak at least three times a day to look for sails. He knew the way well enough that he could carry a lit branch and keep it aflame until he reached his brush pile. Even if he could not, he intended to take Sanura with him. She could produce a flame with her pendant if needed. Of course, that wasn't the only reason he would take her.

He wanted her to see the view from there. He very much wanted her to see the sun setting as he had. It would delight her, he was sure. He wanted to bring her any happiness he could. After all the hardship she must have suffered and the kindness she had shown, she deserved it.

Jeremy was still a bit stiff when he left the pool. He did feel much better, though.

Sanura watched him stretching when he came into the cave. As he laid his shirt by the fire to dry, she took some of the blossom buds of the medicine plant and put them in one of the bowls.

He was grateful for its incense, and she took a few deep breaths of the smoldering greens as well. They say quietly together, listening to the fire and the sound of the night bugs outside and letting the medicine settle upon them.

Jeremy snapped out of his contented brooding when Sanura drew a shuddering sigh. It was quiet, stifled, but he still noticed. She seemed embarrassed, trying to blink away glossy eyes.

Jeremy's heart gave a twinge. "What is the matter?"

Still self-conscious, she shook her head, pinching the bridge of her nose briefly and composing herself with a defiant sniff.

That was too much for Jeremy. He put his hand on her shoulder. "Sanura, please. Can't you try to tell me? Please, talk?"

Discovered, she took a deep breath and a stick from the fire. Her primal artwork produced several human-like figures and one oval-shaped with a circle on one end and two triangles on top of that. As she added to the little images, Jeremy got a smile on his face.

"Is that a cat?" He pointed, making a meowing sound.

This startled her and to his relief, she laughed. "Yes," she said, mimicking the sound.

"That is a cat," he told her.

"*Kedi*," she said. She used a few phrases and clarified, saying, "Zher-ah-mee, Sanura, Klee-yo," and pointing.

"Your cat is named Klee-yo," Jeremy repeated carefully, pointing.

She nodded and sighed.

Jeremy took in the whole picture. "You miss your family. You miss your home."

It took a little time to verify, teach, and learn, but he was able to clarify that was what was upsetting her.

On inspiration and to try to make her smile, he drew. When he was done, he thought he had made a decent image of his brown and white spaniel.

"Louis," he pointed.

"Lu-ee," she repeated.

"Yes, Louis. He is a dog," he said and barked in the way his canine friend did when excited to go on the hunt.

He was rewarded with a brilliant smile.

"Lu-ee," she repeated. "He ees a dow-ug."

"Yes, you've got it!" he exclaimed. He looked at their artwork and tried to make a joke. "Klee-yo, Louis . . . friends?"

"Freend?" she repeated slowly.

"Yes," he said, "ah, such as you and I. You and I talk together. You and I walk together. You and I help each other. You and I are happy together. You and I are friends. Louis and Klee-yo, they can be friends?"

This idea struck her silly. It was as Jeremy had hoped. Perhaps it was the long-needed release of laughter. Perhaps it was the effects of the medicine. Perhaps the idea was more absurd to her than to him. Whatever the reason, she laughed uncontrollably. Jeremy found it infectious and was swept away in mirth as well. They laughed until they had tears on their cheeks and their stomachs hurt.

When Sanura finally calmed, she daintily wiped her eyes and took some calming breaths with a few last titters. Jeremy regained his own composure, his smile still broad, though. Her joy pleased him in a way he would find hard to describe.

Sanura took a stick, a smile lingering on her face, and absently drew over the lines of her picture.

"Zher-ah-mee?" she said after a minute and lifted her rich

eyes to him. "You and I . . . freends?"

"Well, yes." Her question puzzled him. "Yes, we are friends. Of course, we are friends. At least, I hope we are. I want to be friends."

She looked back to the picture and spoke thoughtfully. "Freends. You and I are freends. Dat ees good."

CHAPTER FIVE

The following days melded together for Jeremy. They were full of the routine they had established for foraging, preparing food, and gathering wood. Jeremy included trips up the peak, and Sanura readily accompanied him. As he had hoped, she was thrilled with the scenery. One afternoon they spotted a speck of white on the far northeastern horizon, but it was too far and disappeared before coming closer. A disappointment, but Jeremy knew their chance would come.

On the sixth day after beginning the process, they gauged their fish was fully dried. The sun, wind, and fire had worked quickly. It wasn't anything Jeremy would call appetizing, but it would serve them in a time of desperation. Sanura made use of the cloth-like material that clung to the base of young coconut palms. She wrapped the fish in strips of the stiff, cheese-cloth fibers, and he made a small rack of sticks lashed together to act as a shelf for her to lay them on.

Their language lessons progressed. They spent evenings and rainy afternoons exchanging the words and phrases they needed in their island world. Jeremy still did not divulge anything about who he was or how he had gotten there.

He wanted to trust her, but one thing he had learned was secrets could not be controlled once told, so it was best to keep them safe. He refrained from any such discussion and did not mention anything of his homeland to avoid it leading to dangerous questions. She did as well, either by choice or because she was following his lead, he was not sure. He would have liked to ask her but wasn't sure how without having to reciprocate.

He had decided she was most likely not a priestess. She spent no time other than at sunset on ritual or worship. She made no mention of her god or gods in their discussions, although he hadn't asked. She most certainly did want to return home, so she was not a religious recluse. Now that he had decided who she wasn't, he still had to figure out who she was.

Jeremy was sitting by the fire one evening, watching her as she organized her collection area and pondering her situation. Jeremy had made more racks for her so her treasures could be more easily found and food could be kept up away from insects or the occasional animal that sometimes dared to intrude when they were away. She was wonderfully pleased with them, as simple and crude as they were. It seemed a special gift, and her pleasure would not have been greater had it been made of gold. He wondered about her, asking the same questions he had asked before. He was also scolding himself, trying to force logic upon himself to quell the flame of desire that kindled so readily when he let himself observe and think of her.

Though she was probably not a priestess, she was religious. Religions had strict rules, especially for women. He did not pursue women that adhered closely to belief. Many put on the façade that they did, but he usually found otherwise. If they truly were pious, he respectfully left them as such.

Another point, he told himself, was that it would be hard to believe a woman like her would not be spoken for. Of course, their conversation of family had offered the opportunity to speak of a husband or beau, yet she had never presented the idea. Even so, he thought it impossible she would not have a man in her life.

Another thing Jeremy noticed, perhaps the biggest deterrent, was that she did not seem to be the least bit interested in him. He did his best to appear nonchalant, but he knew she had caught him looking a few times. He had never seen so much as a lingering glance from her. He was as modest as he could be, but their situation excused the usual taboo of nudity. He was liberated by it.

She seemed neither freed nor repulsed. She did not hide from him, but she had never flirted or teased. Her behavior was the same, clothed or not. Perhaps she was not interested in men. Perhaps she was not interested in *him*.

As he mulled over that humbling thought, a new one came to him. Perhaps she was a virgin. She didn't behave like one, but then, she did come from a different culture. Not all people were taught to be shy of their bodies. If she were a virgin, it was a better reason to restrain himself than if she were a priestess. In his own fledgling days, he had imagined it was the epitome of manhood to escort a girl into womanhood. After two times, he knew better. At first, he thought he had done something wrong. His military comrades and his father shared their stories to reveal the female reaction was standard in their experiences. First, there was the confusing mix of fear, coyness, and refusal in words as they physically sent signals to the complete contrary. After a long fight and dance, they would lie nearly motionless with no idea of what to do and no pleasure. After that was the crying and the desperate clinging as they immediately thought they would always be together.

Trying to shake them off gently was the worst, and there was no way to do it. There was always the inevitable display in which they regurgitated everything that had been indoctrinated into them about true love, damnation, and sin that had only been taught to keep them in fear to prevent bastard children. That rarely worked. It just made them want it more.

He was also left feeling a little guilty that his desire to bring them a bit of pleasure was what threw them into what they saw as a harsh and cruel reality. It was frustrating. If they had only been told from the start what it was like, they wouldn't have to be traumatized psychologically and emotionally when their experience didn't match the unrealistic fairy tales they had been fed.

It was different for men, for some reason. Probably because no amount of fear would quell the beast within. That and a poorly timed liaison was not their burden to contend with unless they were fool enough to hang around. Of course, Jeremy had been taught to use the soldier's cloak. The thin sheath made of animal innards was a highly valued commodity among the ranks. It was not as pleasurable to use, but certainly more than being accused of fathering the child of a woman whose name he couldn't remember. In a pinch, he would call his soldier from battle at the last second. It took concentration, but again, it was better than the alternative.

His father had been wise enough to teach him these things rather than to employ the *fear of damnation* tactic. Jeremy saw the wisdom in it, and it was certainly easier to comply with.

This was the other subject he had to be mindful of when battling his compulsions. If he were to seduce this woman, and if, despite his caution, his seed was sown within her, he could well guess she would die from it there. Jeremy certainly wouldn't have a clue how to deliver a baby if she even made it that far. He dreaded to think of being on the island for that long, but it was a possibility. They would have a hard enough time trying to survive without that factor.

No, even if she weren't a virgin, spoken for, or bound by belief, she deserved better than that.

Although he reached this resolution, Jeremy still watched her. He could not help it. Every graceful movement mesmerized him. Seeing a woman radiate such beauty and even nobility in such a simple state was still a novelty to him. He found himself envisioning what it would be like to have the silken threads of her hair splayed across his bare chest as she lay in the crook of his arm with her head on his shoulder.

Sanura stood back from her organizing, obviously pleased. She turned to him, her smile dimming the firelight, and came to sit by him beside the flames.

"Shalfs good," she said. "Sank jyoo, Zher-ah-mee. I fill happy."

Jeremy found it hard to tear himself from his vision to use his voice. "Good," was all he managed.

He watched the fire lest she see what was in his mind. She paused, perhaps expecting more, but moved to kneel in front of the fire. Her hair was still damp from an earlier swim. She pulled it over her shoulder, leaning forward to fan it out before the heat, and ran her fingers through it to encourage it to dry.

Her innocent actions only served to snap Jeremy back into his conscious dream. He could almost feel her lying against him. He wanted to feel the side of her breast against his arm as he traced the gentle curves of her belly with his hand. He wanted to caress the dimple of her navel and draw circles out from it until he could lay his whole hand on her belly. Then he would slide it forward.

He jumped up so suddenly Sanura was startled. His mind might have been convinced, but his body was not. He went outside to find some solitude.

The next day began with thunder and pouring rain. A cool, gusty wind blew mist so far into the cave that Jeremy felt it touch his face now and again. Just when he thought it could not rain any harder, it did. It felt like being at the bottom of a waterfall.

At that point Sanura rose hastily, rubbing her hands on her arms. Going to the fire, she muttered to herself, sounding displeased, and started to kindle the flame. Jeremy let himself stay still for another minute. He should rise, but really, what was the point? There was nothing to do. He felt he could sleep for hours.

He heard Sanura walk toward the back of the cave and to the front again. He looked up as she walked past to see she had a flaming branch in hand.

He sat up, rubbing his eyes. "What are you doing?"

She didn't stop. "Water . . . fire. Ah, water bad on fire," she fumbled, distracted by her concern.

Then Jeremy understood. Their fire and wood were getting wet. He immediately got up and moved the drying rack and kindling. She had moved the fire to where she would feel its heat, but not so close that she had to worry about it setting her bedding on fire. Some of the new wood she fed to the fire made smoke for a brief time. It did get trapped in the back of the cave but was dissipated by puffs of wind that were strong enough to find their way there.

When the last of the wood was moved, Jeremy sat by the fire to ward off the chill he had earned from the spray. Sanura was shivering as she sat with her arms and legs close against her. The minuscule bumps that covered her arms could not be hidden.

"Sanura, here, please take my shirt." Jeremy immediately pulled it off and gave it to her.

She waved it away. "No, no. Zher-ah-mee culd."

"Nonsense. You need it more," he argued.

She refused again, but he got stern. "Now you listen to me. You take this right now, or I shall put it on you myself."

She didn't know the words, but his tone set her back. It forced her to admit she was terribly uncomfortable.

"There, now. That's much better, I'm sure," he said, sitting beside her and helping her pull it on. Without thinking, he put his arm around her and pulled her closer to warm her in a classic maneuver he loved to use at the slightest coolness in the air. It came naturally, though he had no other intentions.

His act was truly as it seemed. As soon as he did it, though, he wished he hadn't.

She was soft, delicate, and her hair smelled of the coconut milk he had seen her washing it with, yet that was only the surface. Just below her feminine shell, he could feel her strength, the telltale signs of a body trained for endurance and agility. He had never felt it in a feminine form before. It was the most erotic sensation he had ever experienced.

Every place on his body touching hers burned with guilt. The gesture alone was harmless, but his compunction had him on his feet before he even realized it. He saved himself from another awkward moment by laying a few more sticks on the fire.

"*Big fire, more warm,*" he said in her tongue, hoping he said it correctly.

It brought only a glimmer of amusement and a nod.

I made her uncomfortable. It was best to prove he meant to keep his respectful distance. He did intend to sleep more but wanted some warmth himself. For a brief moment, he thought of how nice it would be to sleep under the leaves of her bed, spooned together in the glow of the fire. He could definitely not trust himself to behave then. Putting his arm around her had caused enough trouble. There was only one other solution.

It did not take a lot to carefully push his bundle of grass and leaves to the back of the cave. He positioned it so his feet were perpendicular to hers to receive full benefit of the fire and create no uncomfortable proximity. Sanura was already asleep again by the time he had his bedding arranged. He lay watching her through the dancing flames until sleep came upon him as well.

Meals were scanty that day. Sanura used some of the fish they had dried for one meal. She had braved a drizzle to check the bird trap, which was empty. They ate the fruit in their stores for the rest of the day. Jeremy instigated another lesson for a while to spare them boredom. Most of the day was spent napping. In the evening, the wind and rain finally eased, for which they were grateful. They emerged into the sodden world as the sun was lowering. Jeremy thought Sanura would hurry to perform her daily ritual, but she merely watched the last sliver of sun sink among the shreds of clouds.

Jeremy felt restless and would have liked to have gone for a warm swim, but the water in their pool was tepid at best. He was very disappointed by the whole day. He was hungry, restive, cold, damp, and he knew his tinder on the peak was soaked if it hadn't been blown away.

Sanura seemed to be in similar spirits. She was quiet, keeping her arms folded against the coolness and hardly paying any mind to Jeremy at all.

After ensuring the bird trap was still empty and the water still too cold, Jeremy gave up and went back inside to lie down and fantasize about what it would be like to be found. He planned his strategy to contend with his uncle and envisioned what it would be like to be home again.

Before going to bed, Sanura did go through her ritual briefly over the fire in the cave, but did not douse it in the end. As always, Jeremy had a hair or two to donate. He mulled over the procedure as he witnessed it and wondered how Sanura would fit into the visions he was entertaining. He fell asleep still wondering.

The next day was cloudy and windy with a few downpours that drifted by. Jeremy wondered if a hurricane was coming. It was the beginning of autumn, a time sailors knew was dangerous. He watched the skies closely, studying the wind and cloud patterns. Sanura saw his concern. He tried to explain it to her but could not convey his full meaning.

Apparently, she had never learned of the deadly storms or did not understand him.

The weather calmed over the next night, and after a few scuttling clouds in the morning, the sky was a freshly scrubbed blue with a cool breeze. Jeremy didn't doubt that the gods had smiled on them. Either it was a lesser storm, or they had been on the fringes of one of the monsters. Regardless, they had been spared the horrors of a violent storm and the suffering of the aftermath. They were protected enough by the cave and its elevation, but the island would have been blown clean of its fruits and its plants destroyed. Harder times would have come upon them.

They spent most of the day foraging for all of the fruits that had been knocked to the ground. A few had been gnawed, most likely by rats and other creatures he saw scuttling about in the trees, but there were plenty for the two of them. They moved the fire and Jeremy's sleeping place back to where they had been. The drying rack was moved back into the sun and wind. The pool had warmed by evening, so they were able to indulge in that luxury by the end of the day.

After breakfast the next day, Jeremy found himself rather dissatisfied. He was always grateful for the food they had found, for the fire to cook it with, and for Sanura's culinary skills, yet he was growing weary of birds, fish, and fruit day after day. He wanted hot bread dripping with honey and butter. He wanted mutton with gravy. He wanted pies and cakes. He wanted a wheel of cheese and a dry red wine to go with it. He felt unproductive and bored with nothing to stimulate his mind and body but a woman he could not touch. The only way he knew to solve his problem was to get onto a ship bound for home.

After tidying from breakfast, he scaled the rock. As he had figured, his tinder pile was scattered and soaked. He gathered what he could and spread it out to dry. Afterward, he sat looking east, searching for a speck that would give a ship away. He sat, lost in his thoughts until his stomach interrupted his musings and memories.

Sanura was lying down when he arrived back at the cave. She wasn't sleeping, but she did look tired.

"No ships," he reported needlessly.

She didn't respond, but he didn't expect her to. He found some *pistanos* and a *pahpah* in their stores. He sat by the fire to eat.

"I was thinking we could fish this afternoon," he commented after a few bites. "Perhaps we will find some crabs as well."

He knew some of those words were still unfamiliar to her but thought she would understand. She was quiet, either translating or thinking over the idea.

After a minute, she sighed. "No, jyoo can feesh. I have tiredt."

He didn't correct her, suddenly concerned as such a response was so unlike her. "Are you not well? Do you feel sick? Not good?"

Again, she paused. "No, no, not sik. Ah, no . . ." She fought a moment for words and gave up. "Tiredt."

"Is there anything I can do for you?"

"No," she said, perhaps a little curtly. She took another deep breath and turned on her side to end the conversation.

Jeremy couldn't help but feel hurt. Maybe she was mad at him. For what, he didn't know. If that was it, he wanted to make amends. If she wasn't mad, he definitely wanted to make her feel better.

He took his spear and the collecting bag and walked down to the eastern beach. The shore was littered with shells and debris from the storm. Jeremy walked along it, searching for anything that might be of use. He came across some planks of splintered wood. He could not decipher where they came from, but they could be used. He moved the pieces he found further up the beach, so he could find them again if he ever needed them. He found nothing in the sand behind the rock mazes. At the place where they sank into the ground again, he found something exciting.

At the base of the rock was a large wad of stiff white fabric. A sail, or part of one, at least. Jeremy had to work to drag the wet oiled canvas out of its niche and onto the beach. It even had a bit of rigging still laced through the grommets. When he had straightened it out, he looked over it with pleasure. It was uneven, jagged on most of the edges, ripped and torn with holes here and there, yet it was well over two meters long at its shortest and almost half again wider.

"What good fortune!" he exclaimed.

There must have been a shipwreck in the storm. It was an ill fate for those aboard, but at least it was not a total loss. He had hoped to find some crab and maybe another flower to cheer Sanura. This was exceedingly better.

Jeremy thought a moment and rolled up the sail as best he could. It was even heavier then, but he managed to pick it up and get under it to carry it across his shoulders. He took it to the wide, nearly flat surface of the edge of the rock maze. There he unrolled it under the rays of the midday sun. As it dried, he tried his luck fishing. He caught one small fish and got nervous when he caught sight of a shark. He hastened to shallow water after that and searched for crabs. He did find some mussels on the rocks and added them to the bag. He would have done anything for a clove of garlic to go with them.

Between his hunting, he turned the sail over for the other side to dry. He cleaned the fish in the freshwater pool, and when he was done, the sail was satisfactorily dry. He rolled it up, draped it over his shoulders, and trudged into the forest.

It was a long, slow, hot walk. He had to stop several times

in the climb up the rocks. His foot troubled him, but he ignored it. At last, he summited the trail. He sat for a minute, feeling the unhindered breeze wipe his brow, and took up his burden again for those last few meters.

Sanura was still sleeping, so he made as little noise as possible. He set his burden down in the very edge of the shade outside of the cave. He set to work cleaning and preparing the rest of his finds of the day for the cooking shell. He was nearly done when he heard Sanura stir from sleep. She was slow to rise but offered him a tired smile when she did.

"Good afternoon, my dear," he greeted her. "Are you rested now?"

"Yes, sank jyoo," she replied. "Zher-ah-mee find feesh?"

"Yes, and some other fruits of the sea as well. I also found something wonderful — something good!" He got up and beckoned her to the cave mouth.

"Oh!" Her exclamation needed no translation. She had a specific question to ask but did not have the words. "Ese good?" was what she came up with.

Jeremy beamed. "I have an idea. Just you wait."

Sanura nodded, guessing his meaning and stood with her arms folded, looking over the canvas. Her face tightened in what could have been concern or puzzlement as she knelt to examine the rigging. She was probably wondering the fate of the ship as he had. She offered no comment, though. She stood, gave it another look over and went to the pool, still folded in upon herself. Jeremy hardly noticed. He was too pleased with his finds of the day. He went back to preparing his catch.

Later, as their supper cooked, Jeremy went to the sail with his knife to work on it. Sanura merely sat by the fire, her legs drawn under her until the food was ready. She didn't eat much but thanked Jeremy for his work of the day. He did his best to convey to her that it was his pleasure. After they tidied from their meal, she wandered outside, going somewhere Jeremy did not see, as he had immediately tackled his project again.

He had cut off a ragged edge of the material, making it squarer. The rest of the work took a lot of cutting and prying, but he finally finished and carried the canvas into the cave. He laid it out beside Sanura's sleeping place and moved the grasses into the middle of it. Several uses for the fabric had come to his mind during the day. Of all, this seemed the only good use. He had an idea for the section he had cut off but had only one thing in mind for the larger piece. It was too big and uncomfortable for clothing. They had shade and had no use for a sail. It was too small for that anyway. It could be put to other uses if needed, but in the meantime, he was going to make Sanura more comfortable.

He used all of her grasses and some of his. He folded the ends of the sail over the grass lengthwise, threading the rope through the holes he had made along both edges. He pulled it tight, folded the ends over and tied them as well. When it was done, it wasn't the work of an artisan, but Jeremy felt proud of himself. He carefully rolled the bundle over, moving it to where her grasses had been. He pressed on it, pleased with the feel and assuring himself it would stay together. It was not as firm as he would have liked, but another harvest of grasses would fix that.

He was soaked with sweat and went out into the cooler night breeze. Sanura was nowhere to be seen. He had been vaguely aware she had enacted her ritual at one point when he was cutting holes. She had asked for his hair, as usual. He had not seen her since. Though he was hot and the water of the pool warm, it was refreshing. He swam back and forth once, then sat at the edge, pleased with himself and hoping Sanura would find comfort and delight in his creation.

He also felt encouraged. If the remains of a damaged or

sunken ship could make it to their shores in two or three days, it meant he was right in believing ships sailed close enough to possibly be seen. He would go up the peak again tomorrow. His tinder would be dry, or nearly so. He would probably take some more, as some had blown away in the storm.

His mind wandered, living visions of rescue. He dreamed of how nice it would be to show Sanura his home, to sit together and enjoy a table groaning with delicacies. He smiled at the picture of her in one of the embroidered gowns, layered in satin and lace with ribbons and curls in her hair. He would adorn her with jewels of gold and amber, emeralds, and rubies. He thought of her indulging in a bath, a true bath, with soaps emanating pungent scents of lavender, rose, and honeysuckle. He imagined her safe and dreaming in a cloud of down surrounded by velvet curtains. How he wished he could make it so.

Would she even come to his home? Surely, she would seek the first ship to her home, and he could hardly blame her. What kind of life did she lead? The luxuries of his father's manor were certainly greater than most, and he could well wager she had never seen or experienced anything like them. He wanted her to know them. The little voice in Jeremy's head asked why. Though slightly annoyed at it, he did ponder the question. Why was it so important to him that he show her his home? Being rescued and knowing she would be on her way to her own family and home should be enough to make him happy for her.

Reluctantly, he confessed to himself that he wanted to show her his family's estate in order to impress her. He wanted to earn her attention and her favor. She was so intriguing, so delightful, and, of course, so beautiful. She stimulated every part of him, even without being able to converse properly. Perhaps it was because she didn't know he was the son of a duke and still seemed to enjoy his company. Perhaps he truly could not accept her sexual disinterest and wanted his usual accouterments of seduction to win the prize. He hoped not, but that had been his game, his lifestyle, for several years.

Strangely, he felt that if it truly was a game, he did not want to win. No, he decided, he wanted her to truly like him. He also did not wish to send her off with a wave and never a second thought if he ever did win her over.

Jeremy shook his head to force himself back into reality. Those feelings wouldn't do him any good. He had to marry a woman of noble blood. It had already been arranged. It would be improper for him to keep any sort of relationship with Sanura once they parted ways. It would have to be exactly that—a complete parting.

He was spared from wandering melancholy paths by the sound of Sanura returning. She had gone down the rocks but had made a torch of a palm branch with its fronds tightly bound to light her way. Jeremy hastily got out and dried himself.

"Sanura! I am glad to see you!" He smiled. "It is unusual for you to go walking at night. Were you looking for something?"

She approached with her net bag holding some sort of plant material he could not see. "Yes, but I not know . . ." She trailed off.

"That's quite all right." Jeremy had quickly put on his breeches. "Come, I have done something I hope you will like."

Such was his excitement that he took her hand to lead her into the cave.

"Zherahmee!" She gasped when she saw it. In her excitement, she said his name fluidly, which made him even happier.

"You will be ever so much more comfortable," he said,

beaming as he led her to her new bed. "It will need more grasses, but even this is much nicer than grass and leaves alone. I do hope you like it." This last statement was almost a query.

"For me?" she asked.

"Yes, I made it for you." His heart sank when her eyes filled with tears. "What is the matter?"

She controlled a sob as her tears spilled. "Oh, Zherahmee, eet ees good. Eet ees more, too good." She knelt to feel and looked up at him with shimmering eyes. "Why, Zherahmee? Why jyoo make dis?"

"Why?" he repeated, thinking the answer obvious. "Because a lady—you—should be comfortable, happy." He imitated a sigh of contentment with a matching smile. "Because I wanted to."

She brushed her tears away. "Sank jyoo, Zherahmee. Jyoo are good man."

"Well, it's only right, after all," he said, thinking it an empty response when he really meant much more. Sometimes he didn't know the words, either.

The next day dawned hot and clear. Sanura again grew teary as she expressed her gratitude to Jeremy for her bed. He was pleased but wanted to do more. After breakfast, he visited his beacon post. He arranged the tinder and spent some time scanning the horizon with no sighting of a ship. He descended and went into the forest to gather more wood. After another ascent and arrangement, he again watched the waters until his stomach forced him to descend.

He had a lunch of fruits he was quickly growing tired of but still reminded himself to be grateful for them. Sanura went to make use of her bed after they had eaten. She still seemed withdrawn that day, and Jeremy left her alone. He went into the forest to collect fruits and plants he recognized.

Early afternoon found him following the shady side of the tree line on the west side of the island. He spent some time gathering and threshing seagrass from the marsh. It was late afternoon when he returned with his cargo. A dip in the pool refreshed him, and he sat in the shade of the cave with some vine he had found and worked on the second part of his idea for the canvas remnant he had cut away.

When he was done with that, he joined Sanura, lying down on his grasses in the cool of the cave to sleep away the rest of the day. She wasn't there when he woke. After spending a few minutes stretching and rubbing his eyes, Jeremy scaled the peak to look for sails. He expected the usual planes of blue that stretched before and above him when he reached the top. They were there, but the point of their joining was marred with squares of white.

Jeremy froze, hardly believing his eyes. It wasn't a mirage, was it? He blinked, squinted, and still saw the specks.

"A ship," he whispered, having to tell himself what it was. "A ship!" he cried out in comprehension.

He descended swiftly, taking care not to trip and break his neck in his excitement. Sanura had still not returned when he reached the cave.

"She has the amulet," he muttered.

She had taken to wearing it in case of that very situation. Time was pressing, though. Jeremy set one of Sanura's palm frond torches alight and hurried back up the rock. It was more dangerous to make the climb with one hand and open flame, but he did not care. When he reached his tinder, he expected to see the speck gone, a mere hopeful specter of his imagination, yet it was still there.

Jeremy set his torch to the grass at the base of his tinder pile. It immediately set ablaze. He circled it, helping the fire into existence. It went up quickly, the still-damp wood sending a plume of gray into the pristine sky.

Jeremy stood and fixed his gaze on the speck of hope that drifted against the far horizon. He could only hear the crackle of the fire, the breeze through the palms, and the pounding of his heart. For long, long minutes he watched, sometimes certain the ship had changed course, sometimes certain it sailed on. He sent silent prayers to any god that might hear, begging for assistance.

"Zheramee."

He turned to see Sanura, flushed in the heat, stepping up onto the ledge.

"Jyoo see a sheep?" she asked, giving the fire as wide a berth as she could to stand beside him.

He knew "sheep" to mean "ship." "Yes, there, do you see?" He pointed.

"Yes, yes! I see!" she breathed. "Jyoo sink dey see fyre?"

"I don't know," he replied. "They might see it, but they might not know it as a signal."

They stood in silence, fixated on the far-off ship, watching. The fire popped behind them. The breeze ruffled their clothing and lifted the ends of Sanura's hair. They did not notice. They watched as the sun lowered and the ship continued to drift away. The fire collapsed bit by bit. The sails shrank smaller and smaller, then—pip!—they were gone.

Jeremy and Sanura still stood, watching and hoping.

In the morning, Jeremy collected wood as they foraged. Sanura was delighted with the foot coverings Jeremy had fashioned from the scrap canvas. They were far from what he would categorize as shoes, but they did protect their feet from the rocks and hazards of their forest treks. She laughed at his perturbed expression as he scrutinized his feet once he had tied his on with the vine he had laced through the tops. He was more pleased once he set foot in the forest and did not have to tread as lightly.

The sun grew hot quickly that day. Sanura seemed to be more like herself but wanted to sleep after their midday meal. Jeremy heard the contented sigh she gave when she settled in and couldn't help but feel pleased his work brought her a bit of pleasure. With nothing else to do, Jeremy lay down, too. He stared at the rocky ceiling and thought.

He was deep in a waking dream of beef brisket and red wine when it started to rain. It was a sudden downpour that stopped abruptly only a few minutes later. Jeremy rose to look outside. The cloud passed and the sun immediately beat down. The brief respite of cool air suddenly became a steaming inferno more miserable than it was before the rain.

Jeremy sighed heavily and returned to his grasses. He had shed his shirt earlier that morning and rolled his breeches up above his knees. It helped, but it was still warm. Had he been stark naked, he was sure it would make no difference. Sanura had folded her skirt in half and tied it around her waist so it covered her only to mid-thigh. That certainly didn't help *his* heat problem in the least.

She turned to look at him as he returned. "Zheramee," she said, "jyoo wish to slip here?"

He shook his head. "No, my dear. That is for you. I am quite satisfied here," he said, lowering himself.

She did not seem appeased but did not argue. She was probably not sure how. She looked at the rock above. "Zheramee, jyoo are good man," she said quietly after a moment. "I not see many good man . . . in home." She frowned, not having the right word.

Jeremy took a moment to consider what she might mean. "When you say home, do you mean in your family or in your society? The people of your country? Your land?"

He tried to explain. It took some time, but they sorted through the words and what they meant. She picked it up even more quickly now, and her diction with the words she knew was much less hesitant. Jeremy didn't even hope to have that kind of skill with what he was learning from her.

Once the new words were established, she paused in thought. "Some of fam-a-lee, many of . . . soh?"

"Society," he repeated carefully.

She played with the pronunciation a minute before finding a close reproduction.

"What do you mean there are not many good men?" asked Jeremy.

Sanura sighed, thinking. "Men do, men give, to get. Men not do and give because, for good. My fam-lee, yes. Men out of so-se-tay, no." She turned to set her onyx-eyed gaze upon him. "Jyoo are not same as ot-ter men. I am grat-ful."

Jeremy wasn't sure what to do with this information. He gave her an answer for the moment. "I am a gentleman, Sanura. A gentleman tends to a lady, no matter the situation. I am glad to do it. Your satisfaction," he simplified, "your happiness brings me happiness."

She gave him a soft smile before returning her eyes above. "I sank jyoo."

"It is truly my pleasure," he replied.

She sighed, and her eyes blinked shut.

Jeremy lay there thinking as the afternoon passed.

CHAPTER SIX

The next day began like any other. Sanura was finally in good spirits and eager to get on with the day. They breakfasted on fruit and songbird. After, they made a trek through the jungle to the seashore to forage. Sanura found a patch of the medicine plant and harvested the buds from some, but only if they met her criteria. What that was, Jeremy could not guess. Two crabs they had found went into the bag with a good collection of fruits and a new fruit Sanura found.

"*Ahuacatl*," she said, giving the rounded end of the fruit in her palm a squeeze as she grinned at him.

Jeremy attempted the word, making her smile more and leading him to think there was a joke he wasn't privy to.

"*Ahu*, I like *ahuacatl*." She set the heavy fruit with bright green skin in her bag, still smiling.

As it turned out, he was pleased as well. Once the skin was peeled off, the fruit was made of thick, soft, light green meat that faded to yellow in the center, where a round, slimy seed was nestled. The meat of the fruit had a subtle flavor, smooth and creamy. It paired nicely with the crab and some of the stronger herb leaves Sanura mixed in with them. Any change in flavor was good. Jeremy found himself again filled with gratitude for Sanura and her wealth of knowledge.

They napped again in the afternoon. After a rain, it remained slightly overcast, though the storm had passed on. They decided to walk the west side of the island to forage and to cool off in the water. They were looking for shellfish in the submerged grasses in the marshy elbow of the island when

Sanura looked up.

"Zheramee . . ."

He looked to see her attention was toward the other leg of the island that bent to the southwest.

"I smeel fire," she said.

Jeremy tested the wind. At first, he did not smell anything, but then caught the slightest tinge of smoke on the breeze. "I believe I smell it as well."

They crossed the water and walked the beach to the tree line. Sanura paused, smelling, and followed the edge of the trees. At a certain point, the scent was undeniable, though still faint. They donned their shoes and entered the jungle. As they drew closer, Sanura slowed, becoming more cautious with her steps.

"Is something the matter?" Jeremy asked.

"I sink we shoodt have careful," she said.

"Why?" he asked.

He could tell she didn't have the words or the patience to find out what they were.

"We shoodt have careful," she said again.

He complied, knowing he would learn the answers sooner or later. When they came to the end of the trees, Sanura hovered in their shadows and scanned the beach. They saw them at the same time. Men camped on the beach. They were further down, too far away to see details. From what Jeremy could see, he guessed they were sailors, probably merchants, from the far lands to the east of the central sea. There were four of them, a fire, and a dinghy pulled up on shore. There was no ship in sight, but it was still promising.

"A boat!" he exclaimed. "I wonder if they have a ship nearby."

Sanura did not seem as optimistic. She looked troubled.

"Come, we should speak to them." Jeremy led the way, but Sanura held him back.

"No, Zheramee!"

"Why?"

She made a face. "I may know of dese men."

"You know what sort of men they might be? Could you speak to them?" Jeremy was even happier. "That is good!"

"Yes or no. I not know," she replied. She stepped back into the forest and rested against a tree, thinking.

"What is the matter?" Jeremy asked.

She answered his question with her decision. "Zheramee, jyoo go to water," she said, pointing to the other side of the island they had come from. "I come to jyoo after talk. I no come, go to cave. No come here." She took off her shoes. "You take dese, I muss have, ah . . ." She gestured to indicate that she wanted to step quietly.

Jeremy frowned. "I don't like that at all. I'm not going—"

She shook her head vehemently. "No, no, bad for Zheramee. Some men no like men of Zheramee. You so-se-tay. I can talk."

It wasn't a very satisfactory explanation by any means, but Jeremy at least understood he might be in danger. "Still, I would rather—"

Sanura shook her head again, holding up her hand to silence him. "No. You go. I no come. You go to cave," she reiterated.

Before he could argue, she stepped off into the forest. Jeremy watched her go, alarm building within. If it were that dangerous, he would rather neither of them approached the men, yet it could be a way off of the island, and they had to take any chance they could find. Jeremy was conflicted. At the least, he would be damned if he was going to leave her.

He took off his shoes as well and followed her, stepping even more silently than she. When he got close enough to see the men, he found a bush along the edge of the trees and crouched behind it. Presently, he saw all four of the men turn at once, looking to the trees. One shouted—a response it seemed. They paused, then stood. The man shouted again with a longer response. He was a burly man with a thick beard. A ring of gold glinted in one ear. He listened, then called another response.

A moment later, Sanura emerged from the forest. Her arms were out before her, palms open in a gesture of peace. She had fully clothed herself. She was speaking, but Jeremy could not hear her voice. She stopped a few paces away from the men. The larger stepped forward. Sanura backed away, making him stop.

They exchanged dialogue. The other men stood very still, exchanging amazed glances as they listened. The large man held out his hand, obviously imploring her to come nearer. He gestured to the fire. One man held up a basket to show her that it seemed to have bread in it. Sanura was unimpressed, still speaking to their leader. He responded again, this time at length. Sanura still seemed wary.

The large man lunged forward. Sanura bolted, but he reached out and grabbed her in two strides. It took all of Jeremy's will to keep from dashing to her immediate rescue, knowing it would be folly. Then Jeremy saw something astounding. Sanura turned and punched the man. She twisted her arm and wrested it from his grip, but his other arm was already about her waist. Sanura fought like a wildcat—something Jeremy had never seen a woman do.

Jeremy heard Sanura cry out as the man wrestled with her. The other men were there immediately. Once the larger man was able to let go, he did, wiping his bloodied nose with his sleeve. Jeremy again had to stifle himself and a cry of rage as the man seized Sanura by her hair and dragged her up to snarl a threat in her face.

Sanura was unmoved. She set her jaw in defiance, her gaze locked with his, snapping with anger. The man lifted her and carried her toward the campfire. Jeremy immediately moved closer, still hiding in the trees. His gut turned to a hot ball of hate with each laugh that came to him on the breeze. When he came to the closest point, he found a fern to kneel behind. He watched the men and waited for his chance.

There was a flurry of activity around the campfire. Jeremy could not see what was happening, but he could guess. Sanura fought, but they were quickly getting the upper hand. Jeremy's attention was torn from the scene by the only thing that could distract him — his chance.

One of the men was approaching the edge of the jungle where some supplies were placed. He grabbed a length of rope, but when he turned Jeremy sprinted forward and tackled him. He silenced him with one hand as the other drew his knife across his throat. Jeremy knelt as the man fell.

He looked up, making sure he had not been seen. He had not. The others were too busy restraining Sanura.

Jeremy took the sword of the man he had killed. An eternity seemed to pass as he crossed the sand. Thinking him their fallen comrade, the others did not notice him until he drove his sword into the leader's chest with an angry cry. He shoved the man away, withdrawing his sword and turned to pounce on the man holding Sanura's arms. He immediately let her go, fumbling for his sword and struggling to his feet as Jeremy dove upon him, driving the sword into him.

His heart froze at Sanura's cry, but when he turned, she was not hurt. She had shouted in anger as she wrested a leg free to kick the man in the face. Her fists had come next, one grabbing for the knife in his belt. Jeremy moved forward, but she was already thrusting, plunging the blade into the man's chest. She had no fear or hesitation as she forced him to the ground, stabbing again and again until he lay still.

Jeremy stood with his mouth open as she gained her feet. She brushed her hair from her face, issued a curse, and spat to seal it. At that moment, the dam of Jeremy's heart burst. The inundation of a hundred intense emotions overcame him. She turned to greet him as he stepped forward, but he had no words. He enveloped her in his arms and kissed her with all the passion that engulfed his soul at that moment.

He kept her sweet lips against his for as long as he could and broke it to gasp for breath and to press her against him. She responded, returning the embrace, but with less passion than he exhibited.

Reluctantly, he let her go after a moment, but could not help placing a hand against her face. "Are you hurt at all?" His eyes betrayed his fear of the answer.

"No," she said, "I am no hurt."

Jeremy gave a breath of relief, stepping away. "I am sorry. I did not mean to be so forward. Please, I hope you do not think ill of me."

Her expression melted his concern. "Zheramee," she said softly, laying her hand on his arm with a squeeze. "Sank jyoo."

She looked at the fallen men and frowned, cursing again. She looked to the sea, gazing all around. "We muss go. Perhaps more. Muss . . ." She gestured around at their feet. "What is word? Make no see?"

"Hide," he answered. "You are saying we must hide all of this, so we are not found."

"Yes, hide." She nodded.

It took some time, but they did it. Jeremy and Sanura put all of the supplies they found into the dinghy alongside more that were in its hull. They buried the fire, and Sanura covered the bloody sand with clean. In the meantime, Jeremy dragged the bodies of the men to the boat and laid them beside it. He proceeded to strip them of every valuable they had, including their clothes and boots. He was finishing as Sanura approached, having completed her chore. He almost turned her away from the gruesome scene before he remembered she had killed one herself—and with some skill.

He stood, placing the spoils in the boat. "I am not sure what to do with these unfortunate bastards," he said and flinched, sorry to have lost his manners. He wondered if she would care if she knew he had sworn in front of her. She had appeared to have cursed, after all. Still, he was the gentleman.

She didn't know the words but had an answer for him. She pointed. "We take into sea." She picked up some rope in the boat. "Tie dis, boat." She made a motion.

"Pull?" he supplied.

"Boat pull into water. Sharks *hide* them." She emphasized the word with a grin.

Jeremy could not help his amazement which turned into admiration. "My dear, you are certainly not one to cross!"

Understanding his tone, she gave him a modest grin and set to work.

That night they supped on bread and cheese and crab and, best of all, raised a toast with rum in their coconut shells. Paired with the vapors of the medicine plant, it dissipated the aches of rowing the boat around the island and into the elbow marsh to hide it. They carried what they could from the boat. They would retrieve the rest the next day. Jeremy felt giddy with pleasure, even without the smoke and drink. They now had a bit of good food, clothes, boots, weapons, and blankets—two for each of them. It was better than Yuletide.

They were sitting by the fire, digesting and sipping, both with the same pleased smile of content on their face. Jeremy thought of only one thing to improve their comfort. He stood, poking a lit stick into the medicine bowl for one more deep breath. It made him cough a little, but it felt good.

"Come, my dear," he said, "let us partake of the other source of happiness on this island."

Taking the rum bottle and his coconut, Jeremy went to the pool and stripped. He groaned with pleasure as he immersed himself in the dark water. Sanura needed no urging. She stepped in with a similar sigh, submerging herself and surfacing with an expression of pure contentment on her face. Jeremy settled himself into his sitting niche, the coconut and bottle well within reach.

Sanura smiled at him. "Ees good? Zheramee ees good?"

"Zheramee is very good," he said, not having to try too hard to mimic her slurred accent.

They gave each other a smile he realized was one of the most genuine he had ever shared with her.

Sanura turned and started a slow swim across the water. Jeremy watched her with heavily lidded eyes, the smile refusing to dissipate. He should have been horrified to see her kill a man. Rather, he was intrigued by it. Dared he say aroused by it? There was something about a woman so fair providing such a display of strength, of power, of confidence that made his blood quicken. Even watching her there, her head and shoulders bobbing gently in the water, shrouded by a thin mist drifting on the surface, caused his manhood to warm. He also felt his feelings warm.

The emotions of the day surfaced briefly. The utter fear of her being hurt or killed, the amazement that she had defended herself, the elation that she was freed and unharmed, all blended with his gratitude and admiration for her that had grown with each passing day. He realized he truly did care for her. It was wonderful.

He recalled how sweet it had been to hold her, and oh, to kiss her. Her firm body in his arms, the soft lips upon his. Even the memory made him feel heated. His manhood swelled, unable to remain passive when Jeremy was in such a state. He sighed and did not fight it for the moment. It brought him pleasure, although he could not fully indulge then. It was dark. She would not see. He would wait for her to leave, then relieve himself. In the meantime, he encouraged it, letting himself admire the veiled feminine beauty before him.

Sanura partially surfaced to sit on a shallow bit of rock on the other side. The light of the almost full moon caressed the curves of her wet skin as he wished he could. Her full, rounded breasts glimmered in profile as she turned and wrung the water from her hair. He could see where the curve of her waist turned convex and merged with the pool just before giving him a full glimpse of her buttocks. He could see where the water lapped gently between the rounded hills of her thighs, denying him the vision of that tender place that could bring both of them immeasurable pleasure. He envied that water. He wished to be it, rolling over her skin, weaving itself between the silky threads of hair guarding the entrance to her womanhood and gently seep between her soft folds, touching those places that would make her groan and sigh.

Breathing became harder. Each beat of his aching heart sent a pulse of painful desire, of need, through his manhood. He wanted to surround her with his body, his emotion. He wanted to make love, truly make love to her, physically and emotionally.

Sanura had been looking up at the moon and stars. Her attention returned to the pool with a sigh, and he knew she saw him watching her. From what he could see, she returned the observation. She slid back into the water and drifted back.

Jeremy closed his eyes and laid his head back, trying to control the frustration of his throbbing manhood. He could start another language lesson. That would be best. It would give him some time to control himself. There were many things they could try to discuss. He took a deep breath, sorry that the height of pleasure was over. A small, close gurgle of water made him open his eyes to see her gliding toward him.

He only had time to sit up straight before she straddled him.

She wrapped her arms around him and pressed her lips to his. A jolt of pleasure, so intense as to be nearly painful, snapped him rigid. The silken wool of her womanhood brushed the length of his erect member. She gasped with a feminine grunt of anticipation as their skin connected and pressed her hips forward, the outer lips of her womanhood resting on him.

He broke the kiss to gasp and moan with pleasure. He put his lips to her neck, caressing it with full, hungry kisses. His hands caressed her ivory-smooth back. One wandered down to nestle two fingers between her buttocks, the rest splayed to grasp them and press her close.

Sanura gasped, her breath coming quick, full, and hot against his neck. Jeremy pulled her up, bowing his head to take a nipple into his mouth. Sanura cried out, arching her back to give him more access. Her hands combed through his hair, grasping it in ecstasy as he flicked the nipple with his tongue and took the other breast with his free hand. She rocked her pelvis, pressing it against his, teasing him with the caresses of her soft, warm folds.

Just when Jeremy could stand it no more, she rocked back a bit further and caught the end of his member with the hot rim of her entrance.

Jeremy forgot about her breasts. He was about to use a hand to guide himself when she found the angle and let him slide into her depths.

Her gasping words were lost as she seized onto him, embracing him wholly and shuddering with pleasure. Jeremy's reaction to ecstasy was to take a more secure hold of her and press her close. Bracing her knees on the rock on either side of him, Sanura thrust herself upon him over and over.

Jeremy groaned again, grabbing her buttocks with both hands, feeling them undulate in rhythm with his pleasure. He laid his head back as a wave of tension coursed through him. He tasted the steam of the water that danced on his shoulders as it mixed with the cool night air. Pleasure speared through him again as her hot breath blew against his neck before her lips covered it with hungry kisses, deep and solicitous, urging him on to greater heights of pleasure.

One of his hands returned to a breast, savoring its fullness as his fingers found and gently pinched the hardened nipple, rubbing it between them. She gasped, lifting her head, and Jeremy caught her lips with his, his tongue passing between them to find hers. She met him, her mouth matching the movement of her pelvis upon him. She answered his grunt of pleasure and broke the kiss to cry out in pleasure and tension as she increased the tempo of her drive. Jeremy grabbed her waist, groaning as another tremor of pleasure caused him to seize. It passed, but the pleasure did not.

In the euphoric haze, he did hear Sanura whisper, "Tell me," in his ear.

The one remaining part of his brain that was lucid took strong note of that. It seemed only a short while later, too short by his standards, that he gasped, "Now!"

Sanura dismounted and immediately her hand dove in to complete the work. Jeremy tensed and groaned as the final climactic shudders coursed through him. Afterward, he sat in a dizzy cloud, panting as Sanura moved to straddle him again, sitting on his thighs. She laid her hands on his chest and her head on his shoulder. The water fluttered against his skin where her own gasps stirred it. Jeremy put his arms around her, pulling her to press against him. That pleasure was nearly as great as the one he had just experienced.

"Zheramee," she said after a moment.

"Yes, my dear?"

"I am sorry. I do not mean to be . . . for-ward."

Jeremy paused, then laughed, realizing she was trying to

say what he had said when he kissed her earlier. She raised her head, laughing as well. He took her face in his hands and kissed her.

They sat in the pool until their heads cleared a bit and reluctantly got out as their hands and feet showed signs of shriveling. Jeremy indulged in the pleasure of drying Sanura. Every bit of her was soft and firm at the same time. His manhood stirred as he drew the cloth up the inside of her thigh and felt her stiffen against him. He drew her hair aside and kissed her neck, making her cringe and giggle. She was quick to return the favor of drying, letting him know with a glint in her eye that she noted his manly stirrings.

They sat by the fire, setting aside the rum to save it for another occasion. They shared a warm silence of mutual contentment that drew them together more than words ever could. Sanura dried her hair before the fire. As she combed her fingers through the long, black strands, Jeremy watched the firelight on her skin. He no longer had to dream of how it felt against his fingers, how it tasted on his tongue. Now it was a memory. He wanted to fix it even more firmly in his mind.

When her hair was nearly dry, Jeremy got to his knees beside her. She turned but made no protest as he reached out and drew his fingers through her soft tresses. She closed her eyes when he combed them over her scalp, gently brushing her forehead and temples as he did. She moved to meet his hand on the next stroke and the next. After that, he could no longer bear it. His caress drew her hair aside, and he pressed his lips to her shoulder. Her breath deepened as he moved closer to her neck. He placed his hand on the curve of her waist and slid forward until a finger rested in the dimple of her navel. She laid her hands over his, letting him hold her against him. His swelling manhood pressed into the cushion of her buttock. She gasped in response.

Jeremy rose to his feet, taking her with him. He led her to her bed and his heart thumped as she lowered herself into it, her gaze locked with his, pulling him after her. They lay on their sides, facing one another, their hands tracing each other.

"I must confess," said Jeremy, "I have dreamed of this many times. I have seen this in my mind." He tapped his head to clarify. "I have wanted to do this."

Sanura blinked, pleased, but a little confused. "I sink Zheramee no want me. Zherahee, hide? I sink . . . I sink many tings." She shrugged. "I sink Zheramee no want me."

"Oh, no, Sanura dear, no." Jeremy brushed his hand over her head. "You saved me. You are the best thing that could have happened to me. Sanura, I am sorry I made you feel bad. I did not think you were interested or that you wanted *me*. I was doing all I could to contain myself. I did not want to offend or frighten you or make you think I would hurt you. I-I want you to like me."

Sanura smiled. "Jyoo sink I no like jyoo?"

"Well," he smiled sheepishly, "I know now that you do."

"Zheramee like me?" she asked.

"Oh, yes," he said. "Very much. Yes, I like you very much indeed."

Her eyes glittered with pleasure that surfaced in a laugh as he leaned forward to kiss her and draw her closer. "I like Zheramee," she gasped as he kissed his way to her neck.

Only a moment later she let him press her onto her back and lay upon her. Rather than dive into her to satisfy his need, he restrained himself, stoking the fire within her to its hottest point. He caressed her and kissed her breasts, massaging one as he drew circles over the other with his tongue. His hand went from teasing her nipple to trace down her body to her thigh. She jolted and gasped as he passed by the warm mound against his leg. He shifted his weight and drew his hand up the inside of her thigh. She lay still, her eyes closed in surrender to sensation, yet she was tense as a bowstring, nearly trembling beneath him. The moment the tip of his finger brushed the first few hairs of her mons, she jolted again with a mewling gasp.

Jeremy smiled, gently tracing over those hairs a few more times, making her seize with each touch. He pressed his hand against her, forcing her quickening breath. One finger slid between her folds, the sensation not unlike handling a *pahpah* found in the midday sun, yet this fruit was a hundredfold sweeter and would stay warm to his touch.

He caressed her, drawing pleasure in watching and feeling hers. She fidgeted and writhed, driven mad with anticipation. His own made him burn with desire. As he watched, he was amazed at her response. She was completely unhindered, unafraid, trusting. Most women he had been with remained reserved, even in the throes of his passion. She was exhibiting a level of bliss he had only seen at the height of passion in others, and even then, it was brief, if at all.

At last, he could take it no more. He lowered himself upon her, brushing her shoulder with gentle kisses as he held her gates open and presented himself to her. He again resisted the temptation to dive in and nearly succumbed when she contracted around his tip. He caressed her face, making sure their gazes met. Their hot breath mingled as he slowly slid into her. Sanura's eyes rolled back and fluttered shut with a groan. Jeremy sighed in surprise and pleasure as she tightened around him. He drew back and felt her meet him as he advanced again.

He surrendered his consciousness to pure sensation. The observant corner of his mind likened the experience to finding a partner in dance who needed no guidance and rode the music alongside him, driven by the music and the joy of dance alone. Emotion was Jeremy's music, sweeter than any he had ever heard. Sanura, on the same fleeting wings, drove him even further, responding to each motion with a commitment of mind and body he had never known a woman to allow herself. Her gasping cries met and drove his every thrust. She matched him physically, meeting him with as much force as he gave, allowing him to plunge as deep within her as he could reach.

Her passionate, pleading words, unknown to his mind, were the words on his own heart, driving his passion to launch her to a peak that, to that moment, he had never considered. With a gasping growl that expressed the blissful frustration he was driving to relieve, Jeremy pressed himself to Sanura, his arms surrounding her to hold her as close as possible. She cried out louder, her whole body tensing beneath him as he grasped the back of her neck with one hand. Her gasp was released in a scream of ecstasy as he held her fast, doubling the rhythm of his thrusts upon her.

Sanura responded wholly, in a way that drove him mad with pleasure. Grasping him in turn, she was his completely. She tensed, seizing upon his manhood. Her cries were suddenly stifled with a strained grunt, and she released a scream of pure ecstasy as shudders coursed through her body. After, she relaxed with a sighing groan of satisfaction, seizing a few more times as his thrusts sent jolts of pleasure through her. Jeremy was amazed as she fell limp with another moan. It seemed she had experienced climax in the way he did, but that wasn't possible. Was it?

Jeremy's wonder eased the spell of bliss for a moment. He looked down upon her as she lay in a state of ultimate contentment.

He drew his thumb over her face. "Are you all right?"

Her smile grew in answer, her softened eyes opened under a haze. "I am every good dat is," she breathed. "Dere is not more good dan dis." She wrapped her arms around him once more, the strength returning to her body beneath him. "Jyoo make me need more."

She drew him in with a hungry kiss, her lips massaging his, her tongue gently pressed past his lips as she moved her pelvis to allow his manhood entrance again. A wave of heat washed over Jeremy as when walking into the great hall after being out on a cold, snowy day. A painful shot of desire made him want to burst, and he plunged into her, both literally and figuratively, over and over. She rode the wave of passion with him again, reaching that height twice more, each time driving him towards the top of his own peak, higher and more euphoric than he had ever dreamed.

Immersed in ecstasy, he felt the cold wash as he summited the height at last, withdrawing and clasping himself as a violent shudder coursed through him and the wave of ultimate pleasure and relief was released in physical form onto her belly. When the last spasm had passed, he gave a final groan and collapsed over her, having just enough presence to gently lower himself upon her at the last moment. She gasped beneath him. Even afterward, they were synchronized, drawing breath as one. Her heart pounded, singing harmony to his as their sweat mingled, pressed beneath their hot skin.

He nuzzled her, and she immediately responded in turn. Never had he shared such pleasure with a woman.

"Sanura," he gasped, almost inaudible, "now it is I who am at a loss for words."

CHAPTER SEVEN

Jeremy liked the sound of his boots in the hall. The sharp click echoing off of the marbled walls seemed to resonate authority and confidence. Though not an arrogant man, he was in a position of power, and he didn't want to give any impression that he wasn't aware of it. Walking through the hall alone somehow reinforced to him he was his own man with the right to choose the course of his fate. He needed that confidence. He had gone to war, and he had known and commanded battle, yet no military operation was as complicated nor held the chance of such repercussions as the battle that was about to be waged.

Jeremy was going to dinner.

It was a familiar battlefield. As with a true ground of war, it held all the pomp and circumstance that contrasted with the vicious horrors that were the reality of it. Jeremy happened to feel it was worse in this case. He could not wear a sword at his side. To have and be proficient at swords and not put it to use was a frustrating paradox. Yet he reminded himself, if swords had always been utilized at his family table, the population of Nottingdales and their contemporaries would be significantly less.

Heads turned briefly when he entered the dining hall. He ignored them for the moment and went to his place at the table. He paused to take his mother's outstretched hand and bowed to kiss it.

"Jeremy, dear, you're late," she admonished him. "We're almost finished with the soup."

"My apologies to you, Mother, and to all." He raised his voice loud enough to be heard over the murmur of voices and the clink of silver on porcelain. "I was in pursuit of a fox and wasn't going to let the rascal get away."

115

"A good hunt, then?" grunted his father.

"Yes, sir, it was," replied Jeremy, taking his place at his father's right. A steaming plate of soup was set before him. The tang of mutton filled his nose, warming it from the chill of the autumn afternoon.

His father grunted again. "Next time I hope to be able to go with you." He took a very long drink of his wine.

"I should like that, sir," said Jeremy before taking his first spoon of soup.

He looked over the large table. The usual guests were there, engaged in their own conversation. Jeremy had noticed when he first stepped into the room that the chair beside his mother was empty.

"I assume Uncle Ombreux has not yet arrived," he commented.

"We waited as long as we could before calling everyone to dine, seeing as the two of you were absent," replied his mother. "There is no way of knowing what caused his delay, so we began anyway. I expected him by mid-morning at the latest. I do hope he is all right."

"There's no bad weather today," said the Duke. "I'm sure he will be along presently."

Jeremy's mother still fretted. "Perhaps they were waylaid," she said in worry.

"Oh, now, don't upset yourself, my dear." The Duke reached over and patted her hand briefly. "You know I sent some of my finest men to meet and escort them. We've not had a tale of misfortune on the road from port for some time."

"Yes, naturally, you are right," the Duchess conceded.

"Even so, I wager Uncle Ombreux could hold his own," added Jeremy. "Doubtless he would walk away with their gold and leave them thinking they'd gotten the better half of the deal."

This produced the smile he had hoped for in his mother. His father grunted in agreement and disapproval, taking a swallow of wine that seemed to have gone sour, from the face he made. There were laughs from the men at the table with agreeing remarks.

After the main course was served, Jeremy's mother was relieved by the entrance of Ombreux, Duke of Langue. After the ritual of greeting, excuses, and apologies, Ombreux took his place. Room was made for the three companions at his side.

Jeremy's eye was caught by the fairest of the group, a golden-haired lass with rose-petal cheeks and a blessing of bosoms. From the sidelong glances he caught, he guessed he was of interest to her as well. Ombreux and his mother had all those around Jeremy in conversation, and he felt he might dodge the battle. If dinner ended without an exchange and him offering a tour to the young lady, it could turn out to be a very good evening for Jeremy indeed.

It was not to be so.

Reginald Bardeux, Jeremy's cousin on his father's side and near his age, lived near enough that they were regulars at one another's dinners. He was fond of sparking conversation that put Jeremy on the defensive. Jeremy always suspected the reason was jealousy of his position. Reginald intended to elevate himself in the eyes of those at the table and in the mind of the Duke. Nothing could come of it except upon Jeremy's demise, and it would be a reluctant appointment indeed for the Duke to have Reginald as his heir. Yet as the closest kin of blood, it was the natural order.

Ombreux and his gentleman companion, a Lord Welderly, were explaining how they had met on the ship from ports east. Lord Welderly was traveling with his wife and daughter after having visited distant family.

"I daresay the captain and crew of our esteemed Duke Ombreux's ship were the most skilled and accommodating men I have had the pleasure of sailing with," said Lord Welderly, "yet I must still say that sailing, especially in the company of women, is a most uncomfortable and trying experience."

"One feels as a beast the entire time," agreed his wife. "I believe even the beasts were miserable and unfit to bear such conditions."

"Our dear Jeremy actually wishes to seek out such an existence," chimed in Reginald with a sideways glance to Jeremy. "Imagine. The son of a duke wanting nothing more than to be a sailor." He scoffed.

Jeremy's mother sighed gently. His father took another drink of what appeared to be sour wine, to judge from the grimace on his face.

His uncle, on the other hand, chuckled. "Still chasing the rigging, eh, son?"

"Yes, sir," replied Jeremy. "It is something I wish to experience in life. I'm not one to sit on silk cushions looking in the mirror all day. I seek the life of a man."

The nasty look Reginald shot him only polished his pride at having so quick a response. His uncle took the attention of the table with his full laugh. "Spoken like a true Nottingdale."

"Oh, you can't be serious, Ombreux." Jeremy's aunt, his father's sister, set her fork down, she was so agitated. "Don't encourage the boy."

Reginald didn't try very hard to conceal his smirk at Jeremy being called boy. Jeremy merely gave his attention to his plate of pheasant as if he had not noticed.

"It won't be encouraged because it has been discouraged," declared Duke Nottingdale. "Isn't that right, son?"

Jeremy took a moment to stifle his frustration. "Yes, sir," he answered with as much agreement in his voice as he could muster.

"Oh, come now, Nottingdale," implored his uncle. "I can see it as easily as anyone here. Your son needs some salt in his veins. He's a man, and an adventuresome one at that. Perhaps a sailing expedition is just what he needs to get the idea out of him and make him focus. Let him satisfy his curiosity. Let him go abroad and perhaps he'll stop looking abroad."

"We've discussed this before, Ombreux," said Duke Nottingdale calmly. "I'm not sending my son on any expedition. He is needed here."

At this, Jeremy's uncle grew agitated. "Are you afraid he might learn something of this world? Of trade? Of diplomacy? Learning from books is sufficient? Marrying into the royal bloodline is good enough for him, eh? He will be far enough away from the throne he won't have to know any of that nonsense, I suppose. All he is needed for is heirs, each new line bringing the Nottingdale name closer to becoming the monarchy. My apologies for not seeing such wisdom earlier," he snapped, then lifted his goblet to Jeremy. "Salutations, my boy. You've drawn a fortunate lot, indeed."

Jeremy had no idea how to respond in word or deed. Fortunately, his father reacted immediately.

"If your son were to be betrothed to the king's daughter, I doubt you would react differently," he said. "I wouldn't doubt that you'd have the poor boy under glass like a pheasant for all to admire."

His uncle took a new countenance at this. "Oh, come now, Nottingdale. I mean no offense. I simply wish for my sister's son to know as much of the ways of manhood as he can before he represents our families in Court. You had no opposition to sending him to war, after all. We both know he could not show his face in Court if he had not. Imagine the approval if he puts to use the lessons of trade and treaty you have been pounding into his thick skull. The more knowledge he has, the more he will find favor with the king. Don't you agree?"

Jeremy's father still looked disapproving but did not argue, grunting again.

"If I may," interjected Lord Welderly, "I have had limited experience in Court based upon my own specialized knowledge. Duke Ombreux is not wrong. The king has little patience for those who have nothing to offer him."

"You have had time at Court?" Jeremy's mother sailed to his rescue. "Do tell, Lord Welderly."

For a brief time, Jeremy was granted a reprieve. He was thinking he would get through dessert, but the topic exhausted itself, and Ombreux persisted with one more comment.

"You know, Nottingdale, I have heard you are planning a trip to the new lands in summer for your esteemed captain. I have business of my own to conduct there. Perhaps having your captain and myself aboard to have an eye on your Jeremy would offer enough comfort to your mind to permit him to sail with us."

"With pirates infesting the tropic seas? I think not," Jeremy's father immediately replied.

"Perhaps, though, it is a chance for our son to satisfy his wanderlust," offered his mother quickly. "I would hold comfort knowing he is with Ombreux, and I have the utmost confidence in your captain. It is a common route, is it not? Perhaps one sail and no more, then Jeremy can be done with this sailing business and finally settle himself to the business expected of him."

Jeremy's father grunted again, frowning. His mother flashed Jeremy a look that said a hundred things. The response was not yes, but it was not no. Her look told him the subject was not concluded for her.

A moth with gossamer wings broke from a cocoon in his heart as he scooped the last spoonfuls of brulé into his mouth without even tasting them. Was it possible? Dared he hope?

Later that night, he lay with his head between the two pale rounded doves of Annette's bosom. Even as he had played the game of soaring to her rescue from Reginald's after-dinner conversation, giving her a tour of the manor and dropping by at a late hour to ensure her accommodations were satisfactory, the conversation from dinner was in his mind.

He drew a breath, stirring Annette from the sleep of pure content. "I am afraid, my dear lady, that I must bid you adieu. I would be an inconsiderate host to keep you awake past this late hour."

She gave a musky laugh, running her fingers through his hair. "Is it not ruder to leave a guest wanting for anything, even if it be your company for a time longer?"

"I would readily agree," he said with a kiss to support his statement. "Yet, I fear if the other guests of my home, namely your parents, were to find me here, that any future arrangements for accommodations would be most out of the question."

He rose as she laughed again. He slipped on his breeches, gave her a parting kiss, and left, still donning his clothes, to go to his bed and dream of the watery mistress whose bosom he preferred to be near.

Jeremy surfaced to wakefulness with the memory of that night in his mind. It had taken more persuasion on the part of himself, his mother, and Uncle Ombreux, but his father finally conceded. Jeremy felt guilt and regret, not for going, but for falling so easily into the trap.

Anger rose again, and with it, he wanted nothing more

than to take on lessons in trade, philosophy, and law. All of those subjects he normally shied from, but he now wanted to prove he could master them and that Ombreux should have no doubt of Jeremy's rightful place as his father's heir and in the monarchy.

Suddenly, his thoughts were completely distracted. Warm skin moved against his, a body turned beside him, and a breast pressed against his chest. Sanura nestled herself against him, resting her head on his shoulder and laying her arm across his chest. He was already aroused by his memory of Annette — waking to find Sanura naked in his arms made it impossible to subdue. His emotions, both of her and the betrayal, were piqued. He made quick but powerful love to her. She seemed as ready as he was, riding the wave of ecstasy with him, though perhaps not quite to the peak of the previous night before he spent himself.

She seemed pleased, though, laughing gently in the aftermath. "Dis ees how jyoo say good morning now?"

Jeremy held her close, burying his face in her hair as he kissed her neck. "Yes, this is how I say good morning."

"I like more dan words," she said, cringing with a giggle as he found a spot behind her ear.

"I agree," he said, giving her a kiss and rolling over to relieve her of his weight.

She rose and went outside to wash, but Jeremy lingered with gratitude for how comfortable he was. Though still a far cry from his bed at home, he had slept better that night than he had in any on the island. Even with the cobwebs left in his head by the rum, he was content. He would have liked a strong cup of tea, his favorite remedy for such things, but was glad even without it.

The resolve he had discovered on waking surfaced again. Yes, he would have tea again. He would learn all he could about making a fortune in its trade, that and many other things. Until he faced his uncle to exact revenge, he could take his source of wealth from him.

Jeremy would make him curse the day he had moved to take his father's wealth and lineage. He was not sure how he could, but he would find a way.

That afternoon the weather kept them in the shelter of the cave. Though they shared no intimacy, they lay together as contendedly as if they had. Jeremy stroked Sanura's tresses as they splayed over his chest, just as he had fantasized about so many times. He was led to think of how close he had come to not having this.

"Sanura, dear?"

Nearly lulled to sleep by the rain, Sanura took a sleepy breath before answering, "Yes?"

"Who were those horrid men?"

She tensed a little, immediately making him feel guilty for reminding her of them in a moment of such peace, yet she answered after a moment of thought with a word he could not hope to understand. "Dey are no friend to my piple, to my family. Dey take our foods and our tings, our trade, kill men. Dey are, what is word? Not friend."

"Enemy," he replied. "They are enem*ies* of your people. You fight, you have wars, take from one another, kill each other."

She thought, repeating a few of the words. "Yes, eh-neh-meeh." She paused and tried again. "Dey en-neh-meeh to many piple. Dey no like Zer-ah-mee piple more dan me-my piple."

"I am sure I would know who these men are, I just don't know your word for them," said Jeremy. "Do you know how else they may be called, ah, other names?"

She thought again and sighed. "I do not know."

He curled the arm she nestled against around her in

protective comfort. "It is no matter. They are dead, and we have gained from it."

She leaned her head against his chest, and he felt her smile.

A boom of thunder rolled by outside. It faded over the sea, leaving only the heavy patter of rain again.

"I have never seen a woman fight, truly fight, or kill. How do you know how to fight with your fist and with a knife?" He made gestures where he could to help her understand.

She paused, whether not wanting or knowing how to answer, he could not tell. "I must know to live. My family, all fight, even woman — women to keep? Ah, to keep live?"

"Perhaps you mean protect?" offered Jeremy. "When I came and fought the men, I was protecting you from harm, from hurt. Your family must all fight to protect themselves. Ah, each other and their own person." He tried to think of a better way to explain the complicated concept, but she seemed to understand.

"Yes, we must protect all piple and tings when move, ah, from home."

"Travel?" he asked. "When you go from home to other places?"

"Yes," she nodded.

Jeremy turned this over in his mind. What a harsh existence she must have. Given this information, and from what he could decipher from her appearance and what he had been able to understand from her, he could guess she most likely came from the distant tribes.

Jeremy frowned. "How did you come to be here?"

Sanura was quiet again. Thunder rolled lazily overhead. When it passed, she took a breath, paused and said, "Enemy come to sheep. Dey come to take. I fight wit men." She made a motion.

"Fall?" he asked. "You fell overboard? From ship to water?" He made the same motions.

"Yes, fell o-verboart," she said.

"Were they the same men, of the same society, as the men we killed?"

"Yes and no," she said. "I don't know how say. Men we kill and men on ship friends. Both my enemy."

Jeremy nodded. "I understand. They are allies." He took an end of her silken hair and twisted it lazily around his finger. "Why were you on the ship? Where were you going?"

She thought for a while before answering. "What is word for tings in ship dat it carry?"

"Cargo? The goods such as food, gold, lumber, tea, textiles, wine, anything that is taken from one place to another in a ship is cargo."

She nodded. "I go to see cargo give, ah, is give? To where need." She sighed impatiently. "I see men no take."

"Ah! You were overseeing the shipment to ensure the cargo arrived at its destination without being taken or pilfered. You protect, watch, the cargo. You see that bad men don't take it."

She worked through those words. "Yes, I tink is how to say."

"Why, may I ask? Why are you, a woman, chosen for such a dangerous task?"

"Ot-ter men come wit me," she said.

"What were you protecting?"

Sanura laughed, turning in his arms to face him. Her breasts pressed against him, distracting him from his thoughts. "Questions!" she exclaimed. "I want to ask jyoo, Zherahee. How deed you come to be here?" She carefully parroted his original question.

"Oh, well." He gave a laugh of his own, though a knot formed in his belly. He couldn't tell her who he was. If they — when they — finally found a ship to take them home, none could know who he was. Unless it was a ship of his father's or an ally, he would risk being held for ransom or killed. After his experience, he would likely keep himself unidentified for as long as possible even on the friendliest ship.

"I am a shipwrecked sailor," he said, regretting that he was telling a half-truth. "Nothing near so valiant as your tale." He smiled down at her.

He could tell she was going to ask more questions. He did not want to dodge them or tell falsehoods anymore, even partial ones. His body was beginning to distract him anyway. She was warm against him in contrast to the cool air that breathed in on them. He could feel the point of her exposed nipple on his chest. He brushed it with his fingertips.

"No more questions," he said, looking into her dark eyes, "I've no more answers at the moment. You have driven my mind to think of other things."

She laughed in answer and returned his kiss. Clearly it did not bother her to end their discussion there.

Proper clothing and a bit of food did wonders for Jeremy's spirits. He found his thoughts and projections to be more hopeful and confident. Of course, Sanura's acceptance of him was the main source of his buoyed mood. He found life on the island to be ever so much more tolerable. With a few more creature comforts, a supply of and more variety of food, and sure means of passage off the island as he wished, he even thought he could be happy there.

It was not so bad to search and hunt for food. The scenery was beautiful, particularly at dawn and sunset. He could spend time wandering through visions, thoughts, and fantasies rather than cramming his head with study and planning his strategies around every social interaction. There were no parties to attend and feign interest in. He realized the reason for his sexual promiscuity was partly because it gave him something to do, a game, as he was paraded around by his mother from one dull conversation to the next.

He had thought of his two years in the military as freedom, yet nearly every minute of the day was regimented and scheduled. It was freedom from manor life, but it was still a life of servitude, one always connected to his lineage. One that he knew he would have to continue in the future. He had not expected to have to call upon his survival training, yet what he had learned had enabled him to survive. If he could get this far, he could make it home.

This pervasive conviction was at the core of his new daily activities. Driving it to new heights were his emotions for Sanura. He found himself feeling and thinking of her in ways he had never experienced. He had wondered if one day he would know a woman he could care for in such ways. His impetus was not nearly so strong to get his own person off of the island as it was to protect her and to know she would be returned home. He would gladly stay as a castaway if he could be certain she would be safe.

The days passed pleasantly as they could. Sanura did what she could to liven their fare, collecting and adding any sort of plant anatomy to her creations. Jeremy made regular trips up the peak, spending as much time as he could searching for sails. He was aided by a spyglass that had been a reward from the spoils of battle.

Sanura had expressed concern that the men they had fought were a foraging party from a ship and that it would come searching for them. He promised her he would let her see any ship before lighting the beacon. She told him she would be able to recognize an enemy ship.

As the days passed, Jeremy noted the rains diminished and the heat became less stifling in the day. The nights were pleasant, even cool if there was a late rain. Those nights were very happy, spent in Sanura's arms, warming each other in more ways than one.

One morning Jeremy awoke to feel a lightness in the air he was unaccustomed to. The oppressive humidity had eased considerably, giving a vibrancy to the morning. The air even felt cool. Jeremy took a deep breath and stretched to happy wakefulness. He was sorry to find Sanura had risen already. She did have breakfast started, though. She sat by the fire as it cooked, a happy smile on her face as she watched the morning outside.

"Good morning, my dear," he greeted her with a kiss on her cheek. "You should have woken me. I would have helped."

"*Sabilkeer*, no, it is all right. Dere were no birds," she said carefully, though more correctly. They had been spending a lot of time learning each other's languages. She still could not master certain sounds, such as in his name, but then he didn't work too hard on correcting it. All it did was make him want to kiss her, and he loved that. He knew she still didn't grasp everything he said, and he certainly needed her to speak slowly in her language, but despite that, they understood one another very well.

"Oh, that's a shame," he said of breakfast and sat beside her, looking out into a sky bluer than he was used to seeing on the island. "Of course, it would be a sin to kill one of them this morning. I think every one should be spared to lift its voice in praise of this beautiful day. Is it not marvelous?"

"Yes, it feel wun-deer-ful. In my home, the first day of nice wed-der is day of joy and gather to be happy. Is dere word for dis?"

"Perhaps celebration. People gather together to be happy and *celebrate* the good weather."

She nodded. "Yes, dey cel-ee-brit de wed-der." She turned and pushed a small turtle shell from where it sat in the fire. The water within was starting to boil. She dropped flowers from a plant Jeremy knew as *carota* into it.

"I have seen you make this before for breakfast, but I don't think I've seen it in the end. Do you add it to the food?"

"You no — do not know?"

"I thought you were boiling the leaves to eat or making a tea, to drink, but of *carota*? I've not heard of that. Is it customary among your people?"

"Among de women, yes."

Jeremy was puzzled. "Only women? Why not the men? Do they not like the taste?"

"No one really *like* taste. Women muss take. Do women of Zheramee soc-e-tay not drink?"

"Not that I know of. Why must you take it?"

She was smiling at his naivety in kindness. "Jyoo and I, we have caution in love. Dis help."

Jeremy was baffled. Caution in love? Tea helps with caution?

Sanura smiled broader and leaned forward to kiss him. "Jyoo re-member lass night?"

"How could I possibly forget?" He smiled too.

"Re-member we have caution at end? I help jyoo to, I don't know jyoo word, fin-eesh?" She grinned in mischievous pleasure at the memory.

Suddenly, Jeremy realized what she was saying. "Do you mean it prevents pregnancy, ah, a child?" He knew he hadn't used those words before. He rubbed his fingers over her belly. "No child here?"

"Yes, helps no child here."

"Well, I never!" Jeremy knew herbs to have healing powers but had never heard of contraceptive properties. Then again, he had never cared to find out. It was always in his mind that it was his responsibility. The bastard son of a future duke was still the son of a future duke. His father had taught him well to keep matters under his own control.

Sanura smiled and turned away to tend to the cooking. He watched her with admiration, wondering how it was he had been fortunate enough to find this amazing woman.

Jeremy and Sanura reveled in the next few days as it remained not so hot. The rain stayed away, and the sky was clear blue. It warmed again but was still dry. Jeremy noted the change in the weather with concern. The relief from the heat was more than welcome, yet the end of rain meant the end of growing season. They had dried meat and fruits, but it would not last long. The ocean would provide, but it was not always guaranteed. As it was, their fare was minimal at best. Though there would be no ice and snow, winter would be long and scarce on the island.

Jeremy never voiced his fears to Sanura. She only saw confidence and hope in him. He worried over her. She had been marooned longer, at least a month more, from what they could guess. Though she was strong, he knew the scarce diet was affecting her. He had seen the changes in himself. His belly was shrunken, his ribs and pelvis could be seen more easily as he moved. He retained his muscles, but they tired more easily. He constantly felt empty all over. The reflection of his face in the water showed his cheekbones and hollows starting under his eyes.

Jeremy was sitting at his lookout post worrying over these thoughts one afternoon. He was discouraged, as the day before he had seen a speck on the horizon, but it disappeared even as he took a moment to decide if it was close enough to light their beacon. He rose, thinking to go back down to the cave and spend some time searching for food.

He rounded the rock to find his path and stopped, staring. In the western sea was a ship, near enough to see she was a Caramusal and nearly close enough to see the emblem upon her mains'l.

Jeremy lifted the spyglass, barely daring to breathe. He saw the emblem, one he did not recognize, and the figures of men in the rigging.

"Sanura!" he called, "Sanura!" Far below, she appeared at the edge of the pool. He waved her up. "A ship! A ship!"

She disappeared, and Jeremy looked again to assure himself it was not a mirage. He watched until Sanura arrived. He offered his hand to help her up and pointed.

"Look! See there? A Caramusal!"

She sucked her breath through her teeth and knelt, pulling Jeremy with her.

"It's them, isn't it?" he asked with a sinking heart. "It is the ship those men came from."

"Is enemy, not same, but not good," she answered.

"Damn," he sighed. "I can only assume it is folly to signal them."

She fixed her dark eyes to him. "Dey cut jyor troat like a feesh belly," she confirmed.

Chilled by her metaphor—and its truth—Jeremy looked to the ship again. "They won't find us, will they? There are no tracks, and we hid the boat well enough, did we not?"

"I do not tink dey find us," she agreed. "We muss hide."

They kept low and made their careful way down the rocks. Though the presence of the ship was frustrating and unnerving, they made use of the daylight and spent the rest of the afternoon foraging in the forest on the east side of the island. When they returned at dusk, Sanura performed her ritual in the cave as Jeremy looked for the ship from a spot on the rock above the trees. The ship had moved north and west through the scattered islands, moving away from them. That was a relief, at least.

Jeremy had a dream that night. The men of the ship found them, they found Sanura, and he was powerless, frozen as they surrounded her. He woke with a start and a pounding heart. The quiet was nearly as deafening as her screams in his dream had been. He rose as best he could without disturbing her and went out into the cool night. The fronds of the dark palms were lacquered in moonlight. Stars canvassed the night above.

Jeremy sat upon a rock at the edge of the pool and stared up at them. He saw the very ones that would guide him home. He only needed a seafaring vessel. He was convinced in the deepest part of his heart that he would get his chance to leave the island. The question would be when. How long would he have to wait, and what would he have to endure in the meantime? Would he be in a well enough state to be able to take the chance? Would Sanura be with him?

If not, could he come back?

He sighed, looking over the sea, trying to shake the dread that filled him. He was no stranger to death. In his days in uniform, he had killed and seen his comrades fall. A few had been close friends whose demise had given him cause to mourn. None of those had been so heartfelt as his first experience with death several years before.

He'd been in his twelfth year, nearly a man, yet still an innocent child. Both of his mother's parents had suddenly died while at supper one afternoon. His father and uncle were supposed to have joined them. The two had greeted the elder Duke and Duchess and wine had been served. Soon after, Ombreux had asked Jeremy's father to show him a new stallion he had recently purchased before sitting to eat. There were a few minutes late in returning, and when they did, they found the servants in a panic and Ombreux's parents severely ill. When they died several hours later, Ombreux had gone into a rage, searching every servant until he found one with hemlock in his pocket. He was an older man with a sour temperament. It was known he was in danger of being dismissed.

It was enough evidence for Ombreux. He drove his blade into him on the spot, avenging his parents' deaths.

Now Ombreux's last words to Jeremy made a tight ball of cold darkness in the pit of his stomach. Was it he who had added the poison to the wine they drank before eating? Ombreux had been the one to find it in the possession of the servant. He could easily have pulled it from his own pocket. No one would believe a servant over the Duke's son.

What would have been his motive, though? Power, yet he would have it regardless. Surely, waiting a time was better than murdering your own parents. As he had been a child, Jeremy knew of none of the political or business developments of the time. He dearly wished he could speak to his father. He would be heartbroken. His mother must never know. It would be hard enough to know that Ombreux had tried to kill her son.

Jeremy's love for her and his new hatred for his uncle rose within. He could not let him win. He had to avenge his grandparents' deaths and the attempt on his own life. He had no choice but to survive. His honor demanded it.

CHAPTER EIGHT

The next morning the ship was nowhere in sight. Jeremy and Sanura spent their morning outing on the east side of the island regardless. They lifted their gaze often, ready to dart to the trees should a ship or rowboat appear. They were in good spirits, as they had found some useful herbs in their walk to the water and each of them had caught a plump fish.

They had left their collection bag and Sanura's dress cloth on a rock on the beach. As Jeremy put the fish in the bag, he noted Sanura stayed in the water a moment longer, wearing nothing but her amulet, splashing water on her hot skin. His whole body warmed, but it started in his heart, not his manhood, although it was quick to rise there as well. When she came to fetch her dress, he stood behind her and put his hands on her hips, kissing her salty shoulder.

"Must you hide the exquisite work of art that is your body? I wish to admire it all day."

"Only admire, Zherahmee?" she asked with mischief as she wrapped the cloth around herself and tied it at her breasts.

His answer was a low growl of lust as she turned, and he held her against him. "One can admire with more than the eyes."

"Den sink of how fun it will be to take off de dress when we get to cave." She teased his lips with hers before brushing them with a kiss.

"Must I wait that long?" he breathed.

"Den we can lay out of sun and sleep and den love more,"

she said.

"Sweet temptress, I am your slave." He kissed her fully, took her hand, and walked to the trees.

On the way, they passed a *pahpah* tree. They could just see the yellow-orange of a ripe fruit higher up in the tree.

"I think I can reach it," Jeremy said. When he stretched up, though, his fingertips only bumped the bottom of the fruit. A jump and grab did not encourage the fruit to fall. It was still not quite ripe enough for that. His fingers slipped from around it.

"All right, we'll try this, then." Jeremy reached up to grab a lower branch to pull himself up for the second he needed to pull the fruit from the stem.

As his hand curled around it, his fingers pressed into something soft, something soft that immediately squirmed under his fingers. At the same time, Sanura shrieked, striking his arm from the branch. In that second, Jeremy's brain registered the snake. He saw it strike. Sanura screamed again, and he grabbed her, backing them both away. Jeremy watched as the creature raced into the foliage, only catching a glimpse of its tail before it was no more than a rustling in the leaves.

Cold dread froze solid when Sanura dropped to one knee, clutching her arm. Blood trickled between her fingers.

"Great gods, it bit you!" he gasped, kneeling beside her.

Sanura took her hand away for them to see two cuts, each half the length of his little finger in her arm. Jeremy produced a scrap of cloth he used to wipe the sweat from his face. He moved to take her hand away, but she stopped him.

"No, no touch! Hurt jyoo too." She took the cloth and covered the wound, gasping in pain.

Jeremy helped her to her feet, remorseful for having ever seen the fruit.

"Zherahmee, can jyoo carry me?" she asked. "Is bad I walk."

"Of course." He took her in his arms even as he spoke. They were not far from the rocky ascent to the ledge. Jeremy barely felt her weight, nor his own legs as he hurried through the forest and made the steep climb up the rocks. A few times he had to set her on her feet, climb up, then pull her up. He knew as well as she did that if the bite were poisonous, every beat of her heart carried it further through her body—exertion would only carry it faster.

Finally, they reached the ledge. Jeremy hurried her to the pool. She removed her dress and got in, grimacing as she submerged her arm.

"Zherahmee too," she said with a look of concern to him. "Wash bad from Zherahmee."

Jeremy could have cared less but knew it was wise in case he had come into contact with any poison. He stripped and got in, but only had eyes for her. She was pressing her skin, forcing it to bleed more. All this only confirmed his fear.

"You know that snake?" he asked. "Is it poisonous? Like the fish. Poison make sick?"

She did not look at him and did not answer.

"Sanura?" He tried to find her eyes.

She still avoided him. "Yes, poison."

Jeremy went numb with dread.

"Is only here, not like dis." Sanura motioned to show the fangs had grazed her.

Though it was not a true bite, it did not make Jeremy feel any better. Sanura grimaced, releasing her arm, unable to take the pain of squeezing it anymore.

"You need to lie down." Jeremy helped her out of the pool. He carried her to their bed, quickly drying her.

"I—must—sit—Zherahmee," she said, holding her arm close.

Jeremy moved the mattress so that part was leaning against the rock wall. He helped her onto it and in as comfortable of a reclining position as possible.

"Leef, Zherahmee. Bring leefs on top, lass dere." She pointed. Her eyes were heavy and dulled with pain, and her accent grew thicker.

Jeremy ran to fetch the last coconut bowl on the top of the shelf. Within it were coin-sized bits of dark green leaf.

"These?" he asked.

She took one and put it in her mouth. "Now, use rock and water, break some, stir." She made a motion with her good arm. She was not moving the other anymore. "Put on here, den cloth—" She made a wrapping motion.

"Yes, I understand. You rest."

Jeremy quickly did as he was bidden and cut strips of cloth from a shirt. When he returned to her, her eyes were closed, her breath shallow.

"Sanura?"

She did not respond.

"Sanura?"

The urgency in his voice caused her to stir, but only for a moment. He put some of the mixture on the wound and wrapped it carefully. Her arm was hot to the touch.

"Sanura, dear, what else can I do?"

His loving stroke to her brow came away warm and damp. She gave no answer but a momentary sound in a heavy breath. Jeremy's throat turned to stone and tears stung his eyes as he hurried away to get water and more cloth. She took a mouthful of water and managed a whispered *shokrahn*, the word of gratitude in her tongue. He dabbed her brow with a wet cloth.

"Just rest. This will pass soon, I know it. You're the strongest woman I've ever met. You're stronger than most men I've ever met. You can endure this. You will endure this. You can't let my foolishness—" He stopped, swallowing hard. "You will get well. We will leave the island soon. I'm not going without you. I can't be here without you. What am I saying? All will be well. This will pass, I'm sure of it. Is there more I can do? Please tell me what you need."

He stroked her head, combing his fingers through her hair. When she did not respond, he felt a touch of panic and laid his hand on her chest to try to gain her attention. Her heart beat rapidly under his palm.

"Sanura, please speak to me," he begged in a whisper as his throat had closed.

A quiet minute passed, then another as he dabbed her forehead and tried to coax her into consciousness. He was rewarded when she stirred again. Her eyes opened a little.

"*Meesa?*" she sighed. "*Where is Meesa?*" she asked in her language.

"Only me, Jeremy." He took her good hand and answered similarly. "*Sanura, it is Jeremy. You remember? How I help? What you need?*"

Her eyes set on him finally, under heavy lids. "*Zherahmee? Fetch Meesa. I must speak with her.*"

"*I no can. Meesa no here.*"

"Oh," she relaxed in disappointment, "*I must tell her. You must tell her —*"

"*What I tell her?*"

"*Trade is hers. Go to Medar, Zherahmee. Take . . .*" A word he didn't know. "*Sun glass. You . . .*" Another word he didn't know, but she clarified. "*Give look, to any there. They will know. They will help you.*"

"Medar!" Jeremy was startled to hear the word. "*Who I show sun glass to? What — what — how means trade is hers? How I find Meesa?*"

"*Show the glass,*" she said before her eyes closed. "*You must give it to Meesa. She will take my place.*"

Jeremy's innards turned to black bile. "*No, Sanura, you give to Meesa.* Dammit." He changed back to his language. "I won't hear such nonsense. You will give the glass to Meesa. You and

I are leaving this island together, do you hear me? Sweet gods, Sanura, please tell me you hear me."

She might have tried to open her eyes again, but that was her only response.

Jeremy drew a compulsive breath, half a sob, pulling back his weeping. He took the cloth to wet it and dab her warming body with it. It was the only thing he could do.

Jeremy had never had to care for someone who was ill. Though she was not conscious, he did all he could to keep her clean and comfortable. He used a palmetto frond as a fan to try to cool her and continually wet her skin with cloths, letting a few drops past her lips now and again. When the poultice on her arm dried, he made another, rewrapping it carefully, keeping the arm low and encouraging it to drain and bleed. It swelled around the gashes, and the skin there was hot.

As he worked, repeating the same tasks over and over, he talked to her, encouraging her, telling her of how it would be when they were found and how he wanted to take her to his home to show it to her. He had no way of knowing if she heard. It did not matter. Talking calmed him and kept his fear at bay. He only stopped when he used the last of the leaf in the bowl. He put the bowl to her lips to give her the last drops of the medicine. He did not know if it would help. It just seemed the thing to do. He dreaded leaving her side.

"I must get more of this leaf, Sanura, dear. I will return as swift as I may." He kissed her burning forehead and hurried outside into the last of the day before sunset.

He had never paid too much mind to her leaf gathering. She had shown him her discovered treasures, telling him as best she could of their value, but he'd listened more in interest of her knowledge rather than what that knowledge was. This plant he was familiar with, however. He'd had his first taste after some of the fruit were brought from the Southland from a trade expedition his father was involved in. Some of the fruit must have been washed ashore from a shipwreck and taken hold on the island. It bore a fruit quite similar to the smaller *pistanos* he was familiar with. This fruit tended to withstand the ravages of cooking more than its softer cousin and was excellent in thin slices over fish. He knew exactly where the closest plant was. He quickly harvested a few of the large leaves, each nearly a meter in length, and hurried back to the cave.

She was lying as he had left her. He went numb when he saw she was motionless. The seconds thudded loud, slow with his heart as he knelt, never reaching her soon enough. His hand revealed the lie his eyes told him when he laid it on her. She took a breath, the first in what seemed to him to be minutes, yet only a second had passed. His eyes had seen only what he feared.

Her heart had calmed, though not to what he considered a normal rate. Her breath was irregular still, as well, but it came. Jeremy blew out a breath, moving to sit beside her. By habit, he dipped the cloth and gently ran it over her. As he did, he was suddenly overcome with sorrow and fatigue. He lowered his head to his knee and felt tears burn in his eyes. He became conscious of his own condition, and he was irritated at his stomach's selfish vocalization. He offered it a compromise by fetching a *pistano* and eating it swiftly as he continued to tend to Sanura. He had to stay strong so he could care for her. If she died, he would never wish to eat again.

Night settled upon the island outside. Jeremy fed the fire and continued to nurse Sanura. He had never felt so useless in all his life. There had always been a physician or alchemist that could be called for. He'd never had to learn their business. He knew the basic actions to use if a comrade fell wounded in battle, but he never had to be concerned once they were taken from the battlefield. He drew on his memories from illnesses he had suffered as a child. The nursemaid always seemed to know how to comfort him. He never knew what she gave him. He had always taken it all for granted. Now he was alone, the one with the necessary knowledge was the one who lay dying and needed his help. He had so little to give.

He was mixing yet another poultice, frustrated. "Come now, Nottingdale, think," he scolded himself. "There must be something more you can do."

He crushed the leaves with a rounded rock, trying to recall anything she might have told him. He did remember one thing she had said. He paused in his work and went to the shelf that held her bowls of plants. The top two rows held help plants. The bottom held food plants. He looked over the top rows. He remembered the plant she had given him when his foot hurt.

He picked up a bowl. "Yes, that's it."

"Hurt go," she had said about this one. He took a couple of leaves and put them in his mix. He wouldn't know if it would work, but at least he was trying something.

The sky had been black for some time when Jeremy allowed himself to feel a little hopeful. Her breathing and heart had calmed. She was still warm to the touch, but not hot. He covered her now, fearing she would get a chill. He touched her forehead and chest now and again with the wet cloth still. Toward midnight, Jeremy was startled from an exhausted stare when she gave the slightest of groans. He snapped upright as her head stirred.

"Sanura? Sanura, can you hear me?" He was immediately on his knees beside her.

She was trying to speak but could only murmur. Jeremy wet her lips with the cloth, pleading for her to speak. He only caught a few whispered syllables he did not understand, then she fell still. Some time later, it happened again. That time he deciphered the words, "ship," "gold," and "father," in her language.

"Sanura, is me, Jeremy," he said in her tongue. *"You speak to me. I want to help. How I help? Sanura?"*

He caught a glitter of her eyes for a brief moment, then she closed them again with a sigh and was still. Jeremy stroked her hair. Exhausted, frustrated, frightened, Jeremy let a few tears escape. He hoped she wasn't giving up. She had been through the worst, hadn't she? He wiped his tears away and kept praying to any god that would listen.

Later, his mind, exhausted from his fervent, silent pleas, pondered her words. They had finally made a connection, and he could not talk to her of it. Medar, or Meday in his own tongue, was the great empire in the lands south of the common sea whose northern banks were lined by his homeland. If she had a connection there, why had she never mentioned it before?

It could explain how she came to be at sea. Medar was the great trading nation that held all power between the great south lands, the eastern lands of spice and gold, and in recent decades, the newly discovered ports across the great ocean. It was rare for Medar to trade with Jeremy's nation and those of the northern shore of the sea. The traders of the eastern Empire had violent control over all trade from the far lands of the other tribes and beyond. The rulers of Medar had complete control of trade between them and the far south. They had become the center of trade between the Empire and the new lands of the west. Medar had enough wealth generated from the east-west-south artery that they were not desperate to trade with the north. They let those items be filtered through the eastern Empire rather than risk war with them and upset the fragile balance.

All nations on the north shores suffered the price. All goods from the east and south came at an exorbitant cost. The nations of the north shores attempted to establish trade with the south from time to time. It worked occasionally, but never with the dominant rule of the eastern Empire. Any trade from the north that sprang up was squelched by the east. The king of the south had no interest in wasting his men to fight them and did not wish to disrupt good relations with the east. For although formidable in military might, it would be an expensive campaign for the south to challenge the east. Aside from that, there were enormous cultural and language barriers that prevented relations between the north and south. The main reason for the apathy of the King of Medar was that goods from the north came to him at a relatively low price from the east, as he had the upper hand with them. His goods tended to be in more demand, and he had no incentive to maintain direct trade with the north. Given all of these factors, Jeremy and his neighboring nations were largely ignored by the largest center of trade and wealth in the known world.

The amulet Sanura bore must be an emblem of her tribe. Jeremy assumed they had good relations with the King of Medar, so they must be from the south or east. So Sanura had been sent with a shipment of goods from Medar across the ocean to a port of the western lands. That lent even more amazement to her story. With all the tradesmen in Medar, they sent a woman? She had explained before, but he still didn't fully comprehend. It did explain her skill with fighting. Anyone on a caravan to or from Medar had a good chance of getting their throat slit. What was it she had guarded? He suddenly remembered her muttering the word *gold*. Was that it? Yet gold came from the new lands. It did not go *to* them.

Jeremy was too tired to think about it more. After some cursory muddling, he forgot it altogether as he continued to tend to Sanura. Through the night she would occasionally speak to Meesa, instructions regarding trade Jeremy did not understand. She once tried to give him a message for her father but slipped away before she could convey it. She called for her father and mother a few times and for Meesa as well.

Jeremy battled exhaustion despite his concern and fear. He sat beside her, resting his head against the upright part of the mattress as his body felt increasingly ill with fatigue and his eyes closed of their own volition. Just before falling to slumber, he would jolt awake, pain pricking his body, and he would settle to near slumber once more. A vision of a *pahpah* tree with writhing branches was before his eyes when he was startled awake by her voice.

"Zherahmee," she whispered.

He jolted forward before he even realized what he was doing. "*I am here*, Sanura," he responded, though his head was heavy as a rock.

"*Water, please*," she said.

Jeremy gladly provided it, noting the sky beginning to lighten outside. He drew a damp cloth over her forehead.

"Sanura, *what can I do?*"

She took a few full breaths. "*I do not know.*" She turned her head and truly saw him for the first time. "*You are ill?*" Alarm edged in her voice.

"*No, no, I am tired, concerned. I have fear for you,*" he assured her.

"Zheramee muss sleep," she said drowsily.

"No, if you need —"

"I tink bad go. De . . . what is word?"

"Poison?"

"Yes, poison go. I want lay. Jeremy lay too."

Relief brought tears to his eyes. He leaned over and kissed her brow. It was no longer hot. He helped her to move to lie supine and gently pulled the mattress until all of it lay flat upon the ground. He moved Sanura to a comfortable position, covering her with a blanket. He lay beside her, putting a hand on her good arm, and immediately fell asleep.

He woke a few times as the day passed, waking Sanura to get her to drink. After, he would sleep again. It was afternoon when he woke and felt rested. He turned over, his first thought for Sanura. She was sleeping peacefully beside him. He sent prayers of gratitude to the gods as he lifted her hand to kiss it and rose. He went outside to relieve himself, then went to their food stores. She had been drinking, and he knew it was important she continue. He would like to see her eat. He wished he had a broth or soup to offer her. He could make something if there was a bird in the net, but he did not want to wait that long to cook it. Could one make a soup of fruit? The thought was at first ludicrous, but he reconsidered. He took some of the fruits and cut them up into a bowl, taking care to save the juices. He added water and mashed the mix with a stone. Presently, it became liquid, stirred smooth to the texture of a bisque. Jeremy gave it a taste and was pleasantly surprised. He went to Sanura, waking her gently.

"I have something for you," he said.

She let him pull her up, leaning against him as he cradled her in his arm. He brought the bowl to her lips. She drank deep and took a breath.

"Is good, Zherahmee," she said and took more.

She drank most of it, then laid her head on his shoulder. "Sank jyoo, Zherahmee."

Those were the words he would have given his entire birth-right to hear the night before.

He set the bowl down and rested his hand against the side of her face. When she drifted into sleep, he laid her down, kissed her brow, and went check the bird trap.

The concoction of bird, fruits, and herbs he had created was nearly done when Sanura stirred. He jumped up when he saw she was trying to rise.

"Wait, Sanura, what are you doing? You should lie still."

"Muss get up, Zherahmee, I muss go outside," she said.

"Why, oh—" He suddenly understood. "No, I'd rather you didn't. I have—"

She shook her head, fighting to get up. "I can go out. Is not far."

Rather than upset her, he helped her to her feet and assisted her outside. They made their steady way out and to the side of the rock to their private spot. Jeremy helped Sanura to perch herself on one of the rocks there. She leaned against a larger one for support. Neither of them had the first thought of modesty or privacy. It was not an issue in the least for him. If he went away, he would be abandoning her in her time of need. He did take a few steps away and turn his back out of respect. She had never been shy before, so he was not sure if it bothered her to have an audience. He had always suspected she chose this separate place and went deeper into the trees on their walks for this need for practical reasons rather than modesty.

They visited the pool afterward, and he could immediately tell the water felt good to her. He joined her, unwrapping her arm so she could submerge it. The wounds were still red, and an area half the size of his palm was swollen around them.

She grimaced when the water touched her arm. His heart strained in sympathy at the pain in her eyes.

"Be at ease, Sanura," he soothed her, guiding her to sit back. He sat beside her and gently took her arm and lifted it from the water. He scrutinized it, though not knowing what he saw. Her flesh was still swollen, the two angry red slashes glaring at him, yet it was not as bad as it had been.

"*Is it good?*" he asked in her language.

Her soft smile made his soul tremor. "*Yes, Zherahmee. It is much better. The . . .*" She said an unfamiliar word and made a motion with her hand over her arm to imply swelling. " . . . *will be smaller.*"

His own smile returned as he leaned forward to kiss her shoulder. "I am relieved beyond words to hear that," he said.

"You are a good healer, Zherahmee," she said with a sleepy smile.

He shook his head. *"No,"* he said, *"You teach me, I learn of you. No, Sanura, Jeremy no heal. You leaves. They heal. I only use."*

"I still say you are a good healer." She sighed and closed her eyes, leaning her head back.

"You have tired," said Jeremy. *"You need lay."*

"A few minutes more, please?" she pleaded.

He could not refuse her. They sat a short time longer, simply glad to be where they were, then she let him help her back to bed. She ate some of the food he had prepared and after wanted to rest, falling asleep as he covered her. When he lay down beside her later, he was asleep nearly as fast, the core of his being fluttering with relief and happiness. Whether it was his doing or not, she was spared from death.

Over the next few days, Jeremy devoted himself to Sanura, doing all of the tasks necessary for their survival and reveling in the responsibility. Her smile and "Sank jyoo," made the sweat and toil seem insignificant nuisances. He was proud of himself as he concocted a few rather palatable dishes and started to recognize the plants he gathered and their uses.

Sanura slept much of the first day, but when she woke, she was coherent and stronger each time. He always had food and water for her when she did. He kept the "hurt go" leaf under the wrapping on her arm and always had a drink of it ready for her. He also used aloe on her arm to help the wound to heal and to keep her skin from being irritated by the wrapping. He kept the medicine plant nearby, offering her a breath of its smoke if she wanted. It helped the pain and also helped her to sleep.

His new role of servitude felt strangely empowering. Sanura's recovery depended on him, and his own continued survival depended on him. No one was there to tend to his every whim. No one was there to tell him what he should, what he ought, or what he needed to do or learn. He did and learned because he had to and because he wanted to. What he learned directly related to everyday life rather than some far-off promised future of someday-when-you-are-Duke.

The first evening it was apparent that Sanura would re-cover, Jeremy had performed her nightly ritual. It did not seem fitting for it not to be done.

"I don't know who I am addressing, why I offer these items, nor the words I must say, but I beseech ye, god of this woman, Sanura, to hear and see me in her stead," he had said as he held then dropped portions of his harvest of the day as he had seen her do. "I also do not know why I do this." He cut a few strands of his hair. "I offer them just the same as she does." Afterward, he was strangely comforted and peaceful.

Sanura was much better by the third day, moving about on her own and well enough to sit outside for a little while when it was not so hot. She was sleeping when he performed the ritual. She could have done it, but he did not wish to wake her, and the sunset would be missed. He could do it once more. He found he enjoyed it.

He offered his excuses as he had before, enacted the ritual, ending with his hair, then took a moment to savor the peace. It was enhanced by the surrounding canvas of red, orange, yellow, and pink over the dark green waters. Sunset and dawn, when the sun was birthed or absorbed into the horizon, were times of magic and spirits. He made every fiber of his being concentrate on the spell it created. Then, with a snap heard with the soul, the sun was gone, leaving a brilliant sky in its wake.

Jeremy sighed in utter contentment, doused the fire, and rose from his knees. He took up the bowls he had used and went into the cave.

Sanura's voice was as mystic as the display of the heavens he had just witnessed. "What you were doing?"

He looked up to see her eyes, sharp and bright, and a smile knowing the answer and pleased by it. He had set the mattress again with one corner rested upright against a rock so she could sit up if she chose. She reclined against it.

"Oh," he quelled a bashful grin, "I, ah, thought it fitting to continue your ritual. I didn't want your god to be angry." Her laugh turned his core to butter. He went to kneel beside her, taking her hand and kissing it. "I hope I've not done wrong."

"Zherahmee," she cooed, running her fingers over his head and sending a sizzling shot of pleasure through him, "you are . . ." she shook her head, still smiling, "Even in my language, I do not know word."

Overcome, Jeremy leaned forward and gave her a gentle kiss.

Her hands took his as he moved to sit before her.

"What you give?" she asked.

He shrugged. "Bits of what I found today, everything that you do."

Her eye glinted. "Even Zherahmee hair?"

For some reason, he blushed. "Well, yes. You do."

Her full, joyful laugh dropped the bottom of his belly into his groin. He had a flashing image of leaping atop her right then and ravishing her until her passionate screams matched the one coursing through him.

Her eyes sparkled. "Zherahmee, you do much good, but I need, ah, ex-playn, what I do. At night when sun go, I give gra-tee-tud for all good of day. All is gived to me, I show I know and have thanks by give a leetl back to . . ." She made a broad gesture. "Don't know word to all."

Knowing some people were private about their religious affairs, he had never held more than a distant curiosity, but now he had done it, he did want to know more.

"What god do you offer to?" he asked.

"Gohd?"

"Yes, a being. Not a person, but similar that we can't see, but they have power, they work, in our lives."

"Ah," she realized and said a word he did not recognize. She made a face that he wanted to kiss. "Not gohd, but I give to wur-eld, to all. Not be-ying. I don't know. Is hard to say."

Jeremy thought. There were those who believed that god or gods of existence were beyond comprehension and certainly beyond sight. Perhaps that was what she spoke of.

"I think I understand," he told her. "You offer gratitude to the universe. All in the world and beyond for the good that occurs?"

She nodded. "Yes, that is co-rect." She smiled broadly. "I do not tink Zherahmee understand if I say. Try to ex-playn."

"No, I understand perfectly," he said, though it raised many more questions about her. Then he had a thought. "Wait, though, what does my hair have to do with it?"

She blushed and looked down at her fingers as she toyed with his. "I have gra-tee-tud for Zherahmee."

"You have been doing it since the very first day you found me."

She rubbed the tip of her index finger over the back of his hand. "When Zherahmee come, all bad go. Zherahmee bring happy to me."

That was too much for him. He cupped her jaw in his hands and pressed his lips to hers, soft but lingering. Her hands touched his face, driving him to kiss her deeper. One of her hands fell away to rest upon his manhood, gently rubbing and squeezing in her search for it, making him break the kiss and suck a breath through his teeth. His hand moved a half second before his desire overwhelmed him.

"Sanura, dear, I cannot." He took her hand away, kissing its knuckles desperately. "You are not well. It would be most dishonorable."

She seemed to be confused. "I want to plees Zherahmee."

"You do please me, sweet Sanura, you do, and you need not do more than smile to do it. Had I one grain less resilience, I would be expending all the passion in my body upon you even now, but I fear hurting you even with the most care."

"Zherahmee." Her voice and eyes were suddenly musky. "Come." She took his arm, pulling him forward.

"Sanura."

She pulled him slightly off balance as he tried to rise and resist. He was forced to kneel, straddling her, or he would have fallen on her.

"Let me," she said, putting the hand of her good arm in the back of his neck to pull him forward for a kiss. He relented to at least that, sensing her need, hoping to meet it with that least of actions. Her hand left his neck and she began to pull at the ties of his breeches.

He protested, but she stopped him with her stare. "Wait."

His eyes rolled and closed as her soft hand found his semi-rigid phallus. She stroked it, coaxing it to life.

"Sanura . . ." he begged in a whisper.

"Dis is all," she whispered back. "I want to plees Zherahmee."

Finally, he understood. Comprehension shot a jolt of raw heat through him that caused him to solidify.

Her breath caressed his face. "Yes, Zherahmee, I like, too."

Jeremy surrendered to her, letting her hand stoke his fire until it burned all within. Her fingers left searing white-hot trails up and down his manhood. He was vaguely aware when she paused a moment, his glazed eyes saw her dip her fingers in the husk of aloe he kept by her bed, then the brand of her touch coursed through him again. He groaned as she squeezed harder, sliding easily over his full length with the slippery substance. She twisted her hand as she stroked, curling her fingers over his tapered head before pressing it through them.

His strength left him. He braced his hands on the rock behind her for support. He could feel her hot breath on his shoulder.

"Oh, Zherahmee," she muttered with unknown words.

He thought his member might break, he was so hard. One more stroke sent the cold wash through his loins, and his seed burst forth with his groan of relief. Her grip softened, and she caressed him as the last spasms left him, leaving him spinning in the wake.

He would have been glad to flop down beside her and ride the aftermath in a daze, but his first lucid thought was for her. She sat with a pleased smile on her face, waiting patiently for him to recover. He kissed her breathlessly and pulled his shirt over his head, then drew it over her chest, now glistening with the fruit of his passionate release. Only after she was tended to did he fall aside. She curled up beside him, gently placing her bandaged arm on his chest. His hand found hers as they lay between their bodies, and he floated away on a cloud of bliss.

CHAPTER NINE

"By the gods, those are sails!" Jeremy took the net satchel from around his head and shoulder and dropped it in the sand. He retrieved the spyglass from among the leaves and fruits and put it to his eye. "I can't see the marks, but it's a merchant ship. Here, look, can you see?" He handed the glass to Sanura.

She was able to hold it with one hand. The other arm was in a slung. She looked long before frowning. "No, I cannot see. Dey go nort-wess, I tink."

They watched the ship, and it was not long before it was lost behind the rise of an island.

"Do you think it was the same we saw before?" he asked.

"No, we see mark on big sail if is," she said. "I tink is not same, but I don't know what ship it is."

"Nor do I," he said, disappointed. "Well, we must keep sharper eyes, then. Perhaps it will return this way."

"Yes, per-haps," she agreed softly, turning and handing him the spyglass. He smiled. She was getting better at his language and was becoming nearly fluent, though without losing the accent that drove him mad with adoration. He hoped he compared at least a little in his practice of hers. They switched back and forth between the two unconsciously many times. Her need for rest had brought many hours of conversation.

The first rays of the sun to come from over the eastern side of the island fell upon her bare breasts, veiling them with orange light. Jeremy feasted on their beauty as he gathered their things. She continued to watch the horizon until she sensed he was ready to move on. She caught his pleased observation with a smile.

"You do not hide good, Zheramee," she teased.

"Should I hide how I feel? Did you not say it confused you before?" he retorted with a smile.

They walked the waterline.

She tucked her black hair behind an ear. "I tink Zheramee likes to hide his feel. Does he not?"

"Oh, yes, a gentleman does hide his feelings, except when he is alone with the woman that creates those feelings in him," he said happily. "That being the case, my heart is out for the world to see, and I say, let it see!"

He opened his arms to shout his decree to the sky. Sanura laughed, spurring his joy. "I would not care if I were in the market square at the port. I would jump up on a stack of barrels." He leaped up on a rock to illustrate. "Shout at the top of my lungs, I have found happiness! I am driven mad with pleasure by Sanura!"

She was blushing and laughing. "Zheramee! Fall down!"

He gave her a tremendous grin and hopped down. "As m'lady wishes, but I must correct you. The word you need is jump."

"Zhump?" she tried to repeat.

"Yes, jump. I think, then jump." He tapped his head. "Fall is oh, no! I fall!" He gyrated his arms and leaned off balance, making her laugh. "You see? Jump is on purpose. I do it. Fall is accident. I do not want to."

"Yes, I see, zhump and fall," she said. "Deeferent."

His pleased smile faded as he realized something. "Wait, you said you fell from the ship. Do you mean you jumped?"

Sanura became subdued as well, dropping her gaze. "Yes, I zhump." She turned away, but he took her arm. "Bad men come and kill men on my ship. I fight. I only not killed. Dey all come, and I know dey hurt me and den kill me." Her eyes showed a shadowed fierceness when her gaze met his. "I take dey pleasure away from dem."

Jeremy nearly felt ill with the understanding. "You are very brave, Sanura," he said almost without breath.

She shrugged. "Perhaps, but when it happen, I only hayte."

She walked down the beach. Jeremy stepped quickly to take her hand and walk quietly beside her.

She had seemed well the morning they walked on the beach, then she withdrew, staying in bed most of the rest of the day. He worried she had overexerted herself. The horizon stayed clear for the remainder of the day and the next. Sanura remained withdrawn. She tried to sleep, but she was restless. He knew the wound pained her when she was awake, no matter how she tried to hide it. A drink of her leaf potion helped to ease her discomfort, as did the reduction of swelling in her arm, but it would take some time before she was truly well.

Jeremy came down from his lookout post the following afternoon and found Sanura sleeping. He was glad. He took up a spear and the satchel. Though it was midday, the temperature was quite tolerable, even in the sun. He followed the stream to the pool he had slept by the first night. His raft was still there. He again reflected on events since he rode that broken wood.

"Many things have changed, not the least being myself," he said thoughtfully, tapping the wood.

Jeremy turned away and made his way to the rock maze. He was within their walls, spear poised for anything when his eye caught a shadow. He froze in fear at first. It was a shark, yet it was a small one. It was not near the size as the one that had threatened him the day his life changed forever. Courage rose in him quickly, and with a lunge and a jab, the beast quivered against his spear. He pulled it from the water with a triumphant shout. They would have fine steaks that night.

Catching the shark gave Jeremy's spirits a mighty boost. It confirmed his empowerment and his self-sufficiency. After gutting and arranging the shark in the satchel and setting it in a safe place, Jeremy looked for seaweed and crabs he might use. He also found a thin, flat rock the size of a dinner plate and got an idea. Returning to the cave, he found some fruits and herbs that went into the bag.

He smiled at his gatherings when he put the last of them in his stuffed bag. "I may not be at home, but we will eat as well as any duke in the homeland tonight."

Sanura woke as Jeremy was wishing for a clove of garlic.

"*What is that wonderful smell?*" she asked in her language, still drowsy.

"*Our supper,*" he answered, going to her. "*How do you feel?*"

She smiled with a deep breath. "*Tired still, but I am hungry now that I smell what you are making. What is it?*"

"*Shark, ah, I don't know how say, with fruit and herbs. Come, I show.*"

He helped her up, noticing she was protective of her slung arm. He was ready for that and gave her a husk with the medicine drink. She sipped it as he led her to sit by the fire.

"*See?*" he asked, proud of himself and perhaps a little unsure now that his work would be under scrutiny.

Sanura's expression was nothing more than pleasant surprise to see the shark steaks sizzling on the stone in low flame with flecks of herbs dotting their faces.

"*And this?*" she asked, pointing to the carapace holding four square bundles of leaves.

"*Pistano leaves. In leaves are fruit with herbs and crab. I . . .*" He made a motion.

"*Fold,*" she supplied.

"*I fold the leaves and hold with vine. They are on rocks with water in bottom for this."* He pointed to the vapors of steam rising around the leaves.

"Steam," she said. *"Zheramee, I am . . . I feel happy for your good work. Where did you learn to cook like this?"*

"I do not, not really." He shrugged. *"I learn cook in army when I fight for my country. We make food like this way, but not same food. No fish, no fruit. I don't know is good. We will eat and say."*

"I hope it tastes as good as it smells. It will be more than good."

He smiled. *"I hope."* He used another small, flat stone to turn the steaks.

He had no reason to worry. Their meal that night could have easily been served at his father's table. He longed for a bottle of Chardonnay, a loaf of bread and butter, and a round of sharp cheese, but he was not ungrateful.

"Zheramee, that was very good." Sanura sat back and laid a hand on her stomach in content.

"Yes, I am pleased as well," he agreed. *"We have more shark meat. I put on rack to dry."*

Sanura smiled. *"Zheramee knows more than he thinks."*

Jeremy translated her words as she rose and went to the bed.

"I knows more than I thinks?" he tried to repeat.

"Say, I know more than I think," she said carefully for him and he repeated it correctly.

She lay down, moving her arm to a position where it would not bother her. As she settled, Jeremy got a bowl of medicinal herb and a lit stick. He made it smolder for her, and she breathed it deeply.

"My gratitude," she said after a few full breaths and a cough.

"What does it mean, what you say?" asked Jeremy.

She smiled. *"It means what it says."*

She sighed, relaxing as the herb worked its benefits. Jeremy sat beside her to ponder as she fell asleep.

Sails were spotted three times more in the following days. More frustrating than not seeing any was to catch glimpses and not be able to light the beacon in time. Jeremy sprinted to the peak the third time to light it anyway as they determined it not to be an enemy ship. They both sat watching the western horizon where the sails had disappeared until the fire was glowing ash at their feet. They were both very disappointed, but Sanura rallied them first.

"Dey come again," she said firmly. "We see tree time in same place, we will see more."

"Yes, you're right," he agreed. *"I gather more sticks, then."*

After his beacon was restocked, Jeremy did find himself in a better mood. Although they could not hail the one ship, the other held promise. He wondered if one had something to do with the other, since they had been seeing them repeatedly in the western sea.

Sanura improved rapidly. Her walks on the beach with Jeremy became longer, and she foraged more and more. Jeremy actually felt useful now that he knew a bit more of what she sought. He also paid more attention to her teachings about those he did not know.

"How have you come to know all this?" he asked her one day.

She gave him that sultry smile of hers before answering. *"In trade, one must know many things, so you know what is offered and what is value in gold. I see a lot of trade in these lands, so I know what is here and the uses."*

Jeremy took a moment to translate. He also thought of how his father had tried to teach him the ways of trade. He only listened to and learned the bare minimum to bolster his chances of being put on a merchant ship. He regretted that now. His father had been trying to better him, to give him the knowledge he needed to one day take his place, and he had ignored it.

"What you know has much value."

"Yes, very much." She stepped further into the brush after a new treasure.

They walked on the west beach one afternoon, hand in hand. The sun was quite warm, and Jeremy perspired under its rays. Apparently, Sanura was feeling it too, despite wearing her dress as a short skirt. She no longer had a sling or bandage on her arm. Only the marks on her skin told of her ordeal. She had improved greatly over the past week and was able to participate in routine activities.

"Let us hunt for crab, Zheramee," she suggested.

"That is a fine idea."

They left their clothes and the net bag at the water's edge and waded into the warm turquoise water. It was a day of brilliance. The whisper of the water on the sand sang harmony with the warm breeze through the palms on shore. Sea birds gave their laughing cries and circled overhead. The water and sky were bright and radiant with color. Despite being stranded, Jeremy looked around as he stood in knee-high water and felt appreciation for the beauty around him. He turned to bring Sanura's attention to it, and the beauty of nature was eclipsed by what he saw before him.

He had not looked upon her with pure desire for some time. He had let daily concerns distract him from thoughts of passion, as he feared hurting her in her weakened state. Despite smaller displays of affection and the night she had relieved him, he had reverted back to the mindset of restraining himself. Now his need came back to him, full and demanding.

She stepped carefully through the water with the care of a shorebird. Her bronze skin glowed in the sun, dewy from its heat. Her hair shone, its ends caressing her buttocks as she stepped. One hand had slicked it back behind her ear as her sharp eyes searched. Her delicate fingers held her tresses against her neck to keep them from covering her face. She looked up then, her doe-like eyes meeting his gaze from under lashes thick and long as a feather fan.

In two strides, Jeremy had his arm around her waist, pulling her sun-warmed body against his and taking her mouth in a deep kiss. She responded immediately, her knee drawing up against his inner thigh, driving the madness that filled him. He felt her gasp on his lips as his hands wandered over her, caressing her to encourage her. She weakened in his arms when his waking manhood pressed against her hip, only causing it to start rising to attention.

He had one final thought of caution, and only because of his feelings for her transcended desire alone. "Sanura," he breathed in her ear, "I do not wish to hurt you. Are you well enough?"

She interrupted him by trying to pull him closer. "Please, Zheramee, I need you. I need to feel you," she pleaded.

It was enough for him. He clasped the back of her neck and dove into a deep kiss. She responded, mirroring his desperation to join in pleasure with her.

Still holding her close, Jeremy lowered his head to take her nipple, hard and smooth as a pearl, in his mouth. She groaned and tilted her head back, her spine curling under his fingers, and she pressed her pelvis against his. She moaned again as he persisted, teasing with his tongue. She gasped words of her language when his finger slid between her folds, slowly massaging her crevice. She flinched each time his finger passed over her bead of pleasure.

He smiled though his mouth was occupied and opened her folds to gain better access to her nodule. He tickled it with his fingertip. Sanura gasped. Tensing, she gave a cry with each breath. Yes, she was certainly ready to engage with him.

Jeremy knelt, and when the tip of his tongue touched her hardened bud, he thought she would collapse upon him. Her screams rivaled those of the sea birds and were ever so much more beautiful. Jeremy rode her passion, becoming more vigorous even as he drove her mad with the pleasure he brought upon her. He was aware of nothing more than Sanura, her body before him, the intoxicating taste of her, and how he was driving her to the peak of ecstasy.

He freed a hand and found the rim of her womanhood. He drew slow circles around it with his index and longest finger, making her groan. He waited, sensing her tension build in one of many waves he was causing to wash over her. When it was at its peak, he gently penetrated her, going deep into her soft cavern. He stroked its velvet walls as he doubled his efforts on her clitoris.

He achieved the desired effect. The added stimulus at the peak of her wave drove it further, stronger. He refused to let her into a trough again. Her hand grasped his hair as she screamed her delight, and the clenching spasms coursed through her body.

She groaned a sigh of relief as he withdrew his hand and gave her a final kiss. The honey of her passion was sweet on his lips. He stood, taking her in his arms to steady her, kissing her moist skin. She found his lips with a hungry kiss. She lowered herself, pulling him with her. She sat with her breasts bobbing slightly on the undulating surface of the water, and Jeremy kneeled, leaning over her, kissing the valley between them just above where her sun glass lay as his weight settled upon her.

Her hand guided him to her warm folds, and he slid in, sighing with the pleasure of her grasp. The near weightlessness freed their movements, allowing him to hover his weight over her as he drove himself toward ecstasy. The heat within him burst into new flame when she wrapped her legs around his hips and lifted herself to float beneath him. He groaned and slid one hand down her back to the base of her spine to hold her close. She braced herself and kept her head and shoulders above water by leaning back on her hands. The rest of her body was his.

Jeremy dug his knees into the sand to gain more leverage and surrendered his body as well. At first his movement was slow, steady, their bodies rocking together with each wave that passed around them. Through them, it felt. Jeremy's motions became more intense, and they moved the water instead. It seemed to seethe and boil around them, heated by their passion. Sanura ascended the height of pleasure once more. Jeremy, close behind, felt her reach her climax as she called his name. A wave broke over him, and he withdrew, spinning in the dizzying wake as his body released itself into the sea.

After a moment, he pulled himself closer, floating above her to kiss her. He hung his head, resting his forehead on her shoulder to catch his breath, the smell of her warm skin filling his nostrils, his heart.

She ran her hand over his back, giving him a pleasured chill. "Zheramee, dis not hunting for crab."

He laughed, letting his body settle against her. "No, but it is much more enjoyable, is it not?"

"Yes, but now we have more hunger," she laughed.

He laughed again. "I will pay that price for such pleasure."

They kissed, and he rose.

Suddenly, Sanura gasped, grasping his arm. "Zheramee! Look! It is good ship!"

Jeremy turned and saw a ship in the far channel. Even with their naked eyes, they could see the emblems of the sail and the shadows of the men upon her. Her bow was pointing the way to sail right past the island.

"Gods be praised!" Jeremy jumped up, Sanura behind, and they hurried to their clothes. They both kept their eyes to the ship, watching it lest it turn away, or worse, be a vision of their imagination.

Jeremy tightened the laces of his breeches. "Is there any-thing at the cave you do not wish to leave?"

She thought a moment, tying the knot at the back of her neck to make her cloth a full dress. She shook her head. "No, no-sing."

"Neither have I." Jeremy looked again at the approaching ship. "Here is my thought. We go fetch the boat from the reeds and row it out to them. They can't miss seeing us. We can pull alongside and board."

"Yes, good." Sanura agreed, and they hurried down the beach.

Jeremy acted on the compulsion to take her hand. He had meant it when he said he would not leave her behind.

They easily found the spot where the overturned dinghy was hidden. Pure adrenaline had it righted and pushed through the marsh in minutes. As they passed into the deeper waters of the bay, Jeremy motioned to Sanura.

"Get in."

He helped her into the stern and pushed it further into the water. When it was deep enough, he climbed in facing her and took the oars.

"Zheramee, wish me to . . ." Sanura made a motion.

Jeremy shook his head vigorously. "No, my flower. I will row. You keep your eye on that ship and flag her." He ges-tured. "Wave when you think they will see you."

Jeremy pulled with all of his might as fast as he could. The boat was perhaps a bit large for one man to row, but he had no choice. Desperation gave him the power of two. Sanura sat, her fingers clutching the amulet beneath her dress, her dark eyes focused over Jeremy's shoulder. He kept the prow pointed ahead of the bow of the ship so they would intersect. He hoped it could slow enough for them to catch.

Sanura waved her arms. "Zey see, Zheramee!" she breathed. "No stop!"

"Not even if my arms fall off," he panted.

His heart jumped as he heard the sounds of men's voices on the breeze. How odd it was to hear. It renewed his strength, and he redoubled his efforts. The boat's nose turned when they entered the current of the deeper channel. They paralleled the ship as they neared. The sun was broken by the finger shadows of the masts, then blocked by the ship itself.

At last, they were alongside her.

The thump of the ropes landing on the boat sounded surreal. Even as Jeremy grabbed one to tie the boat fast, he could hardly believe it. Sanura tied one to her end. A rope ladder was lowered, and the captain himself descended. His mate followed close behind. Jeremy moved to Sanura's side, taking her hand to reassure himself that he was not dreaming the ship, and he was not dreaming her. He did not want the men to stand before him and see a raving lunatic, starving and exhausted, babbling about a woman that didn't exist.

Sanura had a broad smile on her face when the captain turned to her. He seemed to be in utter amazement. She placed the palms of her hands together before her and bowed her head with a greeting. The captain and his mate made a movement, but she stopped them. With her speaking her language at proper speed, Jeremy found it difficult to keep up. The syllables ran together, and he had no hope of separating them, especially with the abundance of words he didn't know mixed in.

The captain and mate bowed to her, then to him, which he had enough wits to mirror. The captain was speaking breathlessly, still amazed. She replied, and they nodded, stepping aside, offering a hand to help her up the ladder. Once she was up, Jeremy began his climb, still in a daze. Then strong hands took his arms, and he felt wood beneath his feet. Bronze faces showing great smiles greeted him with exuberant words and laughter. He cast a frantic gaze around and found the red beacon of her dress.

Sanura was truly there. The ship was truly there. They were on it together.

CHAPTER TEN

The sound of creaking woke Jeremy. Stale air and darkness were the next things he noticed. At that moment, another sound startled him enough to sit up. A cough. A male cough. He almost fell out of the hammock, but he caught his balance just before he overturned onto the floor. With a beating heart that continued to pound from excitement and joy, Jeremy sat and soaked in the surroundings. By the gods, he was on a ship. Hammocks swayed in time to the gentle creak and groan of timber. In the dim light, he could see men in some of them, sailing men, foreign to his eyes, but he loved each one at that moment.

The smells of humanity filled his nose. Gods, yes, there were smells. Oil from the lamps, damp wood, musty linen, sweat, sour breath, feet, and all the other masculine smells trapped in the hold of the ship with them. A grunt escorted another smell into the hold, one that Jeremy wasn't sure he wished to partake of. His thoughts had gone to Sanura anyway. He swung out of the hammock and quietly made his way to the stairs. It had been so long since he had worn boots, he had forgotten the pair that had been given to him the night before. He didn't want them, but the concept of dignity and appearance had been reawakened in him. He went back and fetched them.

A fresh, salty breeze washed over his face as he went on deck. He stood a moment and filled his lungs. The sight of a ship around him brought mist to his eyes. All around her was the deep, wide ocean. The sails were spread full and wide, gleaming in the morning sun. They had always riled emotions of new places for Jeremy. This morning his heart swelled as full as they with the promise they held of home.

"Jharehme!"

Jeremy turned to see the captain striding toward him with a smile. He remembered his manners, placing his palms together as Sanura had done the day before and giving a short bow.

"*Sabailkeer.*"

The captain mirrored him, seeming pleased he knew that much. He let out a string of words they both knew that Jeremy wouldn't understand but needed to be said regardless. He beckoned for Jeremy to follow him, gesturing and talking as he walked.

Jeremy complied, trying to listen, then forgot about him when he saw Sanura.

She was sitting at the bow, a table and two chairs set there for her. They were crude and worn but were the loveliest he thought he had ever seen. She was dressed in a tunic and breeches with boots, as the ship certainly would have no proper clothing for a woman. Though she could have worn the clothing they had salvaged on the island, she never had, as it was too hot. Seeing her now, dressed as a sailor, dress that signified strength and courage, was one of the most erotic visions of her he had ever seen. The clothes fit her, as did what they represented. Strangely, he now wanted nothing more than to rip them off her.

She stood, her glowing smile dimming the bright morning sun. They enacted a formal greeting. Jeremy sensed it would be inappropriate to even kiss her cheek in front of the captain and all of the other men on board. He took her hand and kissed it. It was a feat not to linger on her taste and smell even in that distant touch.

She gestured for him to sit. "Zheramee, we have proper

breck-fass today." She beamed, sitting. "Look." She named the tea, bread, fruit, and honey on the table as he sat after her.

"It looks fit for royalty, kings," he agreed.

Sanura beamed, turning to the captain to converse as the ship's boy served Jeremy's breakfast. Jeremy was impressed they were being treated so well. These seemed to be kind, genteel people. Sanura smiled at Jeremy as the captain excused himself with a short bow. Jeremy stood briefly to answer it, then regained his place. The ship's boy stood at attention nearby.

"You sleep good?" Sanura asked.

Jeremy smiled. "Yes, I slept very *well*," he emphasized gently in correction, "but my arms felt empty without you," he confessed. She smiled pleasantly. "And you? Did you sleep well?"

"Yes, very *well*." She'd noted the correction. "Lass night I give grat-tee-tud wit-out fire. It was deef-rent, but I feel mos happy."

Jeremy smiled. "Yes, you're right. I suppose that will change now. I was very tired, but I felt gratitude, here before I sleep." He laid his hand over his heart.

She smiled. "Dat is only part dat is im-por-tan."

Jeremy shared a genuine smile with her before savoring a swallow of tea. "It was kind of the captain to surrender his quarters, his room, bed, to you," he said, gesturing to assist with the words she did not know. "He seems a gentleman. All of the men are well-mannered. Who are they?"

Sanura looked thoughtful, as if searching for words. .

This was the first chance they'd had to converse privately. There had been much bustle and excitement once they came aboard. They were taken to the captain's quarters, offered food almost immediately, and after there was much conversing between the captain, the mate, and Sanura. Sometime shortly after dark, Jeremy was shown to the crew's quarters below and given clean clothes and a hammock. He had fallen asleep instantly and guessed he had woken more than twelve hours later. He hadn't even heard the day crew wake and the night crew come in.

"Deese men are of my piple," Sanura said. "Dey trade. I meet, what is word for him?" She gestured toward the captain.

"Captain," supplied Jeremy. "The captain."

Ah." She nodded. "I meet de captain early bef-or in trade. I no sail wit him, but I know him."

"Ah, I see." Jeremy nodded as he chewed on the coarse bread. They knew each other through their work in trade, so there was a reason for his amicability. They were of the same people, so that was another good reason for the respect being shown to her.

Jeremy smiled. "If the captain and crew are Sanura's people, then I am not surprised they are good men."

She looked puzzled.

"Sanura is most beautiful, most kind," he explained in simple language. "Her people must be the same."

She smiled, taking a gentle sip of tea. "I wish to meet Zheramee piple," she answered. "Dey make me smile, muss have big . . ." She tapped her hand to her chest and remembered the word he had used a few times. " . . . harts."

Jeremy smiled at the flattery but felt a small shadow at the thought of some of the people associated with him. The ship had brought back strong memories. "Not all, I'm afraid."

Sanura clearly saw his sudden change but did not press. He certainly couldn't elaborate. These men were friendly, but they could change instantly if they knew they had the son of a northland duke aboard. They might not have ever heard the Nottingdale name before, but they would certainly understand his position and the price of his head in possible ransom. No, he had to remain a castaway sailor in their eyes, no matter the situation.

Another touch of reality darkened his heart more. Returning to his world meant a return to his obligations. Sanura was not among them.

In speaking to Sanura that morning, he learned the ship had been in the sea chasing the very ship that had attacked Sanura's. They had been part of a small fleet sailing back to their homeland from the rich lands of the west. They had hailed the ship they had thought was friendly and were nearly taken in turn. With the assistance of two other ships, they were able to take back the stolen ship, but the enemy ship that had originally attacked Sanura's escaped. The rest of the fleet, with the exception of two ships, stayed to chase down the fiends, but had not had an opportunity to confront them yet when they came across Sanura and Jeremy. They met their companion ship the day after finding them, and the two decided to abandon pursuit and take the castaways home. It was decided the men the two had come across on the island were possibly sailing with the enemy, as Sanura had thought. Whether they were shipwrecked or part of a foraging party, they could not guess. Jeremy noticed the smile that came upon Sanura's face at the confirmation. It reminded him of her courage and skill and made him glad she was not his enemy. It also made him want to be alone with her. That was one thing he found difficult to get accustomed to.

Jeremy quickly acclimated to life aboard ship. He eagerly jumped in to assist in what tasks he could. The men seemed to accept him for the most part, despite their lingual and cultural differences. There were a few who didn't seem to care about him and one or two who outright scorned him, but he ignored them and did what he could to earn the favor of the rest. They were friendly enough and seemed accepting of his abilities. He was grateful to them and wished to be as helpful as possible, working alongside them no matter the task the whole day. He seemed to be genuinely liked by a few, but the entire dynamic changed whenever Sanura appeared.

Jeremy was astounded at the change in their countenance when she appeared on deck. It would be comical if it didn't cause tension for him. They were respectful towards her, perhaps overly so if she came near, bowing low to her, some reaching for her hand to kiss. He could tell their words were full of praise, but they were never forward or overbearing. He knew they sought her attention, though.

If she wasn't near enough to engage, they would work even harder at their task, exaggerating their strength, some even removing their shirts to let their muscles glisten in the sun. Jeremy was amazed at their audacity. Of course, they were sailors, virile men cooped up in close quarters for long periods of time. He could hardly fault their behavior. Hell, he had sometimes acted in similar ways if he sought a woman's attention, especially in competition with another man. It was unsettling, though, to have a ship full of them, since they all seemed to want her attention.

It became obvious that Jeremy was the only one Sanura would seek out, though she accepted interaction and pleasantries from the others. This earned Jeremy dark looks, sometimes even when she wasn't around. Jeremy remained a gentleman, though, ignoring their glares and refusing to participate in their antics. He remained the same whether she was around or not. He might have earned the respect of some of them because of it, but he was aware of their ire as well.

Sanura was either oblivious or didn't care. In the evenings, she invited him and the captain to sit and converse with her. The captain seemed to be inclined to learn Jeremy's language, more so than the crew, who neither taught nor learned. Jeremy and Sanura taught him. They continued to expand their own proficiency with each other as well.

The first few nights, Jeremy was so tired, he excused himself early. Sanura made her excuses as well, so Jeremy and the captain left together, exchanging farewell pleasantries for the evening. Jeremy didn't mind having someone else to talk with. He was glad. The captain was a gentleman, intelligent and kind, yet Jeremy grew impatient that he was always there when he met with Sanura privately.

He at first guessed that the captain, as the leader and therefore the man responsible for Sanura, was being protective of her. He guessed that men of his own culture, perhaps even he, would react the same way were the situation reversed. He and Sanura knew each other, though, and she obviously liked him and trusted him. She did not need guarding from a foreigner.

Jeremy questioned whether that was really the captain's intent. Once rested after a few days, Jeremy noticed the calculating looks he received when he conversed with her. Did he see or was he imagining an abundant, perhaps superfluous charm that came from the captain when he spoke to her? Many times, he would use language Jeremy couldn't hope to understand to elicit a smile or giggle from her. His look would go to Jeremy after the desired effect. Was it an apology for excluding him, or triumph? Was the captain trying to seduce her? The thought soured Jeremy's stomach. He knew it was a delicate situation. He wished to maintain honor, decency, and peace as well. He wanted to stay as neutral as possible, but the desire of the other men only brought his to the forefront. He found himself thinking of her more often than not and was tormented by his memories of being with her.

One night when their evening meetings had become routine, Jeremy found himself at the brink of being unable to contain himself. He had asked himself if there was anything in the captain that Sanura could possibly be attracted to. His immediate answer was yes. He had seen women flutter their fans at his kind. Rugged, mature, bearded, strong, yet with kind eyes, a pleasant smile, and a soothing voice. He had authority as well. Women got soft between the thighs at the mere thought. He should know. Uniform and sword were often enough to attract them. To know him as the heir of a duke, they were clay in his hands.

He was entertaining the idea of blurting out this trump when his senses slapped him into reality. Horrified at what he had even thought, he abruptly stood even as the captain was speaking.

"Please excuse me," he said, recovering his wits, "I am weary. I will bid you a good night," he said to Sanura with a bow. He expected the captain to take his cue as usual, but he did not.

He and Sanura stood, but he spoke to Jeremy. "You have worked hard today, sir," he said through Sanura. "Go, sleep. You earned it well."

Jeremy spent a moment in fluster, then recovered. He was suddenly resigned. It was up to her, regardless. He reached for her hand. "Good night, my dear." He kissed it, paused, and with a final nod to the captain, took his leave.

"I am weary of talking as well."

Jeremy heard Sanura's words as he closed the door, and they brought comfort to his heart. It only lasted a moment. He paused and happened to steal a glance through the crack and felt his heart pierced to see the handsome captain on one knee, his lips pressed to both of her hands with low words to her. Worse, Sanura laid a hand upon his head with a kind smile down to him.

Jeremy felt sick. He hurried to the deck and the railing to steady himself. A cool, salty breeze wiped the sweat from his brow. He took deep breaths to calm himself.

"Concede, Nottingdale, concede," he scolded himself.

"You cannot have her anyway, and you damn well know it."

Oh, the price he was paying for yielding to temptation. Perhaps there was some truth behind the teaching of restraint after all. Jeremy felt as though his heart were being torn asunder. He had wanted nothing more than to see Sanura safe on a ship to be returned home. He had chosen to ignore the truth that once he saw her to the home of her family, he must never see her again. He was betrothed. He had responsibilities. His involvement with a tribal tradeswoman was completely unacceptable.

He hadn't known, though, that his affair with her would only make him burn more for her. He usually sated his need and curiosity, won the prize, then forgot about them. He could not sate his desire for Sanura. Even as he was still spinning from the last of his climax, he always wondered how soon their next joining would be. He realized at that moment that he could never be with her again.

A liquid blackness filled the place where his heart had been. He bowed his head and felt the wind chill a trail of moisture on his cheek. At least, their separation would be easy for her, it seemed. He couldn't decide if it was a comfort or if it hurt more.

I am weary of talking as well.

The captain's reaction could only be interpreted as gratitude, acceptance. She was weary of talking. She wished to do more. Jeremy's mind tortured him with images of the peppered beard abrading her delicate neck, her silken lips, and reddening her breasts. Even now, was he upon her? The displaced captain, of his bed, of his ship, drilling his defiance and triumph into her, driving her to the heights of pleasure so her voice would announce his victory for all to hear.

Jeremy made to stumble to the bow, where the cleaving of the water might silence anything he might hear. He had a momentary vision of throwing himself in to escape his torture. As he moved, a shadow came on deck. Jeremy was startled enough to stop as the figure of the captain emerged in the moonlight to walk serenely up to the wheel to monitor his ship.

Jeremy felt dizzy. He slumped against the rail, still nauseous. She hadn't accepted him. A plethora of emotions rolled over Jeremy. He felt a little ridiculous, then mad at himself, relieved, then sad and angrier. Regardless, he still could not keep her. He was so confused. He was tired and decided to go to bed to escape all of the turmoil.

After his first steps, though, another emotion rose to wash away the others. He had to see Sanura.

Three more steps and the ship's boy emerged, spotted him, and ran to him. He stepped before him with a short bow.

"Sir Zheramee, Sanura bids jyoo come," he said, obviously parroting words with an accent Jeremy recognized immediately.

"*Shokrahn*," he replied, the emotions rising again.

He cast them aside and hurried to the captain's quarters. He paused outside the door to collect himself and to scold himself into maintaining control. He had to keep himself under rein. Things had to be different now.

She immediately granted him entrance at his knock. He closed the door and froze when he saw her on the bed, brushing her hair. She immediately stopped and rose for him. His thoughts and emotions were autumn leaves blown away in the brilliance of her smile. Before one word could return to him, she trotted to him, flung her arms around his neck, and kissed him.

He embraced her, more fully than perhaps was warranted, but he wanted to meld with her, never let her go. Her hungry kiss weakened his knees. She pulled at his clothes, and he could resist no more. He fulfilled his fantasy of stripping her of her sailor's clothes and ravishing her in a mad frenzy of passion.

It was quick. He simultaneously relished it and wished he could have spent some time pleasing her, yet his body was impatient. Restrained and tortured, it took over and did not let him have his senses until it was over.

He fell onto his elbow over her. "Oh, Sanura," he gasped, kissing her neck.

She laughed huskily, wrapping her arms around him. "It has been few days. Zheramee need is great."

"My need is always great for you," he replied, turning to lie on his side.

"I am sorry we no toget-her," she said, raking her fingers through his hair. "Is, ah, is im-por-tan dat we —"

"Sanura, dear, I understand," said Jeremy. "We are among other people now. We must act properly among them."

"You understand?" she asked.

"Yes, I would not wish to tarnish your reputation, ah, make others see you as bad."

This confused her. "See as bad?"

"I'm sorry, I'm not explaining very well."

He tried to think of how to put it, but she laughed. "Zheramee no understand, but Zheramee know manners, and dat is good."

This now confused him, but her kiss made him forget the conversation. His body took over again, ready for her before even he expected. This time he was able to take his time. He would be tired the next day, but he did not care. He did not care about his concern that would come in later days, either. He promised himself that after this he would control himself. He would let himself separate from her slowly. Yes, it would be less painful for both of them. He just hoped he could do it.

It was a relatively pleasant sail to civilized lands. Autumn was well upon them now. The days were mild, sometimes cold after a day of squally weather. As they traveled north and then east on the trade current, the change in the weather was definite. Jeremy reveled in it, enjoying every minute he wasn't sweating in tropical humidity. The last weeks on the island had been tolerable, sometimes pleasant, but he enjoyed the cold. Sanura did not seem to care for it as much as he did. A thick robe, common of the garb of the sailors' lands, had been provided for her. She spent the pleasant days wrapped in it on deck. On the unpleasant days, he hardly saw her at all.

They had been discreet in their affair, but it was common knowledge by dawn the night after their first liaison that Jeremy had the favor of the female on board. After this, most of the men were reserved around Jeremy, accepting his assistance, but not behaving in any overly friendly way. A couple were blatantly rude, showing their spite toward him openly. He was surprised by this extreme behavior, as well as all of their continued efforts to impress Sanura. It seemed they were simultaneously protective of her and also wished to exploit her, but none ever acted on the desire. It was clear they received her attention only at her discretion. Jeremy was baffled. It was not that he didn't feel that was how it should be, but it was unusual behavior for crude sailors, in his eye. He was certain he knew nothing of Sanura's people and their ways.

Regardless, he and Sanura continued to teach and learn when they could. He learned words he needed to know for life aboard ship. They schooled each other in grammar and worked on aspects of pronunciation. As before, Jeremy avoided talk that might lead to questions about his home or who he was. He still did not ask Sanura about herself so he would not have to answer in turn. She seemed content with the simple subject matter.

Jeremy found himself speaking her language almost exclusively. Sanura complimented him often, and he formed cordial relationships with some of the men who did not appear to resent his relationship with Sanura. He did not think of them as friendships, as he was sure that mutual loyalty did not run deep, but he was aware he had the favor of some of the men. He was far from keeping up with their conversation or contributing at their speed, but he was improving.

After a few weeks at sea, land was sighted. Jeremy was overjoyed and ran to fetch Sanura. She stood at the rail with her robe close around her, her smile pushing tears from her eyes.

"It is beautiful," she said in his language.

He had his arm around her in his excitement. It was the first close contact they'd had in two weeks. They had given in to temptation a few times on the ship, but Jeremy had finally started to master himself. The smell, the feel of her was poignant after such a long separation. Distance had not made Jeremy's task easier. It only tortured him. He could barely concentrate on their evening discussions anymore. He always claimed weariness and departed when he could not bear it any longer or when it seemed she would make an advance.

Jeremy felt a lump in his throat, but it was not from the sight before them. He forced his arm off of her.

"I thought you would like to see," he said as his means of excusing himself and went back to the fishing net he was mending. He acted as if he wasn't aware that Sanura was watching him. She left the railing soon after.

"You're a big man, aren't you?"

Jeremy looked up to see one of the men, who clearly didn't like him standing before him, fists on his hips. Jeremy ignored him.

"Hey! I'm speaking to you, big man!" He snatched the net from Jeremy's hands.

Jeremy popped up to his feet in defiance of the brute. *"What do you want? I try to work."*

The man laughed. "*I hope for her sake you fuck better than you speak.*"

"*Had I a cock like my small finger, I still am better fuck than you,*" Jeremy shot back, using the bawdy sailor talk he had picked up.

The man pushed Jeremy. He stumbled back but stood fast and regained his stance.

"*You strut like a peacock,*" growled the man, "*but we all know what you are. You understand, big man? I will speak slowly. You are a thing to play with, then poo!*" He gestured, throwing his hand over his back. "*No good! She is a good woman. She found a lost dog. Aw, lost dog . . .*"

He reached out to pat Jeremy's head, but Jeremy slapped it away.

He laughed. "*She will keep you, lost dog, and play with you from pity. Then, in the land of real men, she will forget you. She has men waiting for her. Captain has been waiting for her.*" His lips curled in pleasure at the jab he was sure he was making. "*In a fortnight, she will forget your name. The only reason she is not with me for her romps is because she is sorry for her lost dog, but I don't worry. On another sail, she will call. She likes —*"

"*Enough!*" The captain strode up, glaring up at the man. "*Get to work.*"

Jeremy's antagonist demurred, but the captain gave him a tongue lashing and drove him off. He gave Jeremy a parting shot. "*Goodbye, lost dog. The big dog must fight for you!*"

Jeremy, his mood now completely sour, snatched up his net and worked again. The captain looked as if he wanted to say something, but didn't and moved on, ordering the men back to their work. Jeremy heard a few laughs in his favor and a compliment, but he ruminated on what he had heard. He wondered if he could swim to shore.

Jeremy went straight to his bunk that night rather than take dinner or spend time with Sanura. Why bother? It wasn't because of what the man had said to him. It was because Jeremy already knew it. He and Sanura had had a fling. It was over. The sighting of land was a harbinger of its end. He had known she had to have suitors. She must at least have a lover. Her experience attested to that. The logical part of his mind was glad. She would have someone waiting for her. This all worked in Jeremy's favor, yet it only made him more miserable.

"The only reason she is not with me for her romps . . ."

Hell, he was on a ship full of her suitors. She was probably eligible to any one of them. Had he understood correctly?

"On another sail, she will call . . ."

Did that mean she had before?

"She likes . . ."

What? How did he know? Jeremy wanted to wretch at the thought that his antagonist had any idea. He wasn't worthy of her glance. She deserved a man with a higher station in life. With her experience in trade, she would probably be better suited for the captain. He could give her a comfortable life.

Jeremy despaired. He wanted to give her the life of a duchess, and she deserved better than even that. It was folly, though. He could not take her from her family or the trade she knew. She had a life planned, as did he. Scream as his heart might, he could not change it.

The ship's boy came. Jeremy dismissed him.

That one night of separation seemed a good breaking point for Jeremy. Land was sighted. It was time to end it. There was no reason to pretend it wasn't upon him.

When Sanura appeared on deck the next morning, Jeremy felt his throat close. He wanted to avoid her. He didn't think he could trust himself to speak to her without professing his undying love. He did owe her at least a few words. He would be a cad if he did not.

As expected, she approached him, smiling, but with

concern in her eyes.

"*Sabailkeer*, Zheramee."

He bowed his head, only catching her eyes for a brief moment before averting his. "Good morning, milady." Could she see his broken heart?

"Are you well?" she asked.

"I must speak with you a moment," he said using his language to deter the open ears all around.

He escorted her to the railing, looking over so no one, not even she, could see his face.

"Sanura, I know you will not understand why I say what I must, but I must say it regardless." He paused, then his words came out in a rush. "The time has come that we must part ways. I will see you home, but we mustn't be alone together anymore."

It was a saving grace that she seemed confused rather than if she understood and cried.

"Zheramee?"

He shook his head. "No, Sanura." He nearly choked as he tried to force the words out. "It cannot be changed."

He gave her a brusque nod and spun about to climb up the rigging, his only means of escape.

He left his heart on the deck. Gods, he had sounded so cruel, so cold. It was how it must be, though. He could not follow through with a tender farewell. He didn't dare look down for fear that what he beheld would cause him to cast himself from the top of the mast.

From then on, when Sanura appeared on deck, Jeremy scampered up the ropes to check the rigging. The ship's boy came every night after dinner, but Jeremy sent him away. He knew she must be confused and hurt. He was sorry, but the very sight of her brought him such pain, he could not bear it. He consoled himself that she was not as heartbroken as he because she did not seek him out herself at night. Yes, it was easier for her. He found himself hurt even more by that.

The ship docked for provisions, and he considered disembarking, but his honor immediately quelled the thought. He was going to see her home safely. It was the least he could do for her. He climbed a mast to get a good view of the island port, but also to avoid everything. He noted Sanura remained unseen. The port would not have been friendly for him anyway. He only heard his newly learned language and others he did not know being shouted on the dock. Of course, the port would be Medaran, and they were not friendly to any but their own. They did not trust outsiders. The ship only stayed long enough to procure supplies. Jeremy had expected they would stay overnight to sate all of their needs, but they left in the late afternoon.

After another few days of sailing, they docked again. It was a completely foreign territory for Jeremy. The men of the ship told him they were close to their destination, so he guessed they were at the very northern shores of the great Southlands. It was dusk when they came to port. By that time, Jeremy felt that if he did not get off of the ship soon, he would expire. Three of the friendliest of the men escorted him ashore with much welcoming fanfare. They led him through the bustling city, and Jeremy was overwhelmed by the sudden influx of humanity to his senses. Bright colors, dry dust, roasting meat, earthy spices, the drone and trill of an exotic language, smelly animals, and laughing children all bombarded him.

His companions dragged him through the dusty streets to a lively tavern. The most unusual music Jeremy had ever heard was being played, drowned out by men's voices and women's laughter. They sat at a table, the sailors talking and yelling. A bottle and small wooden cups were brought.

A libation was poured with the warning, "*This will make you a man!*" Then it was bottoms up.

The searing liquid made Jeremy grimace and cough, but the numbing effect spread through him instantly. As soon as he could speak, he held out his cup. "*Another!*"

The men roared and cheered. If he could not reason his pain away, he was going to drown it, burn it, destroy himself to spite it.

The rest of the night was a blurry haze of song, dance, food, drink, and women. A stunning woman with chestnut hair, skin and eyes to match, took a liking to Jeremy. He was lucid enough at that point to know she was a professional.

"*I am sorry,*" he slurred, holding onto her for balance even though she sat in his lap, "*I have no money.*"

"Jarmee, Jarmee!" hooted his friends, "*This is your pay for work!*" they jested.

One dropped a heavy coin between the woman's bosoms, planting a loud kiss after it to seal the deal. His friends cheered, and the woman took Jeremy's hand and led him away.

Somehow, he ended up in a small room with a crude bed and a single candle. The woman was kissing him as she pulled him in, closing the door with her foot.

When you fall off of a horse, you must get back on, right?

It did not take much for her to push Jeremy over onto the bed. He landed on his back with her straddling him. She smelled of musk. She fished the coin out of her brassiere-like top and set it on the wash table. She proceeded to remove her top. Caramel breasts presented themselves to him. His manhood warmed as he took them in his hands. She made sounds of pleasure as he teased the nipples between his fingers.

She undid the knot of her skirt, unwrapping it from around her. Jeremy's hands fell from her and clarity struck through the liquor like a lightning bolt. That one motion brought Sanura back for him. He realized what he was doing. He wasn't thinking of the woman before him. He was wishing she was Sanura and pretending in his drunken haze. Seeing the woman naked before him left him empty. She was not what he wanted. Sex was not what he wanted.

"What's the matter?" she asked.

Jeremy stroked her thighs, speaking carefully. *"You are a lovely woman,"* he said. *"In all the other times of my life, I would have you, but my heart has been taken by a woman I cannot keep. You can separate the body from the heart, but once the heart is taken, the body cannot act apart from it."*

Though hesitant and accented, she understood his words. She looked as if she were about to weep in sympathy.

He gently moved her aside and rose. He kissed her cheek. *"Keep the coin and stay here for a small time. I will tell them I had a wonderful time, and you do the same, agreed?"*

She nodded but took his arm when he stood to leave. *"No, please, stay. You don't have to leave."*

He shrugged. *"There's nothing for me here. I'm sorry."*

Jeremy staggered back to the main room and slid out a side door. The night air was cool and felt good on his face. There was a fountain in the courtyard with cups hanging on the upper tier. He took several long drinks and sat on its edge. That had nearly been disastrous. Sanura aside, Jeremy Nottingdale could no longer consort with whores. Had he hated himself a little more, he might have done it. *No* – It would feel as if he were being disloyal to Sanura, as ludicrous as it was. He was frustrated at his inability to move on. Perhaps once he saw her home, then he could go back to his old ways. Yes, that was acceptable. It would only be a few days anyway. He just needed a bit more time.

He sat there for a while longer as his head cleared, had a few more drinks, and went back into the tavern. He could not shake the feeling, though, that cavorting did not have the appeal it used to. Not here, not at home, never again. Every woman he would meet from then to the end of his life he would wish to be Sanura.

Jeremy's new friends escorted him back to the ship, teaching him a song about drink, women, and music. It could well have been a song about that very night. They bawled it at the top of their lungs. The four of them had their arms over one another's shoulders for support. They howled with laughter as one stumbled aside to vomit. They serenaded him as he did. He laughed when he was done, wiped his mouth, and rejoined them to stagger on.

When they boarded the ship, Jeremy was sober enough to see the guards in the dark and one robed figure. He stopped with a short intake of breath. The other three didn't see her and started a loud verse about lapping up pussy like honey.

"*Gentlemen!*" Jeremy hissed, elbowing the ones beside him sharply.

They gathered their wits then. They gave her sloppy gestures of greeting, each with a slurred, "*Evenin' m'lady,*" then they went below, dragging Jeremy with them. He saw her turn away. He was horrified when he realized he hadn't greeted her.

He wanted to go to her to apologize but knew he would only make more of a fool of himself. He flopped into his hammock. Dizziness couldn't carry him into unconsciousness fast enough.

The next morning Jeremy felt a bit sore in the head, but after a cup of hot tea, he was ready for the day physically. Emotionally, he was still a mess, but he was used to that by now. Some of his companions weren't quite so fortunate. There was an abundance of chiding and insult among the men as they recovered from their night through the morning. Jeremy seemed the only one who had gone ashore who was not suffering. He had employed the secret of avoiding the curse of the drink, but in truth, he was unaffected by the pains of his head because the pains of his heart so outweighed them.

He worked hard to sweat out the alcohol and the thoughts of Sanura that tormented him. He seemed to have earned a level of respect from his friendlier mates, and their good-natured jesting eased his heart a bit. He focused on the fact that they were almost to their destination. It was almost done. In less than a week, he would be on a ship home. He forced himself to think of his parents, trying to make himself anxious to return to them to deliver the good news that he was not dead and was ready to take his place as the heir of Duke Nottingdale.

The ship's boy did not come for him that night.

CHAPTER ELEVEN

M ore ships were seen now that they were in the busy sea surrounded by civilization. Jeremy expected they would see even more as they neared Medar and he anticipated a veritable crowd in their final hours of approach. The sense of being surrounded by humanity again was a comfort to Jeremy. After the months of isolation, it almost seemed foreign. He tried not to think of what his preference would be were he given the choice of the remainder of his life with civilization around him or with Sanura alone. He knew his mind would not like the answer his heart would give.

It was late afternoon when a ship appeared in their waters that shared the same current. It was a lumbering merchant vessel much more ponderous than the ship they were on. They overtook it quickly. There was some excitement aboard, as it seemed inevitable they would pass close and that the other ship was moving to encourage a meeting. The sailors prepared to slow their ship and pull alongside for boarding.

Jeremy did a lot of the mast work, taming the sails to slow the vessel. When their speed was checked and the other ship neared, he went below to fetch more lines should they be needed. He heard the greetings above, muffled by the wood and thump of boots on the deck. He was lost in the fog of thoughts that followed him when he came back on deck.

Icy clarity speared through the fog to pierce his mind at the sound, the vision that greeted him. The men on deck disappeared. The ship disappeared. The captain disappeared. He only saw the man that stood before the captain and the sword at the mate's side. He pushed through the gathered men, his hand seized the mate's sword, and he drew it to level the blade at Ombreux.

"The Devil!" Ombreux stumbled back, drawing his own sword, his face paling beneath his dark beard. "What spirit is this?" he gasped.

Jeremy pierced him with his stare. "Have at you."

Ombreux's men signed for their god to protect them and leaped back to their ship in terror. Ombreux backed away, sputtering as Jeremy lifted his blade to eye level and twisted it in a gesture of challenge, the point at Ombreux's throat.

"How can it be?" Ombreux finally hissed.

"How stained are your hands, Ombreux?" growled Jeremy.

The captain ordered his men to separate the two men.

"No!" Jeremy's shout froze them. *"I have business with this man. He must answer for the blood on his hands."*

"You speak their tongue!" gasped Ombreux. "What spell?"

"How much?" Jeremy's shout silenced him, still circling with him, locking gazes with him. "How much is that of your own parents?" he spat out.

Ombreux was suddenly very focused. "Insolent whelp," he snarled, "I'll do now what I should have in the first place."

"Of all the blood on your hands, none will ever be Nottingdale. You are not worthy of the honor."

Ombreux raised his sword. "It starts with you, then I'll have your father, and your worthless line will end."

"Your treason ends now!"

Jeremy struck hard and fast.

Ombreux, skilled in his own right, blocked him. The swords clanged sharply over the silent deck. They parried and struck in a flashing flurry of metal. Ombreux batted Jeremy's blade away with a forceful sweep of the arm, twisting the blade to lunge. Jeremy danced aside, sweeping his blade around to answer, but Ombreux guessed it, dodging the thrust. He regained his stance and they circled. Ombreux charged. Jeremy batted the sword away, but Ombreux kept on, bowling over Jeremy, knocking him to the deck. The sword plunged toward Jeremy's chest. Jeremy rolled and the metal struck wood. He stabbed as he gained his feet. Ombreux shouted, limping on the leg that had been pierced. Jeremy thrust. Ombreux blocked, and the flurry ensued again. Jeremy yelped when cold metal sliced through his upper arm. Ombreux had scored, but the stroke left him open for a millisecond. Jeremy lunged.

He felt the confirming embrace upon his sword as it plunged into flesh. He forced it forward, throwing his weight behind it. It scraped bone as it slid deep and true, exacting vengeance as it deserved to be dealt.

Jeremy was only barely aware of Ombreux's agonized cry. He only felt the swell of satisfaction as agony filled Ombreux's face and admitted Jeremy's victory before it fell slack. Jeremy withdrew the sword, and Ombreux fell to the deck, dead.

Jeremy panted a moment, letting his rage feast on the sight before him. He wiped the blade clean with a cloth he carried in his pocket. He threw it onto the body in disgust and spat upon his uncle in farewell.

He turned to meet the captain's amazement. "*His sword and ring belong to his son. Keep them for him.*" He turned and offered the hilt of his sword to the mate with a bow. "*My apologies. I thank you.*"

He made his way to the hold to contend with the trembling that was rapidly descending upon him. There was shouting and scurrying and suddenly, Jeremy was seized.

"*What — what are you doing?*" he demanded.

He heard the captain shouting directions he did not understand. The sailors were hastily releasing the lines that held the two ships. Jeremy was dragged below and down to the cargo hold to a tiny room deep in the bowels of the ship. He was shoved in, the door was shut and latched behind, and the sailors hurried away.

Jeremy sat where he stood, his knees nearly buckling from under him. Of course, they would not understand his action. He would be freed once he explained to the captain. He could not know all, but he would understand if he knew Ombreux had tried to kill him.

In the meantime, the dark, silent room was the only place he wanted to be.

It was much later when Jeremy heard footsteps. By then he had found the wall opposite the door and sat leaning against it.

He had his revenge. He had never killed for vengeance before. After the thrill of victory, he was strangely empty in the aftermath. Though it had been warranted, necessary, and fair, he still resented Ombreux. His death did not mend his betrayal. His threat to his father had only made it worse. It did not bring his mother's parents back. It had only brought another death in the family.

He would have to sort all that out later.

Jeremy stood as the door was unlatched, ready to speak to the captain as a gentleman.

The captain entered with a lamp, making Jeremy squint after the darkness. Jeremy froze as Sanura entered as well.

What was she doing there?

He only met her eyes a moment, certain she could read his surprise before he forced attention to the captain. He did not know what to read in her expression.

The captain hung the lamp on a hook and turned to Jeremy and spoke.

Sanura translated his words. "I am certain you know why

you are here."

Jeremy did not look at her. Yes, of course, she could best converse with him.

He answered the captain. "Yes, sir, I do."

"Explain your actions."

"Sir, I acted according to . . ." He paused, thinking to simplify his words for the sake of understanding. "It is a matter of honor. That man attempted to kill me."

"When? How? How do you know him?"

Jeremy took a breath, sorry for what would come next. "I was a hand, a sailor on his ship. He threw me overboard." His glance flickered to Sanura.

Her face showed her confusion.

Jeremy's heart forced him to speak. "My lady, I apologize. I was untruthful when I said I had been shipwrecked. I have a good reason."

He wasn't sure if she translated that for the captain.

"Why did he throw you overboard?"

"That is the good reason. I cannot explain further."

"*Nonsense,*" replied the captain.

"Zheramee, you know dat man?"

Hearing his name in her sweet accent rent the festering wound in his heart. "Yes, I just said that—"

She shook her head. "I want to say, you know dat man, ah, who he is, name and tit-el."

"Yes." He still would not look at her.

She seemed frustrated.

"Zheramee, you no understand what you do. Ombru very important. If you on his ship, you muss know of what is happen-ing."

He looked up at her. "What do you mean?"

This time she averted her eyes. She spoke quickly, lowly to the captain. He answered, and their words seemed to become heated. The captain turned to him, speaking kindly but firmly.

"You tell all, or you have trouble, many trouble."

"I understand, but I cannot say more. Not here or now," Jeremy replied, and he did understand. The captain was obliged to act as his laws dictated. Jeremy had yet to find out what those were. Until they threatened his life, he would protect his secret. He offered no more response.

The captain spoke to Sanura, and she answered firmly. Then to Jeremy's surprise and horror, the captain seemed to acquiesce. He gave Jeremy an observant, perhaps respectful look, and took his leave.

Jeremy was alone with Sanura.

He did not wish to turn his back on her, but he could not face her. Gods, how he wished to embrace her. He offered her his profile, clasping his hands behind him. Sanura was quiet a moment. She rubbed her hands together, thinking.

"Zheramee," she finally said gently. "Please, you muss tell me re-sohn. You can tell me all. I can help."

She seemed a little hesitant of her last words.

Jeremy was glad to find he could swallow, though barely. "My dear, I am in gratitude of your concern, but I cannot say more." He forced his mind to focus on his problem. Their reaction to his explanation was not what he expected. "Surely, you and the captain understand my actions based on my explanation, do you not?"

"Yes, but Zheramee, dere is more problem." She sighed, frustrated.

"What problem?" He turned a little more to her. "What did you mean when you said I must know what is happening. What is happening?"

"Trade," she answered. "Dat Ombreux making trade from his land to Medar. He speak for king of his land."

"What?" Jeremy roared, turning fully toward her. "He spoke for the king?"

Startled, she almost took a step back.

Suddenly, something connected in Sanura's mind — he saw it in her eyes. *"Of course,"* she said, *"you are Gahlian! How could I not have guessed?"*

Jeremy pressed on. "What has he done? What do you mean by making trade?"

"I cannot say more," she collected herself. "It is of no matter. Zheramee, I muss talk of you instead."

Little did she know that talk of trade, Ombreux, and the king had everything to do with him.

"Zheramee, please tell me, I can help."

"Sanura, dear, this is out of your hands. I know you want to help, and I am much obliged to the captain and the laws he upholds. You even more so, as you are of his people. Is it not so?"

She looked as though she wished to respond but did not. He knew she could do nothing more for him than plead on his behalf. He appreciated her willingness to try, even after the way he had been acting.

"I will be fine," he said, calmer. "You needn't worry about me anyway." He turned away again. "This will be resolved once I speak to the proper leader." He waved his hand, exasperated. "The man I must go to," he finished lamely, pressured by her words, pressured by her presence. "Please, I'll hear no more. If it eases your mind, know that I do it to protect you too."

"Protect me?" She was finally distracted from the topic. "You protect me?"

He raised his arm over his head and leaned it on the wall, his other hand resting on his hip, his mind consumed with the news of Ombreux. "Yes, of course," he said, distracted.

"Why?"

Her question cut through his thoughts and made him look up at her. The light of the lamp illuminated her confusion and mostly the hurt he had caused her that she could not hide. Suitors or no, she cared for him.

"Gods, Sanura," he dropped his head, "I hope one day you can forgive me for all of this. I do not deserve it, but I hope your sweet heart will pardon me. Of all things, I want you to know that you are the most amazing woman I have ever met and ever will meet. You brought true joy into my life, and though our time was brief and now at an end, it is still my obligation to see you safely home. Yes, Sanura, I will protect you however I can until I see you in the arms of your family."

He did not look at her. The silence of the room settled slowly upon him. He wished she would weep, scream, strike him. Anything. After an eternity, she finally turned and departed.

Jeremy sank to his knees, bowing his head. He heard her speaking to the captain but could not make out the words. She became firm, then angry. He couldn't imagine what she could possibly have to say. She probably wanted to pitch him overboard.

Suddenly, they stopped. Her steps marched away, and the captain's slowly followed. They had been kind enough to leave the lamp.

Jeremy didn't want it.

The lamp, a chamber pot, and a blanket were Jeremy's companions the rest of the day. The cabin boy came under guard to bring food. Jeremy didn't want that, either. He lowered the lamp until it was almost extinguished and stared at darkness until sleep took him. It didn't stay with him. He struggled with it through the night, lying awake for hours at a time. He took a little breakfast when it came, but it was dry, tasteless to him. The captain came alone that day and asked Jeremy if he had anything to say. Jeremy only shook his head. The captain bowed his head in respect and left.

Jeremy sat or lay and thought that day. He thought on how he might have to approach his confession, how he should word it. He wondered who he would have to speak to. He also wondered if there was a way to speak with the leaders of trade in Medar. He had to know what Ombreux had been doing. How long had this been going on? Who had he spoken to? What did he say? Was it true he spoke for the king? If he had without the king's permission, it would have cost him his head. What if he did have the king's permission?

That had numerous repercussions. The Nottingdales controlled the southern ports and so the responsibility of nautical trade lay with them. The king would have insulted Jeremy's father had he given Ombreux the right to speak for him in those matters. Ombreux was subordinate to Jeremy's father in that respect. Ombreux's lands were inland. Though he had an interest in maritime trade and conducted some, it was under Jeremy's father's jurisdiction. Ombreux's responsibility was internal trade within the region, among other things. Jeremy's father was obliged to him in those matters. In this way, the power of the two was balanced.

Was Ombreux arranging direct trade with Medar? The thought seized Jeremy's heart. The riches to be had would be astounding, but so would the threat. When the eastern Empire heard of it, they would attack every northern ship. Most were under the rule of Jeremy's father. Surely, Ombreux planned to use this to undermine Duke Nottingdale. There were many questions that left and created, but through the day, Jeremy guessed at what Ombreux's motives could have been. He didn't like a single one.

Next to the hostile Empire of the east and the complacency of the Medaran King, the biggest problem for trading with the south was language. Ombreux had obviously solved that problem. He must have thought himself clever, exclusive. Jeremy didn't have answers yet to the other problems, but he did have the answer to that. With the ability to speak to Meda-rans, he wondered if he might have a chance to break the other barriers as well.

Sitting in the dark with nothing but his thoughts, Jeremy focused his mind on planning. He thought in the way his father had taught him to. He was not yet a duke, but in the coming days, he would have to act as one worthy of one day bearing the title.

The ship arrived in port the next day. Jeremy was sorry he could not see their approach. He heard the commotion on board. It was a long time before footsteps ventured to his dark corner. He rose when the captain and two men entered.

"You come," said the captain. "You make no trouble."

"No, sir. I have no intention of doing so," replied Jeremy.

"I know you good, but I muss . . ." He didn't know the words but gestured and one of the men came forward with rope.

"I understand," said Jeremy, stepping forward and holding his arms out.

The captain looked him over again with what Jeremy thought was respect as Jeremy's hands were tied firmly, but not uncomfortably. The man took his arm and escorted him out of the room.

Jeremy stopped in awe once he stood on deck. He had often seen the port of his father's land. This place made it seem as a fishing pier. There were almost more boats than water in the bay, and hundreds of them squeezed in together like pigs to a trough at the dock. They stretched east to west as far as the eye could see. Men swarmed around them, on them, before them. The port itself was a crush of humanity shouting, yelling, moving, lifting, singing, laughing, arguing, and doing every loud thing humans did. Animals and wagons of all kinds were mixed in with the fray, as were children, who darted among the constantly moving legs of the rest.

Jeremy was nudged and led down the gangway and to the main dock. A cluster of horses waited, all but three with riders. The captain indicated that Jeremy be assisted onto one. After he was up, the captain gestured, and in a moment a figure appeared, robed, a scarf around her head and face. Jeremy's heart twinged to see Sanura. She was closely escorted to the horses but was kept a good distance from Jeremy. As soon as she was up, the captain mounted the last riderless horse and the whole party moved forward.

The way was cleared ahead for them, and they quickened the pace, getting to a canter as they rode through the crowded streets. White buildings with red roofs slid by as did the blur of the faces of those that inhabited them. An enormous building loomed ahead, a palace, surrounded by high white walls. Jeremy gaped. He had never seen such a place. Palms and other trees waved in the sea breeze on its balconies and roofs. Gold and marble adorned its face, so much that were he to have even a portion of it, he would bear more riches than his king.

His gaze was torn away as the riders charged, unchallenged, through the open gates into the courtyard. Fountains and palms surrounded him as the palace stood stoically overhead. Jeremy was assisted to dismount and hurried up wide marble steps and into the palace. Here the wonders did not cease. Statues, gold, marble, and tapestries all flashed by among other beauties and wonders he only glimpsed.

He was led down a long spiral of stairs to a place bare of lavishness and décor. He realized he was in the dungeon. As he was being led into a small room, a realization pierced his very soul.

"*Wait, please,*" he said as he was pushed forward, "*keep me here if you must, but I haven't said farewell to Sanura. Please, I beg you —*"

He received no response. He was let go, still bound, and

his escorts left, closing the door firmly.

"*Wait! Please!*" He rushed to the door, striking it with his fists. "*I must see her!*"

With a quiet cry of remorse, Jeremy sank to the ground and clutched his hair in his hands. She would be gone by the time he was dealt with. He hadn't thought they would be separated without having the chance to speak to one another. The emptiness that had been in his heart was nothing to that which engulfed his soul. He had truly lost her. He was barely aware of the sob that escaped him.

"Not like this, not like this!"

Several hours passed before steps invaded his quiet world. He didn't even rise when the door opened, letting bright light and a figure into his room. He was a little surprised to see it was the captain. He rose. Able to speak his language, the captain must have been sent to talk to Jeremy.

Jeremy gave him a nod but remained silent.

The captain stepped aside, gesturing to the door. "Jyoo muss come."

Dazed, Jeremy let himself be prodded into motion. Two guards joined them, and he was led, bound and guarded, through a palace that shamed the glory of his king's lavish abode. Ombreux had been working fast. For the King of Medar to become involved meant he was vested in trade. Had they made a treaty? If so, Jeremy was a dead man.

Even if the king recognized Jeremy's claim of honor, it would not trump the murder of his ally. If it was true that Ombreux spoke for his king, Jeremy had betrayed him. He felt no guilt for that. If that was true, the king would have betrayed Jeremy's father first. Even so, Jeremy was on the losing end of that argument as well.

Jeremy and his escort ascended through the palace, winding their way through a maze more complex than any hedge garden Jeremy had ever been in. Finally, they were in a long hall with many doors on either side. Two sentries stood at large doors at the end. Though with an arched ceiling, it could not have been a grand hall leading to a throne room. It was relatively narrow, too high and deep in the palace for such a place. Were they in the private quarters of the king?

Before he could speculate further, the doors were opened, and Jeremy and his escort entered. The room was grand. It held the same lavishness as the rest of the palace but also had a feel of having been lived in. Two walls were open arches with white sheers that moved gently in the breeze. The furniture within was for sitting, conversing, perhaps eating. One table looked as though it was a grand desk.

Against the wall to the left of the entrance was a row of chairs, large and comfortable, though well adorned, in a half-ring around a wide empty space filled with an ornate rug Jeremy immediately knew to be a treasure from the eastern Empire. He was led onto it now, the two guards stopping at its edge to kneel. Jeremy and the captain approached the center chairs where three people sat. The rest were empty.

A man, noble and proud, sat in one. Had Jeremy not been told he was being brought before the king, he would know him as such. His black beard and hair were lightly speckled with gray. His olive skin was wrinkled from years of concern and laughter. Jeremy could see his eyes were sharp, wise, and shrewd. He did not fear him, but he also formed immediate respect for him.

To his left sat two beautiful women. The first was older, perhaps a decade younger than the king by Jeremy's guess. Her appearance did not mark her for age. Her skin was smooth and glowing. Her dark hair, wound with green and gold satin upon her head, showed nary a strand of gray. It was her eyes that showed her to be a woman of maturity. They were bright and keen as the king's.

The woman to her left was younger, only more beautiful to him because of her youth. She wore an ornate velvet robe, similar to that of the two beside her, though hers was in red and the other woman's was in green. Beneath were layers of muslin embroidered with gold. Gold hung about her neck, from her ears, and adorned her hands. Jewels sparkled as well, rubies and diamonds that accented the color of her garb. Her black hair was wound in red and gold with a soft veil trailing behind. She was stunning, and his heart felt guilty for considering her at all beautiful when she was not Sanura.

Her eyes caught his, and her face melted for him, warming in a comforting smile that speared his heart.

"Dear gods," he whispered and fell to his knees, "Sanura."

The face of the woman beside Sanura hardened, and she rose. She seemed to float to Jeremy, taking his hands and undoing the ties herself.

"*I will not have the man who saved my Sanura be brought before me as a common criminal,*" she spat out, to the best of Jeremy's understanding.

He was speechless as the woman flung aside the rope and pulled Jeremy to his feet.

"*Now, Jeremy,*" she said, "*you are safe now. Many things have been made clear. Come, speak with us, please.*"

He did not move, confused.

Sanura stood. She smiled gently as he looked to her for clarity.

"*He still does not understand, Mother,*" she said. "*We must explain ourselves first.*"

Comprehension snapped home like a sword to the scabbard.

"*Mother,*" he repeated, and his gaze went to the woman who still held his hands. "*Fair lady,*" he knelt to one knee, pressing her hands to his lips.

"*Captain, you spoke truth when you said this Zheramee is a*" *gentleman.*" She smiled.

The captain bowed. *"Never would I be untruthful to you, fair queen."*

Queen.

Another obvious truth slid home. Sanura was a Princess of Medar. Dear gods.

"You may take your leave now, captain," the king addressed him.

The captain bowed again and departed.

The queen again pulled Jeremy to his feet, bringing him closer to stand before them. She regained her seat, and Jeremy took a relaxed, yet respectful stance before them.

"Sanura says that you have spoken of your service for your country," said the king in Jeremy's language. "I can see it in you."

The king spoke the language quite well. It was heavily accented, and Jeremy guessed at some of the words, but his meaning was clear. He was new to the language but had been working hard at it.

The king smiled and continued. "Yes, you are every bit of the gentleman she says you are. Your demeanor lends you credibility. We have much to discuss, but first, I must know what happened with Duke Ombreux. Speak, Zheramee."

Jeremy's previous fears were dashed away. He had standing in this place. He was now in the most advantageous position he could ever be in. The fate of his family name and perhaps the course of history was in his hands. His mind was racing, considering all the opportunities that could possibly be before him. Still, he could not speak freely yet.

Before he could answer, Sanura spoke. "Zheramee, it is good now." She rose and stepped forward to take his hand. Her eyes, more beautiful than any of the raiment she wore, smiled at him. "All is good. You are safe. You can stay here. I have promise of my fa-ter. I have much to tell you, but you muss tell him all firss."

She was beaming, nearly gushing. *You can stay here.* Gods, she still loved him. He wanted to take her in his arms and hold her, to let her radiant warmth melt his cares away. All the time they had spent apart hadn't done a thing. He still felt every bit of love he had for her. Princess or no, he loved her.

Princess!

He took her hand and kissed it. He could not share her joy. She did not know who he was. Then another thought occurred to him. The enormity of it was staggering, but to him, it made sense. He could not say it aloud. He would not play with her emotions, especiallyif they would be crushed in the end. He let her go and turned to face the king with a bow.

"Majesty, I am willing to tell you all that you wish, but I ask of you, please, allow me to speak to you alone."

This produced surprise from all three, but the king's curiosity was piqued. He turned to the women.

"There is much you two need to discuss. Go, Sanura, join your sisters. They have missed you."

Sisters? *Meesa?*

"Father, with all love and respect—"

He held a hand up to her protest. *"Go. I will join you later."*

"Come, dear," said her mother. *"Let the men speak. We will know all in time."*

At that, Sanura and her mother bowed to the king and departed. As Sanura passed Jeremy, he could see the myriad emotions plaguing her. He hoped he could offer her good news when he saw her again.

In the meantime, Jeremy Nottingdale was about to address the most powerful king known to civilization.

Still adorned in sailor's attire, Jeremy took on the most regal bearing he could and began with a bow.

"Regal Majesty, I am honored to be in your presence. I offer you profound gratitude for allowing me to speak freely before you. I will begin by first offering you my most sincere apologies for not speaking at your first command. I only made the bold request for a private conference to protect the noble heart of your daughter."

"It is at the behest of my daughter that I am even giving pause to hold audience with you," replied the king. "Her tales of your deeds have earned you the least reward of my attention. Now, Zheramee with no family name, speak at last. How do you know the *Gahlian* Ombreux, and why would he wish to kill you?"

"Majesty, the man you know as Ombreux, the Duke of Langue, was my uncle. I am Jeremy Nottingdale, heir to the Duchy of Rosillo in Gahli."

Surprise was an emotion kings were required to suppress. The King of Medar failed to do so at that moment.

Jeremy spared him further awkwardness by continuing. "It is a long story I can tell if you wish, but Ombreux cast me overboard to spite my father and to gain power with the monarchy through his son. He is also guilty by his own confession of murdering his own parents. I was not only avenging his treason against my father and me, but also the deaths of my mother's parents. You see, Majesty, I have a true claim against Ombreux. I am also sure, Majesty, that you will see what this could mean for you and for me. Before I go on, may I ask your Majesty one thing?"

"Yes, you may."

"Did Ombreux truly speak for my king?"

"He bore a letter with your king's seal, and I have received several since," he replied. "He also came with men, goods of your land, and a man who has been teaching me your language. This man is a servant of your king. He can speak to you to prove that he is." He gestured and spoke to a man standing nearby who went to the desk. "For now, I will show you one of the letters."

"So, it is true that Ombreux and the king wish to establish trade relations with you," said Jeremy.

"Yes. They claim to have the naval power to keep the Empire of the East at bay. They interested me with the promise of exclusive trade going east from your lands. I grow weary of the Empire. They had demanded more and gave less in return. I have evidence that they have tried to establish their own trade routes to the southland, intending to sever me completely. I felt it fitting that I return some of their arrows. Ah, here we are." He handed a letter to Jeremy.

He needed only a glance. "Yes, that is the seal of the king," he said bitterly.

He handed the letter back. The servant was dismissed.

"For the time being, I am willing to entertain your claim as truth," said the king. "I will summon the king's man to help me to confirm that you are who you say you are, but you have interested and convinced me enough to grant you audience, Zheramee Nottingdale. Tell me what you think this means for the two of us."

Now Jeremy had to play his cards. "Majesty, I am sympathetic to your position. Let me now present you with a problem you were likely not aware of. My king's maritime power in the south shores of his land is what he must rely on to protect the ships that will travel between our lands. My father commands this power and is followed faithfully by the men. The king has insulted my father by allowing Ombreux to establish maritime trade negotiations without him. My father is a good man, a loyal man, but if ever he were to decide to defy the king, his sailing forces would stand by him."

"Why would your father decide to betray his king?"

"I do not wish to imagine what Ombreux was planning. I can say, though, that he had plans to be rid of my father much as he tried to be rid of me. Now that Ombreux is gone, my father will know of the king's actions, and I know he will take great exception to it."

"How do you know that your father isn't already dead?"

"I sincerely hope not." He cleared his throat. "By my understanding of Ombreux's words to me in our final confrontation, he intended to be rid of me and then would be rid of my father. I believe that if my father were dead, he would have found pleasure in telling me so. Even if he were, a Nottingdale still lives, and I would stand in his place."

"What would you do in his place, Zheramee Nottingdale?"

"*I would speak to you,*" Jeremy answered the king's tongue. "*I would offer you peace. I wish to trade with you. I bring you goods from all lands north. You bring me goods from all lands south. Together, we join men, open roads to the east, around the Empire. The Empire comes to us and asks for trade.*"

The king was so pleased he laughed. "Zheramee Nottingdale, you are brave! You have learned my tongue well from my Sanura."

"I speak the truth, too, good King." Jeremy went back to his own language. "Even now, I wish for you to know that is what I offer to you."

The king's face became more serious, but his eyes still sparkled. "You are sincere. You mean what you say."

"I do, sir."

"How could you possibly? Why should I even entertain the thought?"

"I have had many hours to think on this, and I have decided it is the only decision you could make in order to open trade to the north. Does anyone else of nobility in my land speak your tongue?"

"Until I met you, I thought Ombreux the only one."

"I do, and now you and Sanura speak mine. Rather well, I might add. How long have you been learning?"

"Six months, perhaps. Right after Sanura left on her voyage." He could not help a sad frown.

"I am sure you were conversant only after a few weeks. Our captains and trade merchants can learn swiftly if there is constant contact between us. Our combined naval power could keep the Empire at bay. I am sure you intended to commit men and ships if you made an agreement with Ombreux. Did you not?"

"It is true," he agreed. "Until now, I and the kings before me all felt that the northerners should come to us, and it was their risk on the return. Now that I am done dealing with the Empire, we can send fleets between our lands."

Jeremy nodded. "I will have men for them, too."

"Good sir, I am intrigued, and I must say amused by your thoughts, but you seem to be forgetting your monarch."

Jeremy darkened. "If he was deceived, then my family will continue to serve him. If he was not deceived by Ombreux and knew he was betraying his agreement with my father, then my family has been slighted by him. He deserves no loyalty, and we shall govern our lands and trade without him. If he wishes to trade in the goods of Medar, he must come to the Nottingdale Court to entreaty."

"You would make yourself a king?" he cried incredulously.

"No, Majesty, my father," he answered. "Our family has been in succession for the throne in generations past. My name is not of the land from which I come. In a far land, another descendant of the Nottingdales sits upon a throne that has been the family's for centuries. Monarchy is in our blood. My father's lands and those of my uncle will be our kingdom."

"Your uncle's lands?"

"I fully intended to concede Ombreux's lands to his son, no matter how worthless he is and no matter the injustice done by Ombreux. That was before I learned of all of this. I won Ombreux's sword and ring. I defeated him in a duel. I can claim his title and lands as well. I will give him the choice. He can either retain his title as Duke under Nottingdale rule or face me in a duel. I doubt it will be difficult to persuade him to surrender. He is not unlike his father," he added with contempt.

The king leaned back. "You are certainly acting quickly with the many things you have learned."

"Yes, Majesty," Jeremy realized he had become slightly agitated and calmed himself. "My father would expect no less of me."

"I have one question, though," said the king. "How would I know that I have your loyalty? How could you prove your allegiance to me and I to you?"

Jeremy did not hesitate. "I could marry one of your daughters."

The king leaned back and put a half-curled hand under his nose.

"I realize, sire, the boldness of my statement, and I hope I am not guilty of any transgression," said Jeremy. "Yet we are speaking on the most solemn matters of trade and alliance. Marriage is the greatest, most indelible alliance between two parties, is it not?"

"Indeed, you speak the truth," he answered, still analyzing Jeremy sharply. "You are young, Nottingdale, but you are shrewd. You also do not waste my time with empty flatteries and excess words. I appreciate and admire that." He dropped his hand and sat back. "I can only guess that my Sanura is the object of your intention. I am a man of business and nobility, Nottingdale, but I also care for my daughters.

"I will warn you now that we Medarans are not like many in this world. Though we keep our bloodlines in the aristocracy, we do not marry our sons and daughters off like pawns to gain power and wealth. They must marry, but willingly. We do not silence and hide our women and treat them like property. The queen is counsel to the king, and both princes and princesses learn the business of the kingdom and actively partake in it. I have the final say in all matters, but I consider their words equally to any other's. It is the mind, not the body, that defines a person in my land.

"Sanura is my consult in matters of trade with the West, a new and rapidly growing means of wealth for my people. I'll not have her taken away from me to be stuffed into a stone castle to let her mind rot while she does no more than produce your heirs."

Jeremy's heart was in his throat. He bowed his head to maintain composure. "Wise King, you and I both know that emotion must be stifled when in parlay. Perhaps it shows my youth and naivety, but I will show my heart to you now to assure you I have none but the noblest of intentions and that you may trust me to tell you the truth in all things."

Jeremy looked directly and intently at the king so he would know his next words were the truth from his heart. "Your Sanura is the most amazing woman I have ever met. I found her beautiful, yes, but the beauty of her mind is what captured my heart. She fulfills me in a way no other woman has before, and I would cast myself into the sea before I would stifle her mind or spirit. Though these last months have been full of the most tribulation and trial I have ever known, they were the best of my whole existence because of your daughter. To now, I was sorry they were over, mad as it may sound. I actually regretted being found in part because I know it meant our time together would end, but I tell you, good King, that my only thought was to see Sanura safe to her family. Had it meant living the rest of my life on that god-forsaken island without her, I would gladly have done so for her.

"You may doubt any of my words to you of trade and treaty and military might, but please, do not ever doubt my feelings for her. I love your daughter, noble King, I love

Sanura."

He said the last words specifically, savoring the taste of them even as he realized they were true and yet still did not encompass the scope of his emotion.

The king looked upon him steadily. "Would it change your heart if I said she is promised to another?"

Jeremy bowed his head. "It breaks my heart but does not change it. In truth, I acted to distance myself from her on our return voyage, as I myself am betrothed, yet it is to the daughter of the king I intend to denounce. To my way of thinking, the king has voided all contracts with the Nottingdales." He paused and cleared his throat. "She is spoken for?" He barely managed to ask.

The king gave a quiet laugh. "It was a question to test you. She has not asked my blessing for a union yet. As I said before, Sanura speaks for herself."

Jeremy felt his heart buoy. "Yes, that she does." He could not help a smile.

The king mirrored it. "How would you answer if I told you her first words to me at our greeting were of you?"

"They were?"

"We had not yet dried the tears from our faces when she told me of you and your trouble. 'I want him to stay here, father,' she said, 'I know I cannot marry him, but if he will stay, please allow it. He has done no wrong.'

"There is a word for the position she wished to honor you with. I don't know the word in your language. She wanted you to have a life of royalty, and it was the only way she knew how to give it to you." He smiled. "You would essentially be her companion servant, tending to all of her needs and whims, escorting her in her travels as well. She thought she could give you a life full of wonder and luxury you had never known. I wonder how she will react to know you are nobility."

"Majesty," replied Jeremy. "If we cannot come to terms, I would prefer she didn't know. I don't wish to imagine what it would do to her to know I am qualified to ask for her, had done so, and was denied because of politics. To protect her, I wish always to be known as a sailor to her. Can you promise me at least that, if nothing else?"

The king had become somber at his words. "You truly love her," he said. "As a man who knows love, I recognize my own heart in you. I would live as a pauper for my queen, die a lonely death for her, fall upon my own sword. Tell me, Zheramee, would you renounce your birthright to stay with her?"

This did give Jeremy pause, but the results of such a deed came to him quickly. "My father and our people will need me in the coming times regardless of whether we reach an agreement. I am loyal to my family. I cannot take my place at my father's side if I renounce my position. As a father and king, I am sure you appreciate the value of such loyalty in an heir, and I hope you realize such loyalty would be yours as well should we reach an agreement. I swear it to you now.

"That being said, once all was set to right with my family, I would not hesitate to renounce my birthright to be with Sanura. Yet because she is royalty, I could not marry her if I am no longer nobility. It would do no good, and I must still decline. I would rather throw myself on my own sword, as you say, than be a direct witness to her being wed to another. No worse hell could I imagine. You have confessed your love for your queen, so I am sure you can share my feelings at the thought of living such an existence. I would also not have her marriage sullied by the constant presence of my grief. No, she deserves better than that. I am sure you will agree."

The king looked at him long and thoughtfully. Jeremy's heart pounded. His words were not said to manipulate. He had meant every one. He had no way of knowing if he had the king's approval. The politics of trade be damned. At that moment, the only answer that mattered concerned Sanura.

The king finally straightened. "Well, Zheramee Nottingdale, you give a king a lot to think on. Come, sit beside me and tell me more of your journey, who you are, and your ideas on trade."

His words snapped Jeremy out of his tense anticipation, and with a gracious bow, he did as bid.

CHAPTER TWELVE

L ater that night, much later, Jeremy stood at a marbled balustrade looking over the bright city of Medar, the port with
its scattered stars of ships' lights, and the dark sea beyond. It
was one of the more stunning views he had ever beheld.

He wore clothing from his homeland, the clothing of a gentleman. The king's man, who was teaching the King of Medar
the tongue and the ways of the north, had given them to him.
The king's own tailor had worked swiftly to adjust the gar-
ments to Jeremy's size, as they were a bit large for him as they
were. It was strange to be in the more constrictive clothing,
but it felt good to have a vest and coat and all the other trap-
pings to go with them again.

The weather was cool, so he did not suffer for the layers.
His now long hair was tied back at the nape of his neck with
a silk ribbon rather than a leather tie. He had grown used to
and rather preferred the look.

The king's man of his country had been a decent enough
fellow, though he did not quite successfully hide his displeas-
ure at the change in circumstances. He was able to verify the
answers that Jeremy gave to the Medaran king's questions of
his homeland and its politics that proved his claim as the heir
to the Duke of Nottingdale. He even confessed he had a slight
memory of seeing Jeremy's father in court once and confirmed that Jeremy had the correct answers to his questions
with regard to the customs and players of the scene. It was
sufficient for the king, though he did not seem to need much
convincing. Jeremy guessed Sanura's high opinion of him had

done much to earn him favor long before he was brought before the monarch.

Once the formality of confirmation was done, the king had spared no luxury for his guest. Their talk had taken a good deal of the afternoon. When the day grew late, the king had ordered Jeremy be shown to guest chambers, where he was bathed and dressed appropriately. The king had gone to spend time and to dine with his reunited family. He had promised not to speak of anything to Sanura of their conversations of the day. Jeremy was served his evening meal in his room, and he knew it was because the king wanted time alone with his family, but also because he shared Jeremy's concern to spare Sanura's feelings. Being near her and meeting more of her family in such an intimate setting would do his heart no good, either. After a rest and some time to gather his thoughts, Jeremy had been ready when he was called upon to spend the rest of the evening conversing with the king.

Jeremy had come to like the man, title and grandeur aside. He was a good man, a fair man, yet one he would not wish to cross. He had promised to speak further with Jeremy on the morrow, but when they parted for the night, both were confident and pleased with what had transpired.

Jeremy could not help a smile as the events of the day sank into his mind. He, Jeremy Nottingdale, had just spent the day negotiating with the King of Medar and had been considered. He realized in having acted in such a capacity that such things were what his father had been trying to prepare him for all along. Not only had he seemed to have some proficiency at it, but he had also enjoyed it. All of the things he had been trying to avoid in his adult life suddenly fell into place. He had always dreaded the moment when he would have to step into adulthood. Now, in that very moment, he found he was more than willing to take his childish thoughts and behaviors and cast them away.

Jeremy took a deep breath and let it out in a sigh, as if doing the very thing in the act. He felt free. He felt redeemed.

He was still troubled, though, with the issue of Sanura. The king had left him with more negotiation and delicate talk ahead, only with matters of the heart, not of trade and politics. The latter was easier in comparison.

"You would manipulate kingdoms for her," the king had said, "yet only she has the power to let you."

Now that the full story was out, Jeremy had all the answers to his other questions about Sanura. Her position and place in the culture of Medarans accounted for her knowledge, her courage, her grace, and her skill. It accounted for the men's behavior on the ship, at least some of it. Jeremy felt a little foolish for that, as it was more than the attention and favor of a woman they sought and could possibly be granted. It was that of their princess. He realized the captain was not only a gentleman surrendering his quarters, but he was also essentially obliged to for royalty. He had kneeled in deference before her, not seduction. The ship's boy had not been coming to fetch him because she shunned the hold, he had been delivering a royal summons. It would have reflected badly upon her had she gone down to the mean quarters of the men. Thankfully, he was sure she could understand that he couldn't have known that and wasn't insulting her by his refusal. It was no wonder she had tried to persuade him to tell her his secret. She really could help him at the highest level. Yes, he fully understood her frustration now.

Jeremy wondered why Sanura had not told him. Of course, she likely held the same fears and caution he did. He did find the humor in that, though it made him sad they had not been able to be truthful with one another. He had never liked that.

He turned at a knock at the door. He went inside, calling, "Enter."

A steward came into the room with a bow. *"M'lord, the*

Emira Sanura will see you now."

Emira. He had heard that word before. Princess, he was sure, although he had thought it might have meant Lady.

Princess Sanura. Oh, what a lovely sound.

"Very well," Jeremy returned the bow and followed the steward.

He went over and over the conversation he'd had with her father, the King of Medar. He had a thousand things to say. He wanted to be sure he would remember them all.

Every last one fell out of his head as he was led onto the balcony of her chambers and beheld her standing before the very scene he had been admiring. She ruined the view. Her radiance outshined every light below. The sight of her melted Jeremy's heart.

Even in the dim light, he could see her glance go over him. "Zheramee?" It was more of a breath, a quiet exclamation. The surprise of seeing him in the proper garb of his land must have been as much of a transformation to her as it had been for him when he first beheld her.

She stepped forward, still adorned in red and gold, reaching her hands out to him. He could not move, such was her beauty, such was his desire to claim her, such was his love for her. She took his hands, perhaps a little unsure, though she smiled.

He barely remembered his manners and moved to kneel.

"No," she stopped him, "here we are friends, Zheramee. Here it is same as before."

"I still kneel before you, my sweet lady," he said, going to one knee and pressing her hands to his lips. "Please forgive me. I was trying to protect you. I know I hurt you, and I am sorry. Please tell me I have your forgiveness."

"Zheramee, please, did my father not tell you I want you to . . ."

He shook his head. "I must hear it from you."

She moved her skirts to kneel at his level. He could see the tears in her eyes. "Zheramee, yes, of course, I forgive you. You did not under-stan. I want you to forgive me. I was cru-el. I could not tell you. I know you not under-stan, even now, but I will try."

"Sweet gods, Sanura, you haven't a cruel bone in your beautiful body." Jeremy stopped her, squeezing her hands. "I do understand. Much better than you realize." Her tears made his own eyes burn. "Sanura, dear, I have nothing to forgive you for. I am the one who has done wrong to you. I tried to make myself stop loving you, but I couldn't. I agonized over it because I didn't want to be without you, but also because I knew you didn't understand, and I had hurt you. Please forgive me for how I have treated you."

She blinked rapidly. "Did you say you love me still?"

Jeremy answered by taking her delicate face in his hands and kissing her. He felt her sobbing gasp through it, and she kissed him back, full and tender. Jeremy wished he could die right then, for no greater pleasure could ever be had in the earthly world.

When he finally did break the kiss, he wiped the tears from her cheeks with his thumb and helped her to her feet. "Come, my dear, there is much I have to tell you."

The furthest point of the semi-circular balcony held a marble bench. They sat upon it with a half-moon overhead, clasping each other's hands.

"Zheramee, I could not tell you of me," Sanura blurted out. "It is rule of wisdom. I cannot tell a . . . a stranger unless I have, ah, am safe, with men of my piple. If you taken in fight, the men may do bad tings to you to know who I am, where I go. My men will die before tell, but I cannot expect from you. I truss you. I would tell you, but my father would be very angry. We truss Ombru, but I hide when he come. He could not know I dere. Den when dere was fight, we break rope and hurry to go. It was becoss of me." She squeezed his hand. "I know you cannot under-stan, but I hope dis help."

"Sanura, dear, I understand completely," he assured her. "I did the same thing to you."

He kissed her hand as she gave him a quizzical look.

"Zheramee, I don't tink I under-stan words."

"No, you heard me correctly," he said. "Sanura, you were right when you realized I am from the land that is called *Gahli* in your tongue. My family name is Nottingdale. I am the son of a *Du-chas*." He used a word the king had given him.

Her breasts swelled with her breath. "Zheramee," she breathed, "you are . . ."

She laughed and wept, and Jeremy took her in his arms. Oh, the bliss. She held him tight, still laughing through her tears and giving him cause to chuckle, glad she had found the humor in the situation as well. He felt her tense and let her pull away.

Concern filled her face. "But Zheramee, dat means you have . . ." She looked alarmed. "You cannot stay."

"No, not in the way you asked of your father," he said and hurried on at her further distress. "Let me tell you of what your father and I discussed."

He told her all of their initial conversation. She listened closely, nodding at certain places, seeming amazed at others. As Jeremy neared the end, he felt nervous.

"Your father wanted to know how I could possibly prove my loyalty, and . . . and I—" He stopped.

What if she didn't want him as a husband? Had he over-stepped his bounds? What if she rejected him?

He stood and turned to lean on the cool balustrade. It felt good on his hot palms.

Sanura stood as well. She put her hand on his shoulder. "What, Zheramee, what did you say?"

Jeremy swallowed the rock in his throat. *"I asked for your hand*, Sanura," he croaked the phrase he had just learned. "*I ask him to let you be my wife.*"

The silence after rent his pounding heart. Unable to bear it, he turned to see her hands cupping her mouth, tears sliding down her cheeks.

"*What did he say?*" she whispered.

A small smile touched his lips as he turned to take her hands. "He said that women of your society speak for themselves. He later said he would bless our union, but that I must ask you myself."

Jeremy sat beside her, still holding her hands. "Sanura, *may I have the honor of being your husband?*"

She pressed a hand to her mouth, too stunned to speak.

"I understand if you must think on it," he said, certainly not wishing to press her. "Please know I would ask even if I were not arranging treaty with your father. I would ask if you were the daughter of the lowliest man of this or any land. Your love is worth more than all of the riches of both of our native lands, and the only one I wish for, yet if you decline, I will respect your wish. Your happiness is my only concern. I only hope there is a place for me within it."

He kissed her hand and rose, not taking his gaze from their hands. He could not steel himself to look in her face. "I know this is a lot and is sudden. I will leave you to consider—"

"Yes, Zheramee."

He was startled enough to look at her adoring eyes shining in the moonlight. "What?"

"Yes, Zheramee, I will be your wife."

She gave a teary laugh as he gave no answer but reached to take her in his arms. Jeremy pressed her as close as he could, kissing her long and hard. Something hot traced down his cheek. She would be his. Sweet gods, she would be his.

The smell of jasmine was intoxicating. He left her lips to descend to her neck. She tasted of jasmine, too. He crushed her against him, desperate to meld with her, to truly become one.

She ran her fingers through his hair, gasping at his needy kisses. This only fueled his desire. He suddenly needed to take her. If he did not, he felt he would die. She banished his sudden question of whether it would be proper when she took his hand and led him inside. She hurried him to her bed, overladen and draped in satin, and proceeded to undress him as they lavished hungry kisses upon each other.

He gently pushed her away once they had slid between the cool sheets. She had drawn her leg up between his thighs as they lay. The press of it against his manhood was maddening. He dotted her neck with tiny kisses. She sighed with pleasure.

"This will be as if it were our first time together," he said. "I want to take my time." It was a half-truth. He truly wished to ravish her—his need had been pent up and was now piqued to a height he didn't dream was possible.

He loved her enough, though, that he could not do that to her this time. It was special. He was going to treat it as such. She was going to be his wife. To him, her acceptance of him on the balcony was more of a marriage than parroted words in a ceremony ever could be. This was their true wedding night.

Sanura smiled and lay back, the goddess he had seen before, now amid the luxury he always felt she deserved.

"Do you remember our firss time?" she asked.

Jeremy smiled broadly, leaning over to kiss the sweet skin between her breasts. "How could I ever forget? You surprised me."

She giggled maddeningly. "I know."

He put his weight on an elbow and threaded his fingers through her hair. "What made you do it? Why did you come to me?" He brought the silken strands to his lips.

"You were so handsome and brave. You protected me."

She smiled. "You kissed me. You surprised *me*."

"I couldn't help it," he said. "I had held myself back for so long. I certainly didn't want you to be frightened of me."

"I did tink, Zheramee, dat dere was sometink different about you. You were a zhentleman. I wanted to ask, but I fear you ask of me, so I did not. I sometime wonder why you no ask."

Jeremy let out an exasperated breath. "I did the same."

She laughed. "Now I can see why I tink you different. I wondered if you were god-man of north. I hear dat dey cannot have pleasure and try to make you follow deir god. I not want dat."

Jeremy laughed. "No, I am certainly not one of them. Like your people, I am a bit different than those around me."

"Yes, I like dat. I like you." She slid lower, closer against him, running her hand through his hair again. "You are very handsome when you fight." She frowned slightly, and her arm gently traced the mark on his arm. "I was afraid when you fight Ombru, but when you win, I feel same for you as when you fight bad men on island. I knew I muss have you den. I always wonder why you not come to me after you kiss me firss time," she said.

"I wanted you to trust me and not fear I would take advantage of you," he answered.

She smiled mischievously. "Some times I wished dat you would take advantage of me."

Jeremy slid his arms around her and pulled her closer. "Do you mean like this?"

He rolled more of his weight onto her, pinning her legs under one of his. He held her arms gently and lowered his head to take a pert nipple in his mouth.

Sanura practically screamed in delight. He laved her breast with his tongue, holding her firm despite her pleasured squirming. She was groaning and giggling simultaneously with cries of startled delight in between as he nipped gently and flicked his tongue over her hard bud. His manhood swelled against her leg, encouraged by her wiggling.

Jeremy went from breast to breast, warming her quickly. He surfaced to kiss her, deep and full, as his hand released her arm to trace down her curved torso, through the soft nest of curls guarding her womanhood and slide between her warm, wet folds.

She relented her kiss, gasping as the jolt of pleasure seized her. He didn't let her go, thrusting his tongue further into her mouth to find hers. She responded weakly, trying to sound her pleasure at his touch.

He released her mouth to return to her breasts as he intensified his caresses. She grasped his hair, clutching it in her hands as she lifted her pelvis to meet his touch. She grew hot under his fingers, tensing as she was carried higher upon each wave of pleasure that passed through her. Jeremy fought to calm himself, to focus on her pleasure. Caressing her made his body threaten to expend himself before he had even employed it. Oh, it had been so long. He moved away from her maddening skin. In response, she reached over before he could stop her to grasp his stiff phallus.

He sucked in his breath, nearly losing control, and put his hand on hers. "No, my sweet. Please, I beg you, it will be over before it begins," he gasped.

"Zheramee." Her voice was the purr of a tigress as she turned to face him. "We have all night. You have well shown before dat once is never enough for you."

The seduction in her eyes left him powerless to answer. Even as he tried to form something, her smile grew. She pressed her hand to his chest, pushing him onto his back. She rolled over to lie against him while her fingers stroked the patch of hair on his chest.

"It has been long time, Zheramee." Her lips felt like a

feather upon his. "It is cru-el to make you wait."

"Sanura," he whispered a protest, but she brushed aside the last of his will as her fingers traced down his chest, across his stomach, and down his thigh. Her lips trailed behind them and did not turn aside at the soft hair on his lower belly.

He gasped and seized as his manhood was suddenly surrounded by warm, wet pressure. He moaned as sheer pleasure coursed through him.

She took all of him into her mouth and withdrew slowly, creating exquisite suction. The tip of her tongue pressed upon the underside of his shaft as she drew back and made little circles around the head before her lips passed over it.

No woman had ever performed fellatio upon him before. Most had been shy or nervous of his manhood, and he felt successful just from getting it between their legs. The pleasure of new sensations made him feel like a virgin again. He surrendered to it, yet again amazed by this woman who made his life seem new.

He groaned as she dove upon him again, enveloping him in hot bliss. She stroked him faster, taking in as much of him as she could. Her tongue danced over him, teasing, driving him ever faster to the apex of ecstasy. His entire body tensed beneath her, hard and stiff as his member. She did not give him any chance to relax. He had no control. He surrendered it all to her.

He was barely aware of his cries of pleasure as it seemed she would draw his very soul from him. Jeremy felt he would weep from the overwhelming ecstasy. Pleasure solidified and became tangible. His mind ceased to be separate from his body and soul, and the sweet release coursed through his entire being.

He gave a final husky groan as the violent shudders abated. He tensed briefly a few more times and collapsed, drained of all but the glowing aftermath. Sanura spread out like ink beside him, her hand retracing its previous path. He could only turn his head to rest against hers as it lay on his shoulder. He lay panting in bliss, feeling his pulse as it slowed. Sanura drew up her leg to rest on his thigh. His manhood rested against her as it relaxed. She smiled and brushed her fingers over it, making Jeremy give a weak grunt.

Sanura brushed her lips on his cheek. "You like, Zheramee?" she asked softly.

He summoned strength and wrapped his arms around her. He threaded his fingers through the hair at the back of her neck to press her closer.

"Little did I know the day I was thrown into the sea was the happiest day of my life. Nothing could ever make me let you go now," he murmured.

She laughed lowly, the huskiness still in her voice. "I am glad." She kissed his cheek and laid her head down again.

It truly was only a short while later when the lazy tracing of her fingers upon his skin stirred his desire again. He laid himself upon her, relishing the feel of her skin pressed to his, her body moving beneath his in response to the exploring of his lips and fingers. She was well ready for him when he presented himself to her. He slid into her effortlessly, driving his full length deep into her hot well. She groaned and arched beneath him as he pressed hard against her. He drew his hand over her breast and held it, pressing the nipple between his fingers, making her cry out again in pleasure. He pressed slightly harder as he forced her legs apart with his, putting his knees beneath him. He withdrew slowly and dove into her again, feeling her writhe with pleasure. His thrusts grew more insistent and forceful. His hand left her breast so he could brace himself to drive faster and deeper, taking them both quickly to the heights they sought together.

"Zheramee," she gasped, "no have careful dis time."

He was startled enough to pause. "What?"

She drew herself from the fog of euphoria to meet his gaze and smile. "We no need careful here." She drew her fingers over his face and drew him in for a kiss. "I need to feel you."

Jeremy almost released then. With a groan, he kissed her neck and freed himself upon her. He had no other thought or emotion than making true, passionate love to Sanura. He breached the crest when her body shuddered. With her screams, she reached the same peak. For a few brief moments, they were united in paradise, truly one in a place where nothing else but pleasure existed.

Time began again, and the golden cloud settled over them and they lay panting together, still holding one another desperately. Jeremy felt her relax slowly beneath him as he felt himself melting. He breathed deep her flowery scent mixed with the tang of their passion, kissing her warm skin softly.

She had accepted him, truly and wholly. She would be his bride. He would be her husband. She wanted to bear his children. Even now his seed was within her, accepted. He almost wished for it to take, but not yet. Not yet. They had much to do before taking on the responsibility of children. The very thought of creating a new life with her made him want to take her again, but there would be time for that. There would be lots of time for that.

Jeremy lay in pure contentment, savoring the warm glow about him, the feel of Sanura in his arms, good food in his belly, and luxury all around. He was where he dreamed he could have been every night during their exile, yet in a place and with a future he thought impossible.

Heaven could be no better.

Jeremy was deep in perfect sleep when a weight on his belly called him from his dreamless slumber. One small area on his stomach was pressed in. Then it eased, and a small area beside it was pressed in. That eased, and the first was pressed, then the second, back and forth, back and forth. He became aware of a low rumbling sound, and Sanura moved beside him. She spoke soft words, cooing and loving. Jeremy cracked open his eyes, and they widened at the face that met his. It was furry, silver and white, with knowing, even penetrating green eyes.

"Well, hello!" he said, lying perfectly still. He did not want to scare the creature. He had never seen anything like it in his life.

It was a cat, but such fur he couldn't dream to be possible. It was long, fluffy, groomed precisely according to the cat's specification, he was sure. It was white, dusted with silver, and had silver and black stripes on the forelegs and going from the nose over its head. The fluff of fur nearly hid its short, prim ears and framed a delicate face, wider than those of cats he knew, with a slightly shorter nose, but still of the feminine essence attributed to cats.

She watched him closely, but not alarmed, as she padded her forepaws on his stomach, purring in contentment. Sanura's hand reached over, and the cat met it, rubbing its nose into her fingers and arching its body as her hand progressed over the silky back to a long plume of silver of the tail.

Jeremy smiled. "You must be Klee-yo."

"She likes you, Zheramee," Sanura murmured delightedly.

Jeremy slowly lifted a hand and presented it to the cat. She sniffed and deigned to entertain him, rubbing her whiskers on his fingers. Jeremy pet her, still smiling. "You are glad to have your mistress home, aren't you? I can promise you she missed you, too."

"She try to sleep by me all night," said Sanura. "I surprise she like you, since you keep, ah, moving her."

Jeremy laughed, turning to Sanura's sparkling smile. "I didn't know she was there."

"She run away when you move. She know you tink of only one ting."

"Does she know what I'm thinking now?" Jeremy asked mischievously.

Apparently, she did. The cat turned one ear back and hurried away, tail waving in disgust.

Sanura laughed as Jeremy smothered her, and she voiced her pleasure, encouraging him to drive her further into it.

A while later, Jeremy lay back with a contented sigh, which Sanura echoed.

The sky outside was turning rosy. He also noted, with a smile, that they'd not had much sleep. He traced his fingers up and down Sanura's arm.

"What do you call the kind of cat that Klee-yo is?" he asked sleepily.

"Hm?" she responded. "What kind?"

"Yes, where does her breed, her kind of cat come from? Cats in my land do not look like her."

"She was a gift from the east, very far east. Her kind come from *Korzan*. She was this small when I was give her." She nearly cupped her hands together. "Me and my seesters all have *kadi* like her. De trader have de moh-ter and fah-ter and would trade de—child."

"Our word is kitten."

Sanura smiled and turned onto her stomach to face him. "In language of far south, my name is kit-ten."

"Is it really?" Jeremy smiled too. "Well, then, that explains a lot!"

"What do you mean?"

"Well," he said, drawing her into his arms to make her lie against him. "You are smart, cunning, brave, tidy, beautiful, independent, and confident, as well as soft." He looked down at her warmly. "I know you do not know a lot of those words but know it means you are very much like a cat, all in good ways."

She laughed and kissed his cheek. She looked down to the end of the very roomy bed to the ball of sleeping fur that refused to be disturbed by their romping. "Klee-yo, she does not like ot-ter men," she said, almost hesitantly, but clearly meaning a compliment.

At first, Jeremy did feel a flash of jealousy and anger that any man had lain where he was, but he let it go. He knew that already. She had proven it yet again last night. He should be grateful for their tutoring. He still couldn't help but feel slightly bruised. He did smile, though. "No? Well, I'm glad she likes me."

Sanura lay on her stomach. She toyed with the patch of hair on his chest. She frowned as if she wanted to say something. He waited for her to quantify her thoughts.

"I no tink I could find man I want here always," she finally said. "I like men. I call dem here, but after I make dem leave." Her eyes met his. "I do not want you to leave."

Jeremy drew his thumb across her cheek. He knew she had convinced her father to let him stay as a servant, but now he realized to what capacity she had intended. She had meant to keep his companionship, both physical and mental. It was as new to her to think of a relationship as permanent as it was for him. He realized that she, too, was learning to cast away the convictions of her past to allow herself a better future.

"Never fear, Sanura," he said. "I won't ever leave you. Where I go, I will take you with me. Where you go, I will stay by your side. I love you, Sanura, I could not bear to part from you."

Tears misted her eyes. She leaned forward and touched her lips to his. "I love you, too, Zheramee Nottingdale."

YOU MAY ALSO ENJOY THE FOLLOWING FROM EXTASY BOOKS INC:

Godshollow
Catherine Price

Excerpt

"Mrs Evans, this is my niece, Miss Annabelle Knight. Well, she's not exactly my niece. My husband is her maternal uncle. You know what I mean. Anyway, Annabelle is accompanying us to Bath for the season."

"Oh! How wonderful," Mrs Evans cried loudly, turning to her daughters. "Look, girls, how sweet she is. How lovely, look at her curls. Oh, just darling." She didn't pause for breath, reaching out and grabbing a ringlet of Annabelle's hair. Mrs Evans' tone was the kind one might adopt with regard to a small puppy, which, to these large women, was the way Annabelle must have seemed. They were practically as wide as they were tall, and they loomed over Annabelle. The girl let out a small, nervous laugh.

Oblivious to Annabelle's discomfort, the ladies continued with their assessment. Mrs Evans' daughters, who had been tittering behind her, giggled at their mother's appraisal and added their own.

"Just wonderful," said one.

"So darling," chimed in the other. They both regarded Annabelle with the same shrewd eye with which one would appraise cattle at a market.

While the girls had clearly inherited their looks from their mother, from the brown eyes to the light dusting of freckles over their noses, their accents most definitely came from a Welsh father. It was strong and thick. Annabelle had never heard anything like it, and it took her a considerable amount of concentration to discern what they were saying.

Their mother spoke with a softer English accent that was peppered with small Welsh moments, indicating a good amount of time spent in the country. "These are my twins," Mrs Evans announced. "Carys." She gestured to the girl on her left. "And Gwennyth." She motioned to the other. Annabelle wondered how she was going to remember which twin was which. They were identical, even, unhelpfully, down to their choice in clothing. Both girls dutifully curtseyed.

One of them leant forward and added, "Most people just call me Gwen."

Right. Annabelle noted. So Gwen is the one with the beauty spot beside her right eye. She curtseyed again to each girl as she searched for other unique identifiers.

"Don't you just love Bath, Miss Knight?" Carys asked as though she thought every young lady in the world should have an intimate knowledge of the place.

"Actually, this is my first time," Annabelle admitted timorously.

The twins looked at each other in horror.

"Your first time!" Carys exclaimed, completely aghast, her tone bordering on offended.

"We go every year," Gwen continued, shocked.

"It's just the best place."

"Oh, the very best!"

"Especially for eligible young ladies." At this, both girls dissolved into giggles, laughing at their own insinuations.

Annabelle nodded along, though she couldn't truly

empathise. She knew that Bath was, aside from London, the best place for a young woman to be. But her parents had strictly forbidden her to travel there until she attained the age of eighteen because of its less than sparkling reputation.

"I can't believe you've never visited," Carys said contemptuously.

"How is that possible?" Gwen questioned.

Annabelle made the quick assessment that Gwen was definitely the nicer twin. While that didn't help her immediately, knowing that would help her distinguish which one was speaking.

"I've never had the opportunity to go before now," Annabelle replied simply. "It's something I've always wanted to do. I'm very excited to be visiting. I've read everything about it. There are so many things I would like to do while I'm there."

Gwen seemed satisfied with the answer, though Carys looked more sceptical. Suddenly, the sterner twin was seized by an idea, or at least Annabelle hoped she was — that, or she was having a fit. Carys turned to her sister and began to whisper theatrically. More giggling ensued, and they finally faced Annabelle.

"We have decided," one twin — Carys? — said, with much grandeur.

"That, as it's your first time in Bath . . ." the other added.

"And you'll need someone to show you around . . ."

"And we've been many times before . . ."

"We are the best people . . ."

"To take you under our wings . . ."

"And show you how to do Bath." They nodded in unison and eagerly awaited Annabelle's reply.

Annabelle was so confused by all the sentence-sharing and the back and forth that all she could do was smile weakly and say thank you, though she didn't know exactly what she'd agreed to.

"What a clever idea," Mrs Evans exclaimed, reminding the

young girls of her existence. "Don't you think, Moira?"

"Marvellous." Mrs Daniels nodded. "Of course, Colin and I know the area substantially," she added quickly. "We know it better than anyone, but I'm sure Annabelle would prefer some younger companions to keep her company. Though, of course, she adores us. Don't you dear?"

Annabelle nodded vigorously. Her aunt didn't like to be contradicted and hated even the remotest implication that she wasn't the best at everything.

"Well then, it's settled," Mrs Evans beamed. "Girls, tell Miss Annabelle about the ball."

In the deserted inn, it wasn't difficult for the young ladies to find an empty table. Once they were sat down, Gwen began to tell Annabelle about the upcoming event.

"Oh, it is the best ball," she announced, her boundless enthusiasm giving away her identity. "They have it every year and it is the most wonderful thing. There's tea, and dancing, and card tables, and so many eligible bachelors." Gwen began to giggle girlishly then stopped suddenly. "I know!" she declared. "We must all get ready for it together. Where are you staying? You may be closer than we are."

"I think my uncle said it was St James' Square," Annabelle replied when Gwen stopped to draw breath.

Carys looked disdainful. "Hmm . . ." She paused, her nose turning up at the thought. "It is closer to the ballrooms, but I'm sure it's nowhere near as comfortable as our accommodation in Sidney Place."

Annabelle quickly decided that arguing with Carys would be a bad choice and instead nodded her head in agreement. "I'm sure." she said sweetly. "But we risk less damage to our dresses if we are closer to the halls."

Gwen's head bobbed enthusiastically. "Quite so. And" — she spun on her toes to face Carys —"St James' Square is rather lovely."

The other twin gave no response to this. Instead, she raked her gaze over Annabelle's appearance. "What will you wear?" she asked in a belittling tone.

"Well, I have one dress that's my favourite. I've worn it for years," Annabelle replied fondly. "It's yellow with—"

"That will never do," Carys cut in harshly. "This is the ball of the season, you know. You can't go in wearing old clothes!" She said this with such a tone one would have thought Annabelle had suggested she would make an appearance wearing just her under-things.

Annabelle was too stunned to make an intelligible reply. Luckily, she was saved from having to find a rebuttal by the arrival of Mr Daniels.

"There you two are. I've been searching for you. Bath is still a fair way away, and we really should get going."

Annabelle nodded and rose from the table, happy to escape this odd, insulting conversation. As she left, Carys fired her parting shot.

"Don't worry," the Welsh girl called out. "We'll look through your clothes to find the least terrible gown. And if there's nothing suitable, I'm sure Gwen has something you can borrow."

Annabelle curtseyed politely and followed her uncle out of the room, trying to stop the flush she felt rising in her cheeks. She sat in solitary embarrassment whilst her aunt bid farewell to Mrs Evans and they made plans to meet for lunch the next day.

Annabelle waved from the carriage as the Evanses shrank into the distance, but as she sat back in her seat, once they'd completely disappeared, she wondered just exactly what her aunt's introductions had gotten her into.

ABOUT THE AUTHOR

Amelia is an avid reader and writer of all genres. She has a great love for travel, history, people, culture, languages, and, of course, a great love of love. It is her goal to create likeable, understandable characters and places that the reader can relate to and inhabit out of the sheer joy of being able to do so. Amelia delights in sharing the wonderful places and people she has encountered in her imagination through her writing. She is proud and delighted to be a part of eXtasy Books.